A Very Political Lady

A Very
Political
Lady

A novel by

Judy La Marsh

McCLELLAND AND STEWART

Copyright © 1979 by McClelland and Stewart
Limited

ISBN: 0-7710-4622-7

The Canadian Publishers
McClelland and Stewart Limited
25 Hollinger Road
Toronto, Ontario M4B 3G2

CANADIAN CATALOGUING IN PUBLICATION DATA

La Marsh, Judy, 1924-
  A very political lady

ISBN 0-7710-4622-7

I. Title.

PS8573.A417V37   C813'.5'4   C79-094016-7
PR9199.3.L344V37

Verses from "Evangeline" by Michel Conte
reprinted with permission of the copyright
holder, © Les Editions du Triangle, c/o Intermède
Musique, 82 ouest, boul. St-Joseph, Montreal,
Quebec.

Printed and bound in Canada by
T. H. Best Printing Company Limited

The public settings in this novel are real, and actual procedures of the Canadian parliamentary system have been followed.

The characters are not real. This is a work of fiction in which there has been no attempt to portray real people in real situations.

A Very
Political
Lady

Chapter One

Kathleen Marshal, Canadian Minister of Justice, was restless. She pushed back the heavy oak armchair and stood up, stretching her arms to erase the knot of tension in her shoulders. She had been sitting for too long.

She walked over to the tall windows and paused before pulling the drapes against the gathering dusk. Outside, she could see that the Hill was black with moving bodies, most of them waving placards, shouting and gesticulating. Snow, thick and wet, was falling from the leaden Ottawa sky, and the broad front lawns of Parliament were being churned into a shallow pond of slush by the trampling of thousands of pairs of winter boots.

Street lights around the curving drive were just beginning to wink on, and she caught the cautious movements of the cordons of RCMP as they insinuated themselves between the milling crowd and the tower-topped building that houses the Parliament of Canada.

This demonstration, she thought to herself, could not have come at a worse time. A day-long demonstration in bad weather would impress some of the undecided members. She only hoped her supporters would hold firm.

As she reached to pull the drapes, she caught a glimpse of her own reflection in the window. Not very fashionable, she decided. Her black hair was severely styled, pulled back from her square forehead and braided into fat ropes that she coiled over each ear. It was a dated style, but it was handy. She could wind the braids into place blindfolded if she had to. Her classic scarlet shirtwaist dress was, except for its colour, plain to the point of dowdiness. It suited her height, though – she was tall, almost six feet – and its colour did tell the world that she was a Liberal.

She hadn't had much time lately to think about clothes – or much else except for the approaching vote. Well, tonight would be the end of it, one way or another.

The other four people in the room were huddled in chairs drawn up to a table near the unusable fireplace. It would be their big night, too; they certainly all had as much to gain, or lose.

"My God, Kathleen, have you seen that mob out there? I had a hell of a time getting through – had to come in by the Senate entrance. I know this abortion thing has people riled up, but I haven't seen so many militant pro-lifers in all my years. And in this weather!"

Bob Northcutt, Member of Parliament for Melrose, had burst through the door of Kathleen's office, the shoulders of his overcoat burdened with melting clumps of snow. He nodded to the others, then dropped his coat and his snow-crowned fur hat on a chair. He stamped his feet and crossed the big, oak-panelled room and took the unoccupied brown leather armchair nearest to the marble fireplace.

"Damned useless fireplaces. Why can't Public Works fix them instead of boarding them up? This crazy place is freezing in the winter and broiling in the summer. Kate, when this abortion thing is done, maybe you'll tackle the weather. Ought to be easy, after this."

Kathleen noticed that Bob was still shivering and rubbing his hands. "Bob, there's hot coffee there. Or would you rather have a drink?" Through the windows and the massive stone walls they could hear faint sounds of chanting. "Those people have been collecting out there since early afternoon. They must be freezing. I wonder if I should have something hot sent out to them?"

Bob laughed as he got up and helped himself to coffee. "Oh, come off it, Kate. This is no time to play little mother to a mob that is thirsting after your blood. Maybe we'll get lucky, and they'll get cold enough to go home."

Harry Williams, the only other Cabinet minister in the room, and a man known more for his cynicism and his Herculean liver than his espousal of radical causes, spoke up: "Don't worry. They're here for the night. All day they've been fanning out in groups to lobby any member who is still sitting on the fence and to keep up the pressure on their own so there'll be no defections. There are so many of them that the commissionaires are going to let them in to queue for seats in the galleries. At least some of them will get warm. Anyway, there are probably more flasks out there than at a Grey Cup game."

Kathleen laughed. She was grateful to these five people – four men and one woman – who had worked so doggedly to muster the votes needed. Despite their jokes and bantering, she knew that they were as tense and uneasy as she was. Tonight they would learn the results of two years' work, two years of planning, marshalling forces, preparing the public, cajoling, reasoning, haranguing, arm-bending and horse-trading.

This was their last meeting before Parliament voted to decide once and for all whether a woman had the right to control her own body. Tonight, Kathleen would ask Parliament to decriminalize abortions in Canada, and to leave that surgical procedure, like any other, to be decided by the women involved and their physicians. This section of the proposed Criminal Code amendments had generated so much impassioned dissension in the country, and in the House, that a free, non-party vote had been declared.

Kathleen took her seat at the table and waited silently for the group to focus itself on her. Techniques she had learned early in her career were habits now.

"Well," she said, "you know there are rumours about a demonstration in the chamber tonight. The Sergeant-at-Arms is preparing as best he can, though he doesn't have enough staff for something like a determined rush to the floor of the House. The Commissioner of the Mounted Police has doubled the number of Mounties outside. I don't know what else we can do to make sure the vote goes smoothly. Harry, you were going to worry about that."

Harry swirled his drink. In the few years of his tenure as

Minister of National Health and Welfare, he seemed to Kathleen to have lost his youth and become a grey, driven man.

"I don't know. We'll just have to hope for the best. Remember the guy who tossed the bag of cow's blood on the floor of the House? And the nut who blew himself up in the men's washroom almost over our heads? Of course, security is a lot tighter now than then, but there will always be some crazy who'll come up with something we haven't thought of. But we have done our best to get tickets to our own supporters for the members' galleries and to make sure that they, and our people in the public galleries, get right up to the front seats to keep demonstrators from the railings. But it's first come, first seated; and they've been warned not to cause trouble up there themselves. It could backlash and cost us precious votes. I think from here on in, we simply have to leave it up to the Sergeant-at-Arms and his boys."

Len Avery, the tall and cadaverous M.P. from Medicine Hat, cleared his throat. "How about one last report on the voting line-up? I checked with our Whip just before coming down here, and he expects that all our members will be here to answer the roll-call. You all know that my leader and the entire NDP caucus are firmly committed to this measure."

Martin Cooke, the only Progressive Conservative member in the group, leaned forward earnestly. "Well, Len, you know my leader is also for the bill, and he's been doing everything possible, in his quiet way, to get our guys to go along. But he's taken a lot of pressure from the other side." Martin clasped his hands. Despite the time he had spent with the group, he maintained a formal air. "My latest tally tells me we have forty-five out of the caucus of one hundred and seven. Tops – forty-seven votes. And I have to warn you that some are a little shaky. I hope none of them comes unstuck as a result of that demonstration out there. Some of the newer fellows are afraid of staking their political futures on this, and they are keeping pretty quiet about telegraphing in advance which side they support." Having given the bad news, Marty leaned forward. "How about the Government members, Kate? Has the P.M. gotten to them?"

"I haven't seen any evidence that the Prime Minister has actually lobbied for the nayes, Martin. Anyway, lobbying is out of character for him. He thinks his position is the right one, and he just naturally expects the members of the Liberal caucus to support him."

If it hadn't been for the Prime Minister's sudden change of heart, Kate reflected, those in this room would not be in danger of having two years of their working lives end in ruins. To say nothing of their chances for re-election. But the ways of the Prime Minister, Jean Jacques Charles, were not to be questioned. Enigmatic and haughty, he was like a high priest except that he believed in no one but himself. Charles was a leader and he expected to be followed.

And yet it was just like him to be perverse enough to voice no objection when his parliamentary secretary, Bonnie Costello, became an active supporter of the abortion bill. Bonnie, the new member for Toronto Beaches, was dark and vivacious. Pretty, she was not, but her eyes sparkled with intelligence, and she was usually flushed with enthusiasm for one project or another. She was an unswerving feminist, one of the first of the new breed of parliamentary women, and as yet the male members had not taken her measure.

"It's rather odd, Martin," Bonnie said, "but the P.M. hasn't said one word to me about it, and he must know I'm working with you. He's been a bit cool with me lately, but he blows hot and cold half the time anyway. I think he understands that even if I am his parliamentary secretary, he doesn't own me or my conscience. He knows I'll vote exactly as I please."

"After all, Bonnie," broke in Harry Williams, "Jacques went along with the idea that the vote should be an open one."

"I know. But he's been making cracks lately about ministerial solidarity – says all the Cabinet should go along with him or quit."

"Yes," said Kathleen, "and he's made damn sure some of our other Cabinet colleagues do some arm-twisting, especially Stan Findlay, our peripatetic Minister of Transport. Stan is the man behind the delays and the complications, you may be sure."

"Stan was upset when you replaced him as Minister of Justice," said Harry Williams. "While he held the post he was very anti-abortion. Remember those letters he wrote to federal hospitals, advising them against permitting abortions? Stan is against us; but you can be sure that he's taking direction from Jacques."

Kathleen nodded. It was true that she had enemies, even one or two in Cabinet, but that was nothing new.

"I think we have split the caucus down the middle. My count shows that we have carried about half the Liberal members with us. How does that compare with your impression, Bob?"

Bob Northcutt took a last gulp of lukewarm coffee. "I think maybe we're a bit better off than that. As of this afternoon, I make it fifty-three against us and fifty-eight for us, and I'm including Bonnie, Harry, you and me. I'm also assuming that everyone will show up to vote." He stopped to light a cigarette. "The big surprises are those two very independent young Montreal members. But, on the negative side, your old friend Hume Frazier has kept lower than an old goose in the hunting season."

Kathleen laughed. Hume had kept himself in the closet but she thought of him as more gander than goose. "I don't know why he's turned around on this. There must be something we don't know about."

"That may be," replied Bob Northcutt, "but his attitude is not untypical. I never saw a guy who disappeared so fast when he had to stand up and be counted on something contentious. I often wonder what you see in him, Kate."

Kathleen was embarrassed. Hume had promised his support early on, but now that the chips were down he was terribly evasive. "I think we'll have to count him against us," she ventured. "It's disappointing. I'm sorry – I seem to have struck out with Hume."

As each person in the circle reported, Kathleen carefully noted the totals, and in the end she gave the summary of the discussion. "I make it 135 for us and 124 against. That's pretty close, but not a bad margin considering the issue."

She rose. "There's bound to be slippage somewhere. One or

two votes could make the difference. It is pretty tight – too tight for comfort." It was always like this before a big vote: so tense she felt almost sick. She pushed back the scarlet sleeve of her dress to look at her watch. "It's about seven now. Only an hour to go. If you don't mind, my friends, I could use a little time to myself before we go into the chamber."

"Good idea," agreed Bonnie.

"Shall we meet here again before eight? Then we can just charge across the hall together, no matter how many media types or pro-lifers are around out there."

"Sure, why not?"

"Let's show the flag."

They let themselves out through the carved oak door into the Centre Block corridor beyond.

Already a queue had formed, stretching along the south corridor from the still-locked door guarding the staircase to the galleries overhanging the Commons chamber. It snaked past the line of portraits of former prime ministers, dissolved into a shuffling crowd in the pillared Confederation Hall, the marble-floored rotunda at the main entrance, and then straggled down the steps to the massive doors, and out into the cold wet night.

Steam rose from the clothes of those inside, and the babble of their voices echoed through the corridors. Their placards had been left outside, but most of them wore buttons or ribbons announcing their affiliation.

One woman recognized Bonnie as she stood waiting for the elevator to whisk her to her fifth-floor office.

"That's one of those devils. That's the Costello woman." And suddenly pointing a long arm at the young M.P., the woman, for all the world like a witch mouthing an evil spell, hissed: "We'll get you, you abortionist. You'll never be elected again. We'll see that you're finished."

With the others gone, Kathleen stretched out on the cold, cracked leather of the worn brown sofa. She closed her eyes against the persistent headache that spread from the muscles of her back and neck, and wondered, not for the first time, if the struggle was worth it. But whenever she thought she was really through with public life there was someone to point out that she owed it to the government, or the party, or even the public, to stay around for just one more election. But still she couldn't help asking herself if this time she hadn't gone to the well once too often, if one of the younger members couldn't have organized this vote without stirring up so much animosity.

Then, irritated with herself for thinking about what she might have done, she swung her legs off the sofa and reached for her handbag. She searched around then popped a couple of aspirins in her mouth, hoping to ease the throb of her headache.

Two years ago, she had begun to gather support for the change in the abortion law. It had started with dozens of meetings with women's groups. Despite all her years in politics, and all the times she had heard women talk about this issue, she was still surprised at the emotions it aroused. Women earnest, angry, demanding, even pleading had pushed her to change the law until she felt it was the one thing in her universe that must be accomplished. Tales of unwanted children, unscrupulous doctors, and surreptitious, sometimes fatal abortions had been rained on her like a plague. Then there had been other groups to confront; church groups and clergymen, campus organizations, newspapers and others of the media, the meetings with doctors, psychiatrists, hospital administrators. And all the while, Kathleen had probed for support from her parliamentary colleagues of every stripe. She had known from the first that this issue could not be decided on partisan lines. Gradually, the list of her supporters had grown, and they were as dedicated and as committed as she was to get through a bill at this session. When she judged her support sufficient, she had taken her proposal to the appropriate Cabinet committee. Kathleen had been elated at the ease of obtaining approval there.

As the Cabinet now operated, it was only *pro forma* to obtain approval of the full Cabinet. Decisions of Cabinet committees were routinely adopted, unless one or other of the ministers wrote to the secretariat to ask for a full reconsideration of the issue. She had expected some trouble from Stan Findlay, who had shown himself adamant against abortion while he had been Justice Minister, but she had discounted his opposition, expecting that he would not dare object too strongly. He was a rough, tough Cabinet operator, but he had never crossed the Prime Minister and Kathleen was confident that she had Jacques' approval.

She had been puzzled and alarmed when she learned that there was an objector, and that it was the Prime Minister himself who had asked that the abortion bill be put on the agenda for full Cabinet debate.

"The next item is number three. The Minister of Justice. Kathleen?"

She glanced at Jacques, slumped in the high-backed, carved chair that marked the Prime Minister's place around the enormous oval table. She sat almost directly across from him, the green baize surface between them strewn with the black leather Cabinet books of her colleagues. As she poured a glass of icewater from the thermos jug placed between her and the Minister of Labour, she glanced around the table at her ministerial colleagues. Most looked at her expectantly, some in attentive postures, others pushed back from the table, relaxed in their padded armchairs – all alert for her presentation.

Findlay glowered at her, but as she caught his eye, he looked away elaborately. Harry Williams, from his place at the end of the table to her right, winked encouragement and gave her the thumbs-up sign. She grinned, adjusted her reading glasses, and bent to her task.

"Prime Minister and colleagues: we have already been over the position papers at the last meeting. I have sent along the supplemental material requested. You will find it in your agenda books. Last day, we went over the law as it presently stands – the therapeutic abortion section which the Prime Minister himself introduced less than half a dozen years ago. We also produced the statistics to show how unevenly the law is applied across the country, amounting to a denial of rights to many Canadian women. You now have the resolutions of the Canadian Medical Association and of the church authorities you requested. I have also appended a tally of my mail, pro and con. I have no doubt that you have already discovered that every shade of opinion exists regarding abortion. But although that opinion is divided, there is a likely majority for it in the House, especially as it is to be treated as a matter for the members' conscience.

"I don't know what would be the result in this minority Parliament if it were presented as a partisan bill, with the Whips on, but I believe it would just barely pass, since the entire NDP caucus is committed to support it. In any event, it is an appropriate subject for a conscience vote. After all, it has never been a test of a member of the Liberal Party – or at least it hasn't been, so long as I have been associated with it – to espouse one position or another on the subject of abortion. The party conventions have never passed a policy resolution on the subject, and none of us has ever campaigned on it as part of the party's platform.

"To sum up, Prime Minister: this was originally presented as a section of an omnibus bill of amendments to the Criminal Code. But because the abortion section appeared to be gaining in contentiousness, we decided to present it as a single bill. It can therefore be voted on separately, without affecting the other amendments."

"What will be the cost to the Treasury?" asked Hume Frazier.

She turned to Frazier, the Minister of Finance, grateful for the opportunity to say something positive. "Nothing, so far as the committee has been able to ascertain," she grinned at her colleague. "This time you get something free."

"Kathleen, you know this bill will stir up a hornets' nest. Did you see that CBC program with the picture of a foetus in a jar of formaldehyde? And what about the Government? In a minority position I think we ought to be more cautious. We should let sleeping dogs lie." Bentley Palmer was the most recent member of the Charles Cabinet. He was an Albertan, a tall cowman with a receding hairline and a pugnacious chin. For longer than most around this table, he had been an M.P., but until shortly after the last election he had sat as a Conservative member. Kathleen had been surprised when Palmer had crossed the floor; and even more surprised – at Charles' obvious political dealing – when the next day he announced Palmer's elevation to the Cabinet. There was something so distasteful to her about Charles' cynical selling of the Cabinet position that her previous neutrality towards Bentley Palmer had become strong dislike.

"This, Bentley, is a *Liberal* Cabinet. We must try to get through as much progressive legislation as we can. If we're afraid to do anything, we'll deserve what will happen: first the House and then the country will vote us out of office. There's precious little money for new programs, as Hume keeps telling us, so we are fairly limited in the kind of bills we can expect to pass.

"At the moment, the NDP is supporting us on this, and except for the SoCreds, there is good support across the House. I consider this an important, pressing public issue, a chance to right a social wrong that has existed for far too long. I feel strongly about the matter, so strongly that it was this concern alone which persuaded me to run again two years ago, as the Prime Minister will confirm." Kathleen looked across at Jacques, expecting him to make some comment.

He was toying with his fountain pen, drawing circles on the blotter before him. He lifted his head, but did not meet her eyes. The pause lengthened.

"I suppose you are going to threaten to quit if we don't agree," came a snide intervention from Kathleen's left. "Maybe that wouldn't be such a bad idea, Madam Minister."

Kathleen caught her breath. Findlay seemed to be trying to provoke a fight. Could it be that Jacques had put him up to it? She looked at the Prime Minister, trying to read his silence. Jacques stirred under her gaze, and shifted position.

"This isn't the place for clashes of personality," he said coldly. "Are we agreed, then, that the bill shall go forward? As a free vote to be voted on according to the conscience of each member?" Charles paused and referred to the agenda in front of him. "Then let us pass to the next item on the agenda, Number Four. The Minister of National Defence."

For the rest of the session Jacques avoided looking at her.

As she gathered up her papers at the close of the meeting, Kathleen took her time. Findlay had cornered Jacques, but Kathleen lingered near the door alternating between curiosity about how Jacques would explain his apparent reversal on the issue and resentment at his lack of support. When he broke free, he took her arm, and wordlessly hustled her down the hall to his office.

As they entered the ante-room, several waiting aides sprang up. The Prime Minister waved them aside.

"Give me a couple of minutes. I'll buzz when I am ready." He held the door to the office open for Kathleen. She preceded him and took one of the gold suede chairs facing the sofa. She looked around the big square corner room – the office reserved for the head of the Canadian government. She didn't much like the changes effected since she was its occupant: everything in sight was covered with suede in a muted golden hue – even the desktop and its accessories. There was a sense of richness, of power, of money lavished on the place, but it was featureless and bland. Over there, she knew, the panels hid a bar, and in that corner, was the ensuite toilet and shower; and behind the enormous, grotesque old desk which had belonged to Sir John A. Macdonald, the first Canadian Prime Minister, there was a cubbyhole safe. In this office, as in hers, there was a fireplace that didn't work; it was now panelled over and masked by a suede-covered screen. Pots of gold chrysanthemums delivered every few days from the Department of Agriculture green-houses dotted the room. Air conditioners disfigured the grace-ful windows. Even the expensive thick carpet and the heavy drapes were of the same pale shade. Kathleen felt suffocated by the overdone luxury of it all.

Jacques strode to the desk, dropped his Cabinet papers on the desk with a thump, and stood looking at her over the top of his pipe as he bent to light it.

He was wearing his public face. The hooded eyes set deep in

their sockets, the pebbly skin quite without expression. The face so well known to the people of Canada.

As she looked at Jacques, waiting for him to begin, Kathleen wondered what had happened to the other Jacques, the man she had known so long. His private face was softer, ready to smile, the eyes sparkling in mischief. The full lips could curve in enjoyment, or pout in self-parody. He was very intelligent, but sometimes oddly flighty. He was a chameleon, a witty sophisticate, an amused gallant, a tender husband. Now professor, now prankster, he had the power to fascinate, up close and at a distance. He had enormous energy, but not much stamina. He was athletic, as he loved to display, but in most things, an observer rather than a participant. He never pitted himself against others, only against himself. Jean Jacques Charles, the son of a gracious French-Canadian mother and a self-made English millionaire father, was an enigma.

Kathleen knew the private man as well as the public man, but it seemed to her that, except in his own drawing room, the cold, even cruel face of the public man had more and more usurped the Jacques who had been her friend. And now, even before he spoke, she knew he would try to avoid explaining his real motives.

"Kathleen, perhaps we should have talked about this before, but I've been busy, and I had hoped you would lose your enthusiasm for this abortion thing. I had hoped that the vigour of the opposition in the country would lead you to re-think the matter. I should have known better, Kathleen. You are a stubborn woman, and you like to have your own way. Well, now you have a Cabinet minute entitling you to proceed. I thought I should argue against you in there, and would have if you hadn't reminded me that when I asked you to run again, I approved your plans. But that was two years ago. You know that circumstances change all the time in politics, Kate. And I have a right to change my mind." He paused and then said with deliberation, "I am going to ask you to withdraw the bill."

Before she could think of what to say to this outrageous demand – the Cabinet had just approved the bill – Jacques carried on.

"I want you to know that I will fight you as best I can, if you do not. You are not prime minister now; I am. Will you withdraw the bill?"

"No," Kathleen said. "It's too late. I can't let my people down like that. The members of the House know all about it. And the Cabinet. And it is in the minutes now. It must come to a vote."

"I can demand your resignation."

"You can demand it," Kathleen said, "but you won't get it. If you want to get rid of me you'll have to fire me."

"Then your answer is No?"

"That's right," Kathleen said. "The answer is No."

Since that time they had barely spoken. She was sure that Jacques was behind the endless delays, but he could delay the confrontation no longer.

Kathleen stubbed out her cigarette and noted with dismay how many half-smoked cigarettes filled the ashtray. There was a soft knock, and the satiny black face of her secretary, Barbara Hepburn, appeared around the edge of the door. Seeing her minister up, she edged into the room, balancing a tray containing a white cup and saucer, the cup ringed with gold and emblazoned with the graceful coat of arms of Canada. In her other hand was a sheaf of telephone messages.

Kathleen looked through them absently as she sipped the steaming liquid. "I'm so tired I could sleep for a month. Maybe I will when this is over."

Before the mirror in the washroom, she undid the coiled braids, then rewound them, noticing the ever more apparent onslaught of grey. But the olive skin was still unlined, even if there were shadows of fatigue under her eyes. She touched on bright lipstick to match her scarlet dress.

"Still plenty of life in the old girl yet," she laughed into the mirror. "Enough to beat those bastards at their own game." Even if Jean Jacques Charles was prepared to fire her and buy himself new ministers from across the floor to support his tottering Government. Well, tonight she would show him what a *real* Liberal could do.

22

Chapter Two

Slowly, enjoying the familiar ritual, Stephan Ludvic buttoned his high collar, tied the white tabs around his throat, and drew on the black robe of the Speaker of the House of Commons. From his already gleaming shoes he brushed a few imagined specks of dust. And then, finally satisfied, he smiled at the thought that he just taking care of public property.

When he had first run for Parliament from his grimy, north Ontario riding, he had never expected that the taxpayers would be providing him with his workclothes – even to the garters that held up his long black socks. But the clothes, from hat to trousers, were one of the perks of the Speaker's office; along with this suite of rooms in the Centre Block, and, even more enjoyably, the cozy summer cottage at Kingsmere in the Gatineau Hills.

Ludvic was a big, heavyset man, and as he lumbered from his private dressing room into the book-lined sitting room and office of his suite, he thought once again that he could easily have spent his whole lifetime straining bone and muscle in the north Ontario mines. But two summers in the mines had convinced him to look elsewhere for his life's work.

His chambers were on the north side of the building, and his window overlooked the back lawn and the parking lot, and beyond that, the stoutly fenced lip of the cliff and its long sheer drop to the Ottawa River below.

The snow was falling fast now and piling thick around the window frame. In the parking lot, a white-blanketed car pulled up and three members leapt out, their heads turned away from the wind, and scurried for the shelter of the building.

The door to his sitting room opened. "It's time, sir."

"Thank you, Max."

With a brisker step, the Speaker turned back into his sitting room and snatched up his black tricorn hat. He was embarrassed by the clumsy, uncomfortable headgear that he had to wear each day during the Speaker's parade before the sitting could begin. Every day he walked the same path, preceded by the Sergeant-at-Arms, carrying across his shoulder the gilded weight of the Mace, and followed by the Clerk, his two assistant clerks and their pages. Their route took them along the north, or Speaker's corridor, past the painted faces of his predecessors, right, through the Hall of Honour to the marble rotunda of Confederation Hall, and along the south corridor to the main entrance door of the Commons, where white-gloved commissionaires saluted his entrance. Then straight to its far end, where he would mount the short flight of steps and turn to face back along the chamber. Then he would stow the hated hat, and lead the members in prayer before the public was allowed to enter.

Ludvic had put on the hat by force of habit. He now took it off again when he remembered that there was no need for the stately procession, which occurred only at the beginning of each parliamentary day. It was now evening. The six to eight o'clock recess for dinner was over, and it was time to bring the House to order for the evening's business.

That business was to be the final stage – at least so far as the Commons was concerned – of the bill to decriminalize abortion. Like all contentious bills, the debate on this one had ranged from the boring to the acrimonious. But there were complications to this bill that made it more interesting than most. For one thing, it was about abortion, a subject that made politicians very nervous, and their constituents sometimes very abusive. Also, the bill was being sponsored by Kathleen Marshal, the Minister of Justice, but her own Prime Minister was openly known to oppose it. And not only was it rumoured that he himself was putting on the pressure, but he had sent his chief bottle-washer and hatchetman, Stan Findlay, round collecting votes. Findlay had even made his way to the Speaker's office to make it clear that, should it come to a tie-breaking vote, the Speaker might like to remember whom he owed his job to. And his uncontested seat.

At least, Ludvic consoled himself, tonight would see the end of this bill. And, as he slowly lumbered through the curtained doorway and up the stairs to stand before his tall carved chair, he couldn't help hoping that Findlay would be disappointed.

Ludvic faced the length of the lofty, green-carpeted chamber. To his right were the Government benches and to his left those of the Official Opposition; beyond them were the members of the other parties and the one Independent.

As soon as the Speaker was seated, the doors were opened to the public galleries. There was an immediate swell of sound as the crowd pushed up the enclosed staircase and into the tiered seats of the galleries. Once there, small groups of people, more women than men, broke past the restraining arms of the uniformed guards, struggling to the front row seats at the railings.

The galleries filled with astonishing speed. The small section reserved for the Speaker's own guests and the bank of seats reserved for senators were crowded to capacity, as were the places set aside for guests of Government members and the long gallery reserved for the guests of Opposition members. The television cameras were in place on his right and left, and their hot lights, ringing the chamber, were already ablaze.

Above the Speaker, to his extreme right, the officials' gallery was also packed tight. Even the standing-room areas were crowded with jostling figures. Above and behind the Speaker's ornate chair was the long open gallery with its two levels of desks, hidden from the view of those on the floor below. This was the press gallery, whose privileged members were the only spectators, excepting the officials, who could take notes. The gallery extended the full width of the room. It was packed, like the other galleries.

In contrast to the public, the members filtered in slowly, moving behind their carved, blotter-topped paired desks, to slump in various postures in the green leather-padded oak armchairs. On each side, groups of members hung back, half in and half out of the chamber itself, where they were finishing their smokes before butting them in the sand of the heavy floor ashtrays. Although the rules were clear – no smoking, drinking, or eating in the House – they did not apply to that golden-curtained space behind the rows of members' desks on either side of the chamber. Those who wished to remain in the House to hear debates were free to slip behind the curtains, or pull them wide along the brass rails and to lounge there, smoking, sipping coffee, or talking in small groups.

The Speaker droned sonorously, "Or-der," and some of those lingering behind the curtains pushed forward to take their seats. But the front benches were still almost empty, and none of the party leaders had yet taken their places.

The Clerk called the order of business, and the Speaker put the question.

"All those in favour will please say yea. Those opposed will please say nay."

Shouts of "Yea" and "Nay" arose from the members in all parts of the Commons.

"In my opinion," Speaker Ludvic said gravely, "the yeas have it."

At once a dozen members, many more than the minimum of five required by the rules, stood in their places to challenge the results of the voice vote.

Ludvic thereupon intoned, "Call in the members." At the Clerk's table, a button was pressed and the division bells began to ring, trilling their call through the corridors, anterooms, and offices of the Centre Block. Even in the parliamentary dining room the bells rang. And the last diners wiped their lips on snowy white linen, snatched their bills from the uniformed waitresses, and hurried to queue at the cashier's desk. The elevator outside, only a half dozen stairs and as many strides away, would whisk them directly to the main floor and the entrance to the members' lobbies and the chamber.

The bells rang, too, in the West Block office of Hume Frazier, the Minister of Finance.

The bells rang but Hume Frazier, unlike the hurrying diners or the M.P.s already in their seats, was happily oblivious. With one ear wedged against the leather of his office couch, and the other protected by the warm left breast of his versatile secretary, Molly Paradis, Hume was serenely unaware.

Molly pulled gently away from him and whispered, "The bells, Hume."

Hume stumbled to his feet and, turning his back to her, pulled up his trousers. In the washroom he scrubbed his hands, and splashed water on his face. He was a handsome, almost pretty man, with a strong cleft chin and thick, wavy black hair. As he smoothed it back with the heavy silver monogrammed brush that was – he sometimes remembered to his chagrin after a session with Molly – a gift from his wife, he noted with approval the way his hair was silvering at the temples.

There had been times, when he was younger, that his image had seemed almost too dark, too intense. Now that his face had filled out and his hair had started to turn, he looked more distinguished to himself, a gentle, almost mellow, man. Peering into the mirror he frowned at the red streaks in his eyes. Those startling blue eyes with their unwavering stare had often been used to advantage – whether to discomfit an opponent, or to compel the interest of a new woman. He adjusted his tie, shrugged into his dark suit jacket, and shot his cuffs. Then he left the office, without even a glance at Molly.

While Hume was inspecting himself, Molly had slipped on her bikini panties – bought specially with him in mind – and smoothed down her skirt. At twenty-five, she considered herself to be at the absolute prime of youthful beauty. She wore her ash-blonde hair shoulder-length and artfully tousled – though at the moment it was damp and somewhat limp. With Hume gone, she entered the small washroom and leisurely brushed her hair and reapplied her make up. Then she smoothed her sweater down over her breasts. Twisting this way and that, she looked for wrinkles or other telltale signs of her recent endeavours. Then she pulled her stockings straight, slipped on her high-heeled pumps, and stepped out through the Minister's office. Once in the ante-room she sat down

27

demurely before her own typewriter. As she rolled a new sheet into the machine, she was satisfied that despite his abrupt exit Hume needed her as much as ever.

Like Hume Frazier, Jean Jacques Charles, Prime Minister of Canada, also had company in his office when the division bells began to ring. But unlike his Minister of Finance, Jean Jacques heard the bells, despite the fact that they were muted by a thickly padded inner and outer door, designed to protect the privacy of his conversations.

He was standing behind his massive old desk at the windows, with their sweeping view of the lawns of Parliament, cradled by the long stone arms of the East Block, the Centre and West Block buildings. He had been surprised by the unexpectedly large demonstration. But with the filling of the galleries, the remaining crowd was smaller and less volatile. The trampled lawns were now covered by fresh falls of snow, as if the weather had finally asserted its supremacy over mere politics.

His aides had reported the full galleries. Many, he knew, still waited, more or less patiently, in the corridor queues, hoping that someone might decide to leave. Those still outside would now quickly disperse, to find a nearby coffee shop or bar to warm their chilled bones and await news reports of the voting result. It irritated Jean Jacques to know that some had paid their own way here to the nation's capital from considerable distances, and that their anger at being unable to get into the chamber would embitter them against the Government – his Government. It seemed to Jacques that whatever went wrong in the country, he ended up being blamed for it.

He let the curtain drop and moved behind the high desk chair. "What did you say, Stan?" he asked.

"Yes, sir. I was just giving you the run-down of how we think the vote will go. Here it is in memo form; you'll have time to study it in the House. It's as accurate as we can be, considering that we can't poll the members. But there is one thing that worries me, Prime Minister. There may be some sort of trouble in the House tonight – from the demonstrators, that is. If anything does start, especially if it's by the pro-life people, there could be a backlash against the nays. Of course, if some of those militant pro-abortion bitches start something, that would help us. No matter what, please get out quickly if any trouble develops. We can't get the security men on to the floor of the House to help you."

Jacques glanced at Findlay's anxious face. "For heaven's sake, Stan, this is the Parliament of Canada, not Japan or Italy. Let's go before you have a heart attack just thinking about what might happen."

They walked down the two flights of steps together, the other members hurrying towards the chamber crowding behind them. Beyond the oak door, they found the government lobby full of milling members. Some stared out the windows at the mounting storm. One or two were making last-minute calls in the telephone booths. Members lounged against the outsized tables or in leather chairs or sofas, and the babble of their talk was deafening. As the Prime Minister entered, most got to their feet, and conversation dropped to a murmur. Jacques gave them an absent smile and a wave as they parted to let him through. He mounted the steps and opened the door into the chamber. The Liberals surged in behind him.

Jacques walked slowly down the aisle to his place. He was exasperated to note that the Minister of Finance, who was his seat-mate, was not yet in his place.

"Damn Hume, why is he always late?" he muttered to himself. "Probably drinking again, too. After dinner break, he smells like a goddamn distillery." He turned to his left, as he heard a soft: "Jacques? Prime Minister?" and looked into the face of his Minister of Justice.

For a moment, it was as it used to be. When he saw her friendly, almost handsome face, he was suddenly nostalgic for the times they used to have. It would be so good if they could have one of their old, long chats. But then he remembered and his head jerked away. As his eyes swivelled he took in the crush in the galleries above, noting that every seat was occupied. His glance brushed across Richard Sherwood, the leader of the Opposition. He was sitting directly opposite and his leonine head was bent to listen to one of his supporters. We are as usual on opposite sides of the issue, Jacques thought, so perhaps it is as well that we continue to keep the centre aisle of the green chamber two sword lengths wide.

And then, looking back at Kathleen, his anger stirred again. He wanted to say something insulting, something that would let her know the extent of his outrage at her treachery in bringing this stupid bill to the vote. He had tried to slow the bill down, to sidetrack it, but it seemed to have taken on a life of its own. And Kathleen had pushed it hard, determinedly collecting every one of the IOUs outstanding from her stint as P.M. He glanced down at the forgotten memo clenched in his hand. His eyes roved down the list of figures: it was going to be close, very close, but it looked as if Kathleen's attempt to cross him was bound to fail.

"Jacques," Kathleen repeated, more insistently this time, "do you expect any trouble here tonight?"

"Trouble? What kind of trouble?"

"Chanting, interruptions – that kind of thing – from the galleries?"

"Not from the pro-life forces, I don't. You can speak for those abortionists of yours better than I."

She wanted to protest that none of them were pro-abortion. They felt they were for freedom of choice. But the words died on her lips. She was startled to see the unmistakable signs that his anger was boiling beneath the surface. His eyes glittered, and his facial muscles worked, drawing the pebbly skin over the high cheekbones. Even the high dome of his forehead was flushed.

She had seen him in a temper before. When he kept it under control, his words were icy, cutting. But when it exploded, the words would come ripping out in one long, sneering stream. Neither manifestation of his anger was pretty to watch, and both were bloody unpleasant for the recipient.

It was clear that Jacques was spoiling for a fight. Well, she thought, it takes two to fight. And I'll be damned if I'll be the butt of his abuse, in full view of the cameras. She turned away.

The Government and Opposition Whips advanced, side by side, along the floor of the chamber to the Clerk's table, where they halted and bowed solemnly to the Speaker. At that signal that they were ready to vote, the bells stopped ringing.

Hume Frazier slipped into his seat at the desk on Jacques' right.

"Timed it just right, I guess."

The Prime Minister grunted in disgust, his nostrils assailed by a mixture of alcohol, peppermint and the ministrations of Molly Paradis.

"Rutting," Jacques said aloud. "Screwing in the office again." He turned away in disgust.

The Clerk of the House raised his pen and poised it over the tally sheets on which he would record the voice votes as members responded to the roll-call. The Deputy Clerk stood beside the table, facing the Government benches, prepared once more for his unique *tour de force*: he would call out the name of each new member as he or she rose and bowed to the Speaker, never confusing one name with another. The members, in appreciation of his prodigious feat of memory, invariably responded by pounding the flat of their hands upon their desk-tops. Most of them could not, even after many years, recognize by name all of their fellows. But within days, at the very first roll-call of a new Parliament, the Deputy Clerk was expected to have the list memorized – new members, new constituencies, all perfectly integrated into his roll-call.

He cleared his throat, ready to begin. First in English, then in French, he called: "All those in favour?"

Suddenly there was the sound of hundreds of small thuds, as throughout the public galleries, men and women leapt to their feet, banging their wooden seats against the padded chair-backs. They stood, almost as one, hundreds of them. And from their hands suddenly cascaded long ribbons of red; they fell over the railings and hung down into the chamber, almost touching the heads of the members below.

The streamers bore messages: *"Don't let them kill," "Stop abortions," "Right to life," "Vote down the murderers," "A foetus is a person."* And then the bright ribbons were dropped all at once to the floor of the House. They curled about the members' desks or fell limply to the carpet where they lay like bloody stains.

Arms linked together, the demonstrators began to sway and chant their slogans in unison. The huge room was filled with the mounting sound.

A single voice rose above the others: "Parliament has no right to decide!"

Just then a flash of reflected light glittered about the chamber as a silver-coloured object arced through the air, thrown from a seat near the railing of the north public gallery. It spun, end over end, catching the myriad brilliant lights of the lofty room.

The shining cylinder hit the floor exactly midway between Jean Jacques Charles and Richard Sherwood. It shattered and a thick, brown nauseating gas billowed from its canister.

Members on both sides were at once affected by the noxious fumes, and eyes watering and throats seared, they began to scramble out of the chamber.

His ornate ceremonial sword banging against his knees, the Sergeant-at-Arms rushed to assist the Prime Minister. Jacques, handkerchief muffling his nose and mouth, was led quickly from the House, followed by the Minister of Finance. Kathleen, slower to react, stumbled to the curtained doorway beside the Speaker's throne and followed the black-clad House officials to the north corridor beyond.

The brown gas eddied near the floor of the House, then began to rise. The press gallery emptied rapidly, and at the far end of the chamber, the technicians who handled the acoustics system and the instantaneous interpreters in their booths fled from the poisoned air. In the galleries, officials and observers pushed and shoved each other and the guards in their attempt to reach the corridors – anywhere to escape the choking, burning effect of the foul-smelling gas. Within three minutes of the canister's explosion, the great green chamber lay empty.

Kathleen, Hume Frazier, Harry Williams, Richard Sherwood, and Bonnie Costello, along with six other members, found themselves in the north corridor, unable to reach their own offices. The Speaker invited them to take refuge in his quarters until the air was cleared. Jacques and the Sergeant-at-Arms were nowhere in sight.

Ludvic ushered his guests into his book-lined office, turned on the lamps, and poked the dying wood fire into new life. His was the only working fireplace. But Public Works wanted to close it up, too. He threw on a couple of logs and fussily readjusted the firescreen. Then he invited his unexpected guests to give his steward their orders for drinks, while he returned to the ante-room to check the operation, already underway, to cleanse the air of the chamber.

Kathleen took a chair near the fire. Facing her was the leader of the Official Opposition, Richard Sherwood. Beside him was Bonnie Costello, and on the arm of the sofa, Hume Frazier perched. Harry Williams sat to her left, sharing the sofa with Alcide Morin, a bearded Liberal backbencher. Two Conservative members, the veteran Bill Hendry, and a freshman member, Wallace Foy, chose the armchairs at the end of the chesterfields, facing the fireplace. Terrence O'Neal paced up and down, scanning the bookshelves. Ben Goodman, the thin, bald, excitable member for Ottawa East, apologetically inserted his bony frame between Bonnie and Richard Sherwood. The conversation, understandably, was of the demonstrations, and especially of the gas bomb that had interrupted the work of the House and so precipitously cleared the chamber.

While they talked, the Speaker's steward moved among them, taking their orders. He soon reappeared with cut-glass tumblers tinkling with ice, for those who had ordered long drinks, and two hand-blown balloons shimmering with golden brandy for Kathleen and Hume.

With nothing else to be done, they settled down with their drinks and soon the desultory conversation gave way to more animated anecdotes. Kathleen, overtired but relaxed, found herself watching Hume Frazier.

He seemed to be enjoying himself hugely. Repeatedly his deep laugh boomed out; and Kathleen remembered how well they had once got along. He was, she admitted, not only remarkably handsome, but also, despite his ambition, extremely personable. He had a way of making a group of people come alive, and even, she remembered, of inspiring confidence. Though since he had married Sybil she hadn't had a good talk with him.

But that last talk, the one before his marriage, was one she wouldn't forget. It had been a sharp, windy fall night, and he had stopped her as she was leaving the House and invited her to join him in his office for a nightcap.

Hume had ushered Kathleen straight into his private office, and told the eager Molly Paradis that she could leave, as he had no further need of her. He broke out a decanter of brandy and two glasses, and they settled comfortably for their talk.

"Kathleen, I'm going to be married."

Confused by the worried expression clouding his face, Kathleen had hesitated, unsure exactly how to respond.

"That's great news, Hume. Let's drink to that! But who is she? When did all this happen?"

He passed his hand across his forehead. Then he answered slowly: "She's Sybil Montgomery. She's from Vancouver. Her dad's a big shot in one of those big lumber firms – Clement's, I think. And I really don't know how it happened. I'm still a little dazed. I didn't tell you before because I didn't know myself."

"What do you mean, you don't know how it happened? When did you meet her?"

"A year or so ago. Before the election. I was skiing at Whistler, and I met her with some other kids from Vancouver. We sort of noodled around together for the few days I was there, but I honestly never gave her a serious thought, and she certainly didn't act as if she saw me in her future. She was just a nice, pretty kid – a little touch-me-not. Anyway I couldn't get to first base with her. But she was a good skiier and she liked to dance; and I enjoyed myself with her.

"Well, she wrote later to congratulate me on my election win, and on the Finance portfolio, so when I was in Vancouver at the Ministers' Conference, I looked her up. We had a couple of very modest nights on the town – nothing special – and when I took her home that last evening, she invited me in. I thought she might be amenable by then to a little smooching, but that wasn't at all what she had in mind."

Kathleen had cupped her hands to warm the brandy in the glass, listening intently.

Hume went on, "I was absolutely floored when she told me that she was too old to fool around casually. She's only twenty-four. She told me that she wants to get married and start raising a family. She wants a serious man who is going somewhere. She told me I qualify, and her parents are willing. And then she gave me an ultimatum: declare myself, or stop calling on her! She gave me all the arguments: we have matching backgrounds and families; both of us are Roman Catholics; we get along well and would have beautiful children. It was high time for me to marry, and politically wise. She said she knew I wanted to be prime minister, and that she felt herself the perfect wife to further that ambition. She has a little money of her own, and will someday inherit a lot. In the meantime, her parents approve of me. She'd already asked them and her father said that he would give us a house as a wedding present and pay for servants until I'm in a position to take that over! She had even spoken to the bishop, and he had promised to intercede at the cathedral to arrange an early wedding date. To cap it off she had already considered who her attendants should be, and suggested that I give some thought to a list of my own."

Hume tossed off his brandy and poured another. He then confessed to Kathleen that he had been taken totally by surprise. As Sybil talked on, he had sat there mesmerized, and he had found himself falling in with everything she had proposed. When she took him to the door, she planted a warm, virginal kiss on his lips, then pushed him outside – engaged to be married! And the next week, following her suggestion, he had mailed her from Ottawa a much larger sapphire-and-diamond engagement ring than he could possibly afford.

As her plans for the wedding went forward, Sybil had

phoned him every evening. Until one morning his secretary had placed before him, without comment, a thick cream envelope. When he opened it, he learned that the marriage would take place within a month.

"What do you think, Kit? Am I making a terrible mistake? You know I'm a Catholic – although I don't work at it much – and I wouldn't ever want to have to go through a divorce. I can't afford to make that kind of mistake. It would be politically disastrous. It would really be fatal to my chances for the top job. Do you think I'm ready for marriage? What should I tell my mother and stepfather?"

Kathleen had struggled to conceal her amazement at his blurted tale. What incredible gall Sybil had shown! What a determined, wilful, managerial type she must be! And – she couldn't avoid the thought – what a great revenge for all the women Hume had so casually seduced and cast aside! But she couldn't say that to Hume.

"What about the girl, Hume? Sybil, did you say her name was? How do you feel about her? Is she smart? Is she attractive? Are you in love with her?"

"I just don't know, Kit. Oh sure, she's pretty enough – a cool blonde; I think she has brown eyes. She's slender, athletic. I'm told she rides a horse well. She sails. She's travelled some, I think. I don't know how bright she is. We've never really talked. I guess I am in love with her – I must be. But, Kit, I've only seen her three or four times, and we've never been – well, you know – intimate. I suppose she's still a virgin, but I know she wants babies. And I don't know whether I am ready to take on a wife, much less kids. Of course, I always meant to get married – being prime minister would be awfully lonely without a wife – but that would come later, I thought." Hume helped himself to another drink. To Kathleen he looked like a little boy who'd been caught playing doctor with the girl next door.

Hume put down his snifter, then asked Kathleen directly.

"Look, Kit, would you talk to her – to Sybil? Maybe ask for a little more time, until I can be sure."

"Oh no, Hume. I couldn't do that; nobody but you can talk

to her about that. And the wedding invitations are already in the mail! Do you realize what a mess it would be if you jilted her now or even postponed the wedding without a damn good reason?"

"I suppose you're right, Kit. Maybe these are just the kind of jitters any man feels when he's facing marriage. It'll probably be all right. But it happened so fast. I feel as though it's a dream. I don't really know how I got myself into this, or how to get out, or whether I really want to get out." He pushed back his cuff, glanced at his watch and went on. "Look, I've got to get back to my apartment. Sybil will be calling me inside the hour. I'll have to make up my mind by the time I talk to her tonight. Thanks for your help, kiddo."

As Kathleen had left Hume's office to pick up her coat from her own office, she heard a rustle in the ante-room. Molly Paradis was still there.

"I thought you had gone, Molly. Was there something else?"

"No, Minister, I just thought I should stay in case you needed me, after all. If you are leaving now, I'll be going too."

"Perhaps I can drop you off somewhere on the way?" Hume asked, and turning back to Kathleen, he called softly, "Will you come to my wedding, Kit?" With a bashful smile: "I think I would feel better if you were there."

Without waiting for her answer, Hume was off, head down, hands jammed deep in overcoat pockets, long scarf flying, busy with his own thoughts. Behind him Molly Paradis, on her ridiculously high heels, struggled to keep up with Hume's long strides.

A few weeks later Kathleen had entertained the Bachelor's Club in honour of Hume's marriage and his new status as a club graduate. Sybil had been furious at being excluded from the members-only affair, and since that time Kathleen had seen her old friend and colleague much less often.

Remembering Sybil's amazing and audacious capture of Hume, Kathleen speculated on how the marriage was working out. Every year there had been a child and Sybil certainly seemed happy. But still, Kathleen had heard rumours about Hume and his pretty secretary – among others – and he was known to hit the bottle a lot more than he once had.

To her embarrassment, Kathleen realized that she had been studying Hume for rather a long time, and she became aware that Richard Sherwood was watching her, a puzzled look on his face. Just as she was trying to think of some remark to explain herself, Speaker Ludvic entered the room to announce that it was now possible to use the chamber once more, and that after consultation with the Prime Minister, he had decided to recall the members at once.

It was now ten-thirty P.M. Kathleen and the others finished off their drinks. The division bells began to ring again, and they could hear the members hurrying down the corridors in answer to its summons. The public – those who still remained in the rotunda – had been roped off from the corridors around the chamber, but most of those who had crowded the corridors of Parliament two hours earlier had given up and gone out into the wintry night. The chamber filled rapidly, members sniffing the air for reminders of the dark, nauseating gas. They took their seats, subdued as they gazed around at the empty galleries. Even the press gallery was vacant; the newspeople would have to watch the vote on television from the Press Club's amphitheatre across the road. The only gallery in use was the official's gallery; there, aides, staff members and department officials had returned to be ready for a summons, awaiting the outcome of the vote.

As soon as the House was filled, the business began and the aye votes were called. Kathleen stood, made her perfunctory bow to the Speaker, and resumed her seat, as the Deputy Clerk intoned: "Miss Marshal." Then she watched the remaining aye voters rise, one by one, to bow to the Speaker, to be recognized by the Deputy Clerk, to be recorded on the long tally sheets. Up, down, up, down, up, down – like so many dominoes, she thought. Liberal supporters were called first; then the Conservatives, led by Richard Sherwood, who smiled at her as he sat down; then the NDP, following their leader, who had bobbed up and down in his customary jerky style; lastly two young SoCred members.

Suddenly she realized that she had forgotten to keep her

own tally and would not know who had won until the Clerk announced the official tabulation. She could not catch the eye of Bonnie Costello and the impassive faces in the officials' gallery gave no hint of how it was going.

When the nays were called, Jacques was the first to rise. There was a hush: such confrontations between members of the same Cabinet were rare. As Jacques moved his chair to stand, Kathleen noticed to her surprise that Hume Frazier was not in his place beside Jacques. He had not voted on the amendment! He had absented himself – ducked out – when the final bells began to ring.

Curiouser and curiouser, thought Kathleen, but forgot the matter as she watched the Liberal nays, the Conservatives, then the SoCreds and one Independent at the far end of the chamber.

Every head in the room was now turned towards the Clerk's table. The Clerk was carefully totalling the results. Then he stood, and in a flat, neutral voice, announced:

"The ayes: one hundred and thirty. The nays: one hundred and twenty-three. The bill carries."

The Clerk's tally was followed by the Speaker's announcement. "I declare the motion carried."

A clerk assistant bobbed up. "Third reading of this bill."

Whatever he said after that could not be heard. Members streamed towards Kathleen from all parts of the House. Bob Northcutt was pounding her on the back.

"We did it, we did it! Oh, Katie, we did it! We lost a few, but we made it."

Bonnie Costello launched herself at Kathleen, kissing and squeezing her, followed by Mary Margaret McMahon, a west-coast Liberal backbencher. Others who had voted aye pressed close. And wedging through them came the arm of Richard Sherwood, the Leader of the Official Opposition.

"Congratulations, Kathleen, it was close." As she bent forward to hear his words, her eyes locked with those of the Prime Minister.

Jean Jacques Charles was standing, his papers gathered

under his arm, coldly staring at her. His face twitched and the veins at his temples stood out like knotted ropes. For a moment he stood, glaring at her; then he turned and stode swiftly away.

Chapter Three

.

"Kathleen. Oh, Kathleen, I must talk to you. Can you come over?"

Kathleen struggled to wake up. The insistent ring of the telephone had dragged her from a deep sleep.

"Evangeline? Is that you, Angel?"

"Kathleen, I'm so afraid. Jacques and I fought all night. He just doesn't understand how terrified I am. I *am* going to die, I know it, I am. Oh, Kathleen, please come."

Kathleen threw off her covers and sat up, alarmed by the tone of Evangeline's voice.

"Evangeline, what's wrong? Are you alone? My dear, of course I'll come. I'll be there as quickly as I can. Go wash your face and calm down. And stop such silly talk. Of course you're not going to die. I'll be there in half an hour. Better order us some coffee."

"Thank you, *chérie*. Please hurry, I'm so frightened. I must talk to you. Hurry, please."

Kathleen hung up the receiver and pulled her robe around her shoulders. The room was cold, the way she liked it while sleeping, and as her toes found her slippers beside the queen-sized bed, she shivered. She pulled back the overdrapes and the pristine white sheers billowed into the room, spilling brilliant sunlight from their folds.

The night-long storm had ended and the sky was a startling blue. She caught the dripping sound of melting icicles and thought that it must be late. But the bedside clock said only ten minutes after nine; Evangeline must have called as soon as Jacques had left for the office.

41

As she dressed, Kathleen tried to imagine what could have happened. Evangeline was usually so optimistic and cheery. And Jacques, whose temper was famous in Parliament, seemed invariably gentle with her, able, with at least this one person, to restrain his temper.

Kathleen took a quick look round the apartment, found her handbag and car keys, then was out the door and standing in the hall, waiting for the elevator. Soon she was driving her rented Ford up the wet incline from the garage into dazzling sunlight. She turned right and across to Elgin Street. Up Elgin to the War Memorial, right in front of the Chateau Laurier, then a left on Sussex. The streets had already been ploughed, and the drains were rushing with water. But the sidewalks were as yet untouched, and all along the way, she had to be careful to avoid splashing slush on pedestrians struggling through the drifts.

The whole city was covered in a sparkling new blanket of white. Kathleen rolled down her window and filled her lungs deeply. This was the kind of weather she loved in Ottawa, the occasional half-dozen sparkling sunny days that almost made up for the rest – the snow, the fog, the rain, the summer's humid heat. The cold air made her feel suddenly fresh and alive, as if the exhausting toll of the past few years had been suddenly wiped away. Driving slowly through the cold white city, sun glaring on the windshield, everything was forgotten.

And then she arrived at 24 Sussex Drive, wheeling the car past the low sentry gates and up the shallow curving drive in front of the stone mansion. She parked the car to the north of the Prime Minister's residence, leaving the keys in the switch for convenience. Striding to the front entrance, she smiled and called a good morning to the alert young Mountie stationed there.

"Madame Charles is expecting me," she explained to the carrot-topped maid in black and white uniform who answered her ring. The maid took her coat, and led her up the curving stairs from the public area to the private family quarters. She left her in the sitting room, where a fresh fire had been laid but not yet lit, to announce Kathleen to her mistress.

In a moment a barefoot Evangeline, still in a nightie and matching robe, flew to her, wrapping her arms around Kathleen and burying her face on the taller woman's bosom.

"Oh, *chérie*, you've come, you've come. I knew you would."

Kathleen looked down at the crown of tangled, tawny hair and put up her hand to smooth it. Although she was not much older than Evangeline, she had always felt protective of her. Kathleen could feel the trembling of the slight body and, as Evangeline looked up at her, was shocked to see how the strain had aged her. The great topaz eyes swam with tears which spilled down the wan face. Below her eyes were violet shadows as vivid as bruises. The full pink lips were torn, as though gnawed. As Evangeline fought to hold back more tears, she pushed back the thick hanks of long gold-brown hair that fell over her face. Like a child, she wiped her eyes with the backs of her hands.

"Sit here, Kathleen, by me."

Evangeline tucked herself into the corner of the pale yellow linen-covered sofa, and held out her hands to Kathleen. The older woman sat beside her, clasping the cold slender hands in her own broader, squarer ones.

"Now, Angel, what's all this fear of dying? Start anywhere you like. Unless I know what's bothering you so terribly, I can't be of much use, can I? Let's get some coffee and light the fire. You haven't even put on your slippers. You must be freezing." She pulled a yellow mohair throw from the arm of a rocking chair at the fireside edge and placed it over Evangeline's lap and legs.

Evangeline tucked the robe around herself. "Coffee, yes. Just pull that bell-strap and Marilou will bring it up. I asked her to have it ready. And yes, please, do light the fire. It's cozier."

By the time the kindling had started to burn, the maid had entered. She threw a delicately embroidered cloth over a small coffee table, and placed the heavy silver tray with its gleaming coffee service before them. Marilou poured her mistress's coffee in the French style: two streams, one of hot milk and the other of coffee, splashed into the translucent Beleek cup.

43

"Just plain black for me, please, Marilou. No milk, no cream, no sugar." The maid passed Kathleen the white cup and saucer and one of the initialed napkins, then left the room.

"Kathleen, I just don't know where to start. Jacques and I have been arguing all night. I've been half out of my mind. This morning he left the house without even speaking to me; and he hasn't called. I haven't slept at all. I don't know what to do or where to turn. Forgive me for dragging you into this, but there's no one else I can talk to."

"Now, Angel, don't worry about dragging me into things. Isn't that what friends are for? But what's wrong? What's happened?"

Evangeline sipped from the delicate white cup, then leaned forward to put it down. She sat back, pushing her long hair behind her shoulders.

"Kathleen, you've never been married, I know. Forgive me – I don't mean to pry – but have you ever been pregnant?"

"No, I haven't," Kathleen answered, puzzled by the question. "Angel, you're not pregnant, are you?"

"Yes, I am," Evangeline said softly.

Kathleen's thoughts raced, putting together the complaints of sickness, the violet shadows beneath her eyes.

"Are you sure? Have you seen a doctor? Does Jacques know?"

"Yes, yes. I have seen a doctor. Though I put it off for weeks. And Jacques does know. That's what we were arguing about all night. I told him last night when he came home."

"But why should you argue about such happy news? I thought Jacques would be delighted to have children. He seems so good with them."

"Kathleen, it isn't Jacques who doesn't want a baby – it's me. Do you know how old I am? We were married just after my fortieth birthday. I'm forty-two now – that's old to have a child. The statistics are against it. The babies are often not healthy. Did you know that?"

Listening to her friend, Kathleen felt torn by different emotions and memories. Of course, she knew what the doctors said; when she had been in her forties, still unmarried, she had read reports on late childbearing with a kind of morbid fascination. And yet she knew that since then it had become both common and fashionable for women to have their first child after their careers had been established.

"I know it's a little bit riskier, but lots of women have children at your age. And, Angel, you can have the very best doctors. What do they say?"

Evangeline took a sip of coffee. "I wish it was that easy, Kathleen. But my doctor is alarmed. He has sent me to two specialists. They agree: I should not try to have the child – or children really. Kathleen, they think I'm carrying twins! They said it would be dangerous for me, and perhaps even for the children. They advise an abortion."

"An abortion! Have you thought of seeing another doctor? You're still young; and your health seems perfect. And how disappointing for you – and for Jacques." Suddenly through her mind flashed Jacques' frozen glare of last night. No wonder they'd fought – if Evangeline had said she'd wanted an abortion.

"I told him last night that I was pregnant, and that I needed an abortion, and we argued and argued; but he is adamant. There will be no abortion, he says, ever. Kathleen, he was absolutely out of his mind. He paced the floor. He threatened me. He wouldn't listen, wouldn't try to understand how afraid I am. He mocked me – said I was useless to him if I wouldn't have children – said we were finished if I didn't go through with it. It was as if he was possessed. Kathleen, I don't want to lose him. I can't. But I'm terrified. I don't want to have a child. I know that if I do, I shall die. I know it, I know it." And she shuddered, fighting again for control, tears spilling down her cheeks.

"Jacques won't talk to my doctors. He says that they'll just tell him what I want them to say. He will *not* agree to an abortion. What shall I do? Tell, me Kathleen. Help me to find a way."

Now she was sobbing out of control. She dropped her face into her hands, the curtain of tawny hair swinging forward. Kathleen reached out to her and pulled her close, her arm around Evangeline's shoulders.

45

Her mind whirled. What advice could she offer? How could she intrude on something so personal between these two? Jacques was such a deeply private person. In all their years of friendship, he had rarely disclosed anything of his personal life. How would he react to the intrusion? And especially now, after last night! An abortion for his wife! What a grim joke that was. Surely it was the very last subject she could talk to him about. He would simply refuse to discuss it with her.

"Evangeline. Evangeline?"

"Yes, Kathleen."

"Now look, Angel, you're a long way over twenty-one. Jacques can't stop you getting an abortion, not if you really want to. It's your body, not his. If the doctors are really alarmed, there's no problem. I can put you in touch with people who will help. Or your own doctor will arrange it. All you have to do is give him the word. You needn't even tell Jacques until it's over. He'll get over it, you'll see." But the doubt in Kathleen's voice betrayed her words.

"But I couldn't do that. He knows now, and he wants the children. And he was so insistent. How could I ignore his feelings? How could I hurt him? And yet I'm so afraid."

Kathleen took a cigarette from the porcelain box on the table. It was so unlike Evangeline to be fearful of anything.

"Angel, you are sure you'll die if you have this baby – babies? Did your doctors tell you that? Is that where you got this idea?"

"No. They just said it would be dangerous. But I keep having a dream – a nightmare really, a terrifying nightmare that's been haunting me for over twenty years. I've always known that I will die if I attempt to have a child."

"Ah," said Kathleen, snatching at a glimmer of an idea. "Then it's not medical advice, but only a dream. Perhaps if you were to see a different kind of doctor?"

"A psychiatrist, you mean? Oh, Kathleen, I'm sorry I'm being so melodramatic. You must think I'm crazy. But I'm not. There's nothing a psychiatrist could do, or even a priest. I've had the same dream, over and over and over and over. I *know* that I will die." She looked at Kathleen, her bright eyes wet with tears.

46

"How do you *know*?"

Evangeline, in a gesture reminiscent of her husband, shrugged. She bent to pour herself another cup of coffee. She seemed suddenly evasive, unwilling to meet Kathleen's eyes. Kathleen, following an instinct that had served her well throughout her years in court as counsel, let the silence deepen, waiting for Evangeline to fill the void.

"There's something else," Evangeline finally said.

Kathleen waited.

"Look, there's something only the doctors know. I've never told anyone else – not even Jacques. Do you promise not to tell him?"

"I promise," Kathleen murmured.

Evangeline stood up, shook her rumpled nightclothes down around her slender body, pushed her hair back from her face. Then she moved to a brightly painted rocking chair beside the hearth. She sank into it and lifted her bare feet toward the warmth of the fire.

"Kathleen, sit across from me, where I can see you. Maybe what I have to tell you will help to explain. And I promise not to let myself go again."

Kathleen took the facing armchair – the one she had so often seen Jacques occupy. This was his chair, the place where he settled with his wife for a private, pre-dinner glass of wine to exchange news of their days apart. Sometimes he had sat here, by the fire, reading, and she had caught his loving glance resting on Evangeline where the two women were engrossed in a game of backgammon at the nearby cardtable. When their glances had met, he had smiled over his reading glasses at Kathleen, happy that his wife and his political colleague had become such fast friends. He had counted on her, Kathleen knew, to ease Evangeline into her public role in Ottawa and in the country, leading her through the labyrinth of protocol, giving her thumbnail sketches of political leaders, helping her to avoid political pratfalls in this, her new country.

Evangeline had been so eager to learn, to be the perfect wife, that both husband and friend found it a joy to indulge her. She was so beautiful, so warm and sweet and unaffected –

no wonder the country had fallen in love with her, as she had with it.

In this room they had been truly happy. Long hours of talk and laughter had been passed here. Often they had eaten in front of the fire, while listening to music from Evangeline's huge collection. What Jacques and Kathleen loved most to hear were Evangeline's own recordings – the folksongs and country music of Acadia which had brought her an international following and made her wealthy in her own right.

"Kathleen, you're not paying attention, and I want to tell you something. Please listen."

"I was just remembering the lovely times we've had here together. It's odd, but I don't remember nearly as many happy times when I lived here alone, as prime minister. I'm sorry. Please go on."

Evangeline leaned forward and began. "You know I was born in Louisiana, in the bayou country, of Acadian stock – Cajuns, they call us. We were poor, but I don't think I really noticed it. The country is so beautiful – on a tributary of the Mississippi – oak and cypress and Spanish moss, flowers and meadows and slow-moving dark water. Dirt roads and oxen and horses. Not much different, I suppose, from the way it looked when my ancestors found their way there by boat after *le grand dérangement* in the mid-1700's. I really *am* of Acadian descent, and my name really *is* Evangeline, you know. That's probably why I love Nova Scotia, the early home of my people, so much." Her voice trailed off. She got up from her chair and poured herself more coffee, then looked at Kathleen as if she was about to confess the utterly unthinkable and began again.

"I was married at fourteen, to a neighbour's boy. He was tall with silky skin and long, sleek muscles. His name was Lajeunesse – like Evangeline's Gabriel in Longellow's poem. He was sixteen, and I was crazy about him and his curly black hair and big grin. He had a job driving a beat-up old truck, and one night the brakes failed and he went over a bridge. It was two days before anybody thought to come and tell me. And then I found out I was pregnant. I didn't have a penny. I had nowhere to go, nobody to stay with. So I did what anybody in that situation did – I had an abortion. A cheap abortion, done as a favour by an old Creole woman. It turned out badly, and I nearly bled to death. It was months before I was back on my feet, and I've never really been right – down there – since. Otherwise I've always been healthy. You've got to be, to survive. I took a job wherever I could get one, and learned to pick the guitar and play the songs of my people. My voice is nothing special, but it suits the songs I sing. I've been playing professionally for over half my lifetime now, but it was only six or eight years ago that my career really took off."

She paused for a moment and then straightened her shoulders.

"People think I'm just a cream-puff – a nice, gentle girl. But I'm not, Kathleen. After a life like mine, you get tough. It's a dirty business sometimes, as, I guess, politics is. And it's no place for a weakling. But I liked it. I'm a survivor, like the rest of the Acadians. I never expected to give it all up, until I met Jacques.

"I knew what I was doing when I left the entertainment business to marry Canada's Prime Minister. I knew that the marriage had to work. I would ruin his political life if I left him. I wanted it to be a good marriage. And for two years, it has been. I have been so happy with him – until now. I love him so much, and I won't hurt him, no matter what it costs me. If he won't let me have an abortion, I think I shouldn't; or I would be going back on my own promise – not so much to him as to myself. And if I die . . . "

"Angel, why do you keep saying you're going to die?"

"Ever since I had that abortion, I've had this dream that keeps coming back. In it, I'm in childbirth, writhing and screaming. The black angel of death is standing there with his dark wings spread out over me. He has ridiculous ruby red eyes and white teeth, and he keeps calling to me. I always wake up screaming. Sometimes my shouts have wakened Jacques, but I've never told him what the nightmare is. And now I am afraid to sleep, because the dream comes so often."

"After all this time, you still haven't told Jacques? Why don't

you? It will help him to understand. He wasn't always so adamant about abortions. After all, it was Jacques who introduced legislation to permit legal therapeutic abortions. The
last two years have closed his mind. We had quite an ugly
scene about it not many months ago, and he seemed very bitter last night when the abortion bill was passed."

"Oh, Kathleen, it passed? Last night? Oh, what a fool I am!
I've been so distraught these last few days I had no idea it had
come to a vote. No wonder Jacques was late, and so cold to me
when he came home. And I had to choose last night to tell him
about my condition! How could I have been so stupid?"

"Now calm down, Evangeline. Where is that tough little lady
you were telling me about a minute ago? Jacques would have
no reason to believe that you chose last evening to tell him just
to grind his defeat in the House in his face. Don't be silly! He
knows you better than that. He loves you, and he knows how
deeply you love him."

Evangeline, who had started to cry again, now wiped her
face. "Kathleen, he has been very curt whenever I mentioned
you these last few months, and he always says he has work to
do when I want to invite you over. Is there trouble between
you?"

"Only over the abortion bill. He was truly angry last night,
but then, you know, these things blow over. Usually," she added. "But it means that he'd probably refuse to discuss an abortion with me, at least right now." As she talked Kathleen
began to wonder if she would, after all, have the courage to
confront Jacques about his wife. "How far along is the
pregnancy? Can you afford to wait a few weeks?"

"No. The doctors say that if there is to be an abortion it must
be done now."

"You know, I really don't understand Jacques' adamancy
and his sudden change from pro to con on the abortion issue.
Is it because of Church dictum, or is it something more personal to him. Do you know?"

Evangeline lifted her head: the topaz eyes were troubled,
and a frown drew the thick, pale brows together.

"Yes, I think I know, but I doubt that anyone else alive does.

The Church is very important to Jacques, you know. I suppose it was the influence of his mother, who was, at least in Jacques' account, next to a saint. She died just after we met, but they were very close. She had a powerful faith. I am not sure that I should disclose his secrets, Kathleen."

She paused, took a deep breath, and then slowly continued: "Jacques was one of twins. When he was born, his sister – Adèle, I think – was stillborn. And his mother lay near death for months. Her doctors had advised her not to have the twins. It was late in her life, and her other children were all grown and no longer even living at home. Jacques' father agreed there should be an abortion, but she defied him and the doctors and went ahead with the pregnancy. She didn't tell Jacques about it until just before she died. She said that if she had listened to the doctors, he would never have been born. She told him that he must never . . . "

Evangeline's voice was stilled. Her eyes widened in alarm. Kathleen whirled in her chair, following the direction of Evangeline's stare. At the door of the sitting room stood Jacques – a Jacques she had never before seen. His eyes were slits. They glittered from a white mask, the mouth working grotesquely. He was breathing in shallow gulps, fighting for self-control.

Jacques took several steps into the room, then stopped almost between them, staring first at one woman and then at the other. He held his arms rigidly at his sides, and spoke first to Kathleen, who recoiled at the venom of his voice.

"Well, if it isn't my longtime friend and colleague, the Honourable Kathleen Marshal, herself. Or no – forgive me, *madame*," and he made a derisory bow, "that should be the Right Honourable Madam, not to forget you were once allowed to play at being prime minister. Tell me, Right Honourable Madam, what are you doing in my house, closeted with my wife, who, as you can see, is ill and half out of her mind?"

Kathleen stood up. She was mystified by the cutting sarcasm, unsure how to, or whether to, reply.

Jacques turned to his wife, and said coldly: "You should get

51

back to bed. Look at you. You're upset." Then to Kathleen: "You'd better go now. As you can see, Evangeline is not herself. If she were, she would never have disclosed such private matters to you. Please go now."

"But, Jacques, I asked Kathleen to come."

"Be quiet, Evangeline."

Kathleen intervened, trying to maintain a reasonable tone. "Jacques, she has just told me that she's pregnant. A woman likes to share such news with another woman, and you know Evangeline has no other women friends in Ottawa."

Jacques rejoined, in an even voice: "She has me. That's all she needs."

"But that is just not true," she argued, "or she would not have invited me here this morning. You know how deeply troubled she is about this pregnancy. And from what she tells me, her doctors agree that she is in danger. Won't you even discuss it with her – reconsider a therapeutic abortion?"

"No."

"But, Jacques, you could be risking her life. Surely you'll at least see her doctors?"

"No. And stop interfering, Kathleen. It's none of your business. I won't discuss it with you."

He turned back to Evangeline: "Now, my dear, I'm sure we can settle this problem without bringing outsiders . . . "

"But, Jacques, it's Kathleen." Evangeline moved towards him and grasped his arm pleadingly.

"Especially Kathleen. I know already what she thinks about abortions. If you left it up to her, no woman would ever have a child. I won't have her poisoning your mind."

"Jacques, that is totally unfair," protested his Minister of Justice.

"Unfair, is it?" His anger came flooding back, his voice rising. Jean Jacques Charles didn't like to argue, and he didn't like to be crossed once he had made up his mind. "I have already asked you once to leave. Now, I'm telling you: Get out. Isn't it enough that you have defied me in public, divided the party and the country and threatened the life of my

Government? What kind of viper are you, to come crawling into my house to poison my wife's mind with your blasphemous ideas about abortion? You are corruption itself, destroying everything you touch! And I have had enough of you."

He put his arm around Evangeline, drawing her closer. To Kathleen he said, "I want you out of this house, and at once. I want you to have nothing more to do with my wife."

Evangeline started to interrupt, to break into his tirade. He grasped her other shoulder and whirled her around to face him. "You are never to see this woman again. You will not have her here in this house, you will not meet her elsewhere, you will not talk to her by telephone. You must swear never to have contact with her again. She is evil. She has poisoned my Government, and I will not permit her to poison our marriage. Do you swear?" He stood over his wife, the knuckles of his fists clenched white, his face thrust forward into her face. "Do you?"

"What are you doing?" Evangeline's face was in her hands. She was shuddering, unable to look at Jacques.

He swung back to Kathleen. "And are you still here? Why? I am not speaking in French; I am speaking in the plainest English. Get out, you bitch, and do not come back! You goddamn poisonous stupid bitch. Go on. Get out right now."

"Jacques, I –" Kathleen was in a state of stock. She had never seen anyone so consumed with rage. He had totally abandoned himself to his anger. Its aura seemed to shimmer around him.

"Will – you – go?" He forced the words out between his gritted teeth.

Kathleen moved towards the door. "Of course, I'll go, and I'll go now, if you will just get the hell out of my way."

He stepped back, with a sudden mocking bow.

She placed her hand on Evangeline's shoulder, murmuring, "Be brave, I'll be in touch."

"What did you say?" He howled in a new burst of rage. "Be in touch? Oh no, you won't. You stay away from my wife, you hear? I mean it! And stay away from me. I hope I never see your face or hear your voice again. You are fired from my Cabinet! As of now, you are no longer my Minister of Justice. You're finished, you damned meddler. Get out! Out of my life, out of my wife's life, and out of Ottawa and my Government. Go and peddle your bloody abortions somewhere else."

Chapter Four

Shocked by Jacques' outburst, Kathleen stumbled into her car and, without conscious direction, drove the familiar way to the Parliament Buildings. There, she parked her car and walked up the stairs from the members' entrance to her office suite. She met no one, nor did she notice the commissionaire's salute. It was Friday afternoon. Many of the parliamentarians had already left for the weekend; and those whose designated House Day it was would sit restlessly through the next few hours until the five o'clock adjournment, paying scant attention to the debate before the House, their thoughts already occupied with weekend plans.

Kathleen, unwilling to face anyone who might be waiting in the ante-room, entered her private office through the locked door off the public corridor. In the aftermath of last night's vote, she had purposely left today without appointments. But this afternoon she didn't want to run into anyone by surprise, especially someone from the press.

She pressed the buzzer to summon Barbara.

"Will you ask Gordon to come in, too, please. And we won't want to be disturbed, Barbara, so ask someone else to take any calls. I'd rather no one knew I was here."

As she waited for her two closest aides to join her, Kathleen felt suddenly sad and alone. She took out a sheet of her private stationery and quickly scribbled a letter of resignation. Then, sitting back in her chair in the big office, she thought about Barbara Hepburn and Gordon Neville, and the debt that she owed them.

Barbara had come to her rescue not long after Kathleen's first election. As a freshman M.P., Kathleen's office had been near chaos – the muddle only made worse by the succession of girls – and they *were* girls, not women – the Whip had sent her to try out as her secretary. Some knew no shorthand, some had no organizational ability and all were hopelessly incapable of turning out literate, legible letters in the volume required by Kathleen's already-swelling correspondence. And, of course, they all hated to do filing. For the most part, in fact, they had been cast-offs from other members who had seized the chance to get rid of unsatisfactory staff.

But Barbara had been perfect. Miraculously, the files were in order, the correspondence caught up, the phone messages neatly written. Barbara's efficiency delighted Kathleen. And the young woman's dark beauty had attracted the attention of some of her colleagues, who had buzzed about Barbara like flies after honey. But Barbara, too sensible and discreet for such games, kept her own counsel, and held the members at bay with a laugh and a quip.

And Barbara Hepburn had become a friend – a woman friend Kathleen had badly needed. When she had first been elected to Parliament, both Houses were dominated by men. There were only three other women members – one a member of the Cabinet – and otherwise women held no staff jobs except those of typist or translator. Kathleen and Barbara had hit it off from the very first and their friendship had continued to grow. The curly-haired secretary had stayed with Kathleen after she was appointed to the Cabinet, and ever since, during her short term as caretaker prime minister, and for the six years since, the last two of which she had spent as Minister of Justice.

Her association with Gordon was not quite so close, nor of such long standing. But Gordon, too, had worked his own brand of miracle when she had taken him on as her executive assistant. One of Alexander Sinclair's staffers, he had come to her after Sinclair's death to ask for a chance to make a career step-up. Gordon, despite his ambition, had proved to have sound and cautious political judgement, combined with a swift grasp of policy options. Despite his despairing wife's objections, he worked long hours, was somehow prepared for every crisis, and even professed to love his job.

"Barbara, Gordon, I'll have to start with the bad news. The Prime Minister has demanded my resignation, effective immediately. Of course I must comply. Here I have a draft of my letter. Take a look at it, please, Gordon."

He took the extended paper. On it was written, in an agitated scrawl quite unlike Kathleen's usual forceful handwriting: "Prime Minister: In accordance with your request, I hereby tender my resignation as Minister of Justice and Attorney-General of Canada, effective today."

Gordon slowly took off his reading glasses and looked at her across the desk. "Is that all, Minister? It's pretty bald. The press will be hounding us for the background on this. Is there anything else I can tell them?"

"No. It's plain enough. The Prime Minister has fired me. If they want a detailed explanation, they can go to him. In fact, if he gives them a reason, I'd be curious to know what it is. I also have to send a note to the Governor General. That's protocol, part of the fiction that a minister is one of Her Majesty's Canadian advisors, holding office through her representative, the Governor General. Please draw up a formal resignation – no reasons – just a one-line affair. And then have Barbara type it up for my signature. Please do that yourself, Barbara. I want no premature leaks. Gordon, we'll need a short press release. Attach copies of the two letters. I'll write a personal note to Their Excellencies, since the *pro forma* resignation is so curt."

"But what will you do now?" blurted out Barbara.

"This weekend, I think that I'll go down to Toronto. You can make the plane reservation for this evening. Leave the return date open. I am not resigning as a member – not while there's a minority government. I'll hang on until the next election, whenever that may be. However, I'll have to move to a smaller office as soon as the P.M. appoints a new minister – I'll bet it will be Findlay, damn it – so while I'm away, you'll have your hands full, putting my personal things together. Be especially careful not to leave my correspondence files on abortion. If they should fall into Findlay's hands, they could compromise a lot of people.

"Now," Kathleen said, looking at Gordon and Barbara for the first time, and grinning, "about your jobs. For as long as I'm here, I hope you'll both stay with me. But since the election could be anytime, I think you should start looking around for new, permanent assignments. In all likelihood, I will go back to practising law, and I won't be able to afford your salaries. If an attractive offer comes up before I leave, I won't expect you to stay on. I know that my former colleagues will scramble to hire you, as soon as they hear that you are free."

Despite everything that had happened, Kathleen felt as if somehow she had failed them and should have somehow done things better.

"No long faces now! Barbara, please bring in the letters when they are ready for signature. Meantime, I'll write that note to the Governor General. And Barbara, see if you can get Mr. Wickstrom on the phone. You'll probably find him in his Toronto office."

Barbara left her chair and came around the desk. She kissed Kathleen's cheek, wordlessly, then left the office. Gordon stood awkwardly, reluctant to leave without some indication of his personal distress.

"Well, Gordon, it isn't the end of the world, you know. I've been anxious to leave Parliament for seven years, even if I foolishly let myself be talked into staying. It will be a relief, when I get used to the idea, to be a private citizen again.

"Now let me have the letters and the draft release as soon as possible. I'd like to get them delivered to the press before six."

Alone again in the office, Kathleen sat thinking for a moment, her hand on the telephone receiver. Then she flipped through the desk directory and placed a call to the Prime Minister's private number, herself. She asked for Jacques, identifying herself to the answering voice. There was a pause, then, in an embarrassed voice, the young woman reported that the Prime Minister had left for the day and could not be reached. But she did offer the information that a senior aide was standing by to transmit Kathleen's expected formal letter of resignation to the Prime Minister.

Even in the Friday night crowd at the airport in Toronto, Andrew Wickstrom was easy to spot. Well over six feet, with a black hat and a wide, smiling face, he was, to Kathleen, like a reassuring image out of Canada's past. Years ago, when she had first met him, he had lived in Winnipeg, and she still saw him as a rangy, easy-going man from the prairies.

As they drove out of the airport, Kathleen watched Andrew's hands on the wheel of his Cadillac Seville. Square and strong, quietly capable, they symbolized everything that attracted her to him.

"Andrew, Jacques gave me my walking papers today."

This as they were turning from the airport road onto the crowded highway that streamed traffic into the city.

"What happened? Did you have a fight about the abortion bill?"

"It was partly that." She smiled to herself in the dark car. It was like Andrew, a newspaper publisher, to see politicians as a bunch of children whose disagreements could be ironed out by common sense and, at worst, a firm spanking.

"He was in a terrible temper," she added.

"Have you talked to him since?"

"I tried to phone him."

"What happened?"

The secretary's embarrassment that had seemed so galling in Ottawa was only faintly comical now.

"Nothing much," Kathleen said. "He said he wasn't home."

As they left the highway and started down Avenue Road, on the way to the Park Plaza – Kathleen's favourite hotel since her days as a university student – Andrew asked Kathleen more questions and, gradually, she told him the whole story of her conversation with Evangeline, and Jacques' discovery of them. As she talked, Kathleen watched Andrew. His face showed almost nothing of his reaction. He nodded from time to time, swung the heavy car through the traffic, sometimes shook his head in sympathy. And then they were at the hotel.

"You want to come in for a drink?"

"Of course," Andrew said. He turned to her and suddenly Kathleen felt the strain of the past days undermine her resolve and, burying her face in Andrew's coat, she started to cry.

On Saturday afternoon, hidden away from the press in the comfort and security of Andrew's Rosedale home, Kathleen read the weekend papers. They were filled with speculation about her firing, and the way it had directly followed the passage of her abortion bill. There were pages of pictures of Jacques and Kathleen. Their early careers and their rise to prominence were recounted. Articles rehashed the events that followed Sandy Sinclair's sudden death, when the Liberal Cabinet and caucus had chosen her – the one senior Cabinet minister who did not aspire to the newly vacant leadership – to lead the country until a new leader might be elected.

Not only had she been the first woman ever to be prime minister in Canada – only the third in the Commonwealth – but she had also been at the centre of party workings for most of the last decade. One admiring columnist wrote, "She was Jacques' most valuable ally: a tough, independent woman with guts and courage, a fighter who had won most of her parliamentary battles. Now he has fired her without comment. Is there any explanation he dares give? Or are there more dark secrets buried in the Cabinet minutes?"

There were even pictures of her at Christmastime at Harrington Lake, the Prime Minister's retreat in the Gatineau Hills.

Sitting in Andrew's house, away from Ottawa, the pictures brought back memories of a beautiful interlude she had spent in the rambling, refurbished old farm house.

It had been her own, private, special Christmas holiday. Every morning she had slept late in the high, four-poster bed, its crisp white sheets warmed by strategically placed hot-water bottles. Each morning she awoke to the aroma of hot strong coffee and the sight of freshly squeezed orange juice in a long-stemmed goblet placed on a tray beside the flames of a fresh log fire.

The balance of the morning was spent in reading the despatches and briefing books that no head of government can escape for long, and after lunch at the long trestle table in the windowed alcove of the beam-ceilinged, rustically furnished living room, she turned again to work. In the late afternoon there was time for a tramp along the edge of the lake, breathing deeply the sharp, pure air, and then an early dinner.

Kathleen rarely had company in the evenings that week but she wasn't conscious of being lonely. She liked the unaccustomed privacy, and she knew there were security people near by at all times. If she put down her book or her knitting to gaze out through the large windows, she might catch sight of a guard as he patrolled in the night, or hear a low whistle to the great black dogs who shared his guard duty.

She filled the silent rooms with soaring music, and sometimes, during a break while another record dropped into place, she heard the young Mounties moving about the big, bare kitchen. She could catch the rumble of their voices as they talked quietly, warming stiff fingers and cold toes, cupping great mugs of coffee or hot chocolate.

Restless on a night made brilliant by the full moon, she surprised two of the young men in the kitchen. Their padded jackets had been laid aside, and they were tilting back in the kitchen chairs, sipping coffee.

"Corporal, I have a request to make. I want you to take me for a ride on the snowmobile. Just for an hour or so, around the fields. The night is so beautiful, I'd like to be a part of it."

"Ma'am, I don't think we are supposed to do that. What if we had an accident out there, and you were hurt? I'd catch you-know-what for that."

But she coaxed him into ignoring his duty, and when he had reluctantly agreed, she left the room, returning in a moment in a zippered Inuit muskrat parka, high boots over thick socks, her hands in warm, furry mittens.

She had climbed aboard the snow machine, her arms around the Mountie's waist, and he had gunned the engine as they took off over powdery snow.

It was so cold the air seemed to crackle with the frost. She dipped her freezing face into the comfort of the fur framing the parka hood, and clung breathlessly to the sturdy young officer. They had flown over the rolling surface to the far end of the lake.

"Will you cut the motor for a minute? I want to listen to the silence." Across the snow came the sound of ice-laden branches creaking in the woods, and then a sharp crack as one fell, split off by the iron cold.

That peaceful week at Harrington Lake had punctuated the crammed schedule of Kathleen's five-month term as prime minister. There had been no time to make plans – the responsibility had been so suddenly laid upon her. She had, in fact, only weeks before his sudden death, gone to her leader, Alexander Sinclair, to tell him of her plans to resign. But she had been startled, once in his office, to see how his face had become drawn and furrowed, his hair thinner and much, much grayer. Sandy Sinclair had told her that he, too, wanted to retire, but that he felt it would be a dereliction of duty while the Government he led was a minority one.

"We'll talk about it, Kate. But please don't resign – not yet. It will be too difficult to replace you at the moment. The other women members need more seasoning. I'm just too tired to wrestle with their conflicting claims just now. Let's talk about it again, soon. There's lots of time."

But there had been no time for Sandy Sinclair: a fortnight later he had suffered a sudden and massive heart attack.

The House, next morning, was subdued when it met. After brief eulogies from the other party leaders, Parliament adjourned for a week.

Kathleen's responsibilities as Secretary of State in Sinclair's administration had included state funerals. The precedents were few: never before had a Canadian first minister died in office. The hasty arrangements were a blur in her mind: the repeated low roll of swathed drums, the streets cordoned by lines of soldiers, seamen and airmen. Wet-eyed people lining the sidewalks as the cortège rolled through. Ottawa draped in crepe. Sandy's red and white flag snapping in the golden October day of Indian summer, at half-mast. Another new Canadian flag draped across the simple coffin. The black cushions bearing Sinclair's medals and honours. A sense of mourning overtook the country. The people who had never granted him the mandate of a majority now appreciated him belatedly in death.

But the business of government had to go on. The Cabinet met under the chairmanship of the most senior of Sinclair's ministers, a long-time member who had contested Sandy for the leadership and lost. He declared that he would seek the leadership again. When it had become clear that most of the senior Cabinet were prepared to throw their hats into the ring, it was agreed that, to be fair, someone who did not intend to run should become the interim leader. The party had been unable to contract for convention space until early April, almost six months away.

It had been Jacques who had suggested Kathleen. There had been some hesitation while her colleagues considered the implications of choosing a woman as their interim leader. But it seemed the best solution, so they had presented their decision to the caucus, which had concurred.

On a gusty night while Hallowe'en goblins roamed the streets of Ottawa, Kathleen was sworn as Canada's first minister at Rideau Hall. Their Excellencies, the Governor General and his friendly, energetic wife, had tendered to Kathleen and the assembled members of the re-sworn Cabinet their condolences at Sandy's loss, and the Governor General had taken her aside for a few private minutes of congratulations and encouragement.

"My dear Kathleen, it is a heavy task you have taken on. I want you to know that you may call on me at any time for help. It's a very lonely job, and sometimes it helps to talk things over with someone above the political fray. That's what I'm here for. We will, of course, meet once a week so that you can keep me informed, just as the U.K.'s Prime Minister meets with Her Majesty. But feel free to come to me informally, as a friend." He paused, and then added wistfully, "Sandy popped over here often. Did you know we were friends from the time we were schoolboys? I'm going to miss him. And, Prime Minister . . . "

Kathleen started. That was the first time anyone had called her by her new title. The distinguished old diplomat noted her reaction, and smiled reassuringly.

"I was just going to say 'thank you,' on behalf of the country, for filling the gap in this crisis, just in case no one else remembers to. Now, shall we join the others?"

They had all sipped sherries, exchanged pleasantries, posed for the news photographers, and then Kathleen, surrounded now by security officers, stepped into the government limousine to return to her Metcalfe Street apartment.

Next day, she had presented her new Cabinet to the reassembled House. And that night, she spoke to the Canadian public through the national television networks. The nation had studied the tall woman with the grave, square face and imposing demeanour and their unease at being led by a woman had lessened.

But there was no discounting it – unease there was, in many quarters. Kathleen, lulled by her ready acceptance by the Cabinet and the Liberal caucus, had not anticipated it. Many opinion leaders were sceptical; some, downright hostile. For weeks, letters-to-the-editor columns were filled with strong-minded opinions as to whether a middle-aged spinster could possibly have the intelligence, the drive, the health, the judgement, to lead the country. Editorial writers struggled for objectivity. The columnists were divided. The issue, as all issues do, ultimately faded, but there was an uncomfortable undercurrent, nonetheless.

"Now, what about dinner? This is Saturday night, when a fellow is supposed to take his girl out to celebrate. Where do you want to go?"

They were sipping cocktails in Andrew's firelit study as the last rays of the weak March sunlight slanted through the drapes.

During the afternoon Kathleen had talked again about the scene when Jacques had fired her. And they had spoken about Evangeline, recalling her first introduction to the Ottawa scene, and the night when both of them had first been touched by a sense of wonder in their enjoyment of one another.

She was grateful that Andrew hadn't asked her, in so many words, what her plans were. She knew he was aware that they were still half-formed, and would be dependent upon how long the current Parliament would last. She also knew that, because of this, he hesitated to press his suit. It was up to her to signal when the time was ripe to talk of marriage; but when she did, she must be sure that she really wanted to leave public life for good.

A month ago, when they had very briefly discussed the idea of marriage, Andrew had made this clear.

"Kathleen, I have always avoided the public eye, and I have no taste for trotting after a wife in politics. I know I would resent playing second fiddle. When you are sure that politics is out of your system, then we'll make our plans. But first I want you to be absolutely certain."

But other than that simple statement, Andrew had exerted no pressure and given no ultimatums. He knew that she had to make up her own mind.

Kathleen had first met Andrew Wickstrom in Winnipeg. As interim prime minister, she had attended a series of Liberal fund-raising dinners held in Halifax, Montreal, Toronto, Winnipeg, Calgary, and Vancouver. The party officials had quickly put them together to provide the money needed to finance the leadership convention to come in the spring and to provide a platform where party regulars and the general public might assess the declared candidates.

At the reception following the dinner in Winnipeg, someone had brought up to her a very tall, burly man, with a train of three equally tall young people, who were introduced as his children.

"It is a very great pleasure to meet you, Madam. My unruly children" – and the three had exchanged impish grins – "insisted on meeting you. My daughter Ingrid, here, is a very fierce feminist, and she said we just had to meet Canada's first woman Prime Minister."

They had chatted briefly. She had not remembered the children's names, but an impression had remained with her of four pairs of startlingly similar, lake-blue eyes, and an easy, warm camaraderie among the siblings and their obviously proud father. But there were so many other people she met, in those crowded months, that it was hopeless to try to fix names and faces in her mind.

It was a month or so later that she encountered Andrew Wickstrom again, this time in Ottawa. To help keep the country on an even keel while it awaited its new leadership, Kathleen had instituted a series of dinners to which were invited groups of industrialists, businessmen, labour and ethnic leaders, publishers, editors and journalists of stature, scientists, academics, economists and thinkers. The dinners were held at the Prime Minister's residence at 24 Sussex Drive, on the bank of the Ottawa River, and across the road from Rideau Hall, the residence of Canada's governors general.

In the role of hostess, Kathleen had been at her best. Her guests found her relaxed, but attentive. The food was chosen with care, the flowers and table appointments perfect. Over cocktails and dinner, the conversation was very general, but after they had dined and withdrawn to the drawing room, as she served coffee and brandy, and cigars were passed, she brought the conversation around to a discussion of their special concerns. Her guests were eager to talk of public issues and to make their own suggestions. She listened intently, sometimes making a note. While she assessed her guests and their views, she knew they were also making judgements of her. Of course, the conversations were sometimes spirited. There were inevitable clashes of opinion, but she never allowed an evening to end in rancour.

Andrew Wickstrom had merely been a name on a guest-list for a dinner at which most of those invited were publishers. But when he arrived, Kathleen had remembered their previous meeting. Physical size alone would have made his a commanding presence, but it was obvious that many of the guests also deferred to his very definite opinions.

As they lounged against the stiff aqua brocade of the uncomfortable cushions in the formal drawing room, the other newspaper publishers urged Andrew to state their case. When he did so, his words were thoughtful and his ideas progressive. She liked him, and once or twice, turning her head unexpectedly, she found his eyes on her, appraisingly. His conduct was impeccable, but she had an intuitive feeling that his assessment of her was more personal than that of an opinion leader assessing his prime minister.

As she had bade goodnight to her departing guests, Andrew Wickstrom had dropped back from the knot of men shuffling into overcoats and rubbers. Over his shoulder, outside the open door, a line of gleaming limousines glided up for their passengers.

The Winnipeg publisher had taken her hands in his, dropped a light kiss on her brow, and murmured, "You're some woman, Kate Marshal."

She remembered that as she drifted to sleep, she had smiled at the memory of that unexpected human warmth. It was good to be seen as a human being, something other than a national monument. She had hugged the remembered moment for months afterwards.

"Kate, a penny for your thoughts. What are you smiling at? I am still waiting for your answer to my question. It is very hard to play the gallant when your lady doesn't pay you any attention," he complained, in mock-seriousness.

"Andrew, I'm sorry. I was thinking of our first meeting. Remember the dinner at Sussex Street?"

"Of course, I remember," Andrew replied. "But tonight's dinner is, I think, a more pressing problem."

"Dinner? Oh, no place very public, not tonight. Not even your club. There are bound to be inquisitive people around, probing for the inside dope."

"Well, I'm sure there must be steaks in the freezer. Mrs. Gorman usually leaves bowls and dishes of things in the fridge, in case I'm at home alone on Sundays. Shall we go exploring? Would you like that – dinner here, alone, with the old man?"

"Some old man!" As he reached to pull her from the chair, she went into his arms. "Oh, Andrew, I'm so lucky. What if I had never called you to take me to the Parliamentary Ball? You know, I nearly lost my nerve! What would I do, without you?" She lay her head in his cardiganed chest. He held her close, waiting. It could be now, Kathleen thought; we could talk about marriage now.

She lifted her face to his and kissed him lightly.

"Which way to the kitchen?"

As she busied herself, tearing crisped greens for a salad, slicing tender scallions and meaty radishes, mixing oil, pepper and salt with fresh lemon juice for dressing, heating the grill and nicking the fat edges of the defrosting steaks, sprinkling basil over the too-pale slices of winter tomatoes, tossing snow peas and mushrooms in light oil in the wok, Kathleen's thoughts revolved about that memorable night, when for her and, she had since learned, for Andrew, love had bloomed. That's a dated expression, she laughed to herself: Love in bloom! Wasn't it Jack Benny who used to play that tune on his violin? Well, old-fashioned or not, it was an evening that even in retrospect carried an afterglow of love.

It had been only two years ago, after the second election under Jacques' leadership, on the eve of the opening of the new minority Parliament.

"Jacques, I know you don't like unsolicited advice. As an old friend, and from my experience in leading a minority government before you were chosen leader, I would like to offer some thoughts. Do you mind?"

Jean Jacques Charles had suffered an unpleasant jolt. This second election had been entirely different from the first. Then he had simply danced away with the country. The press had called it "Doing the Charleston." Every move he made had seemed absolutely right. Out of a sense of experimentation, he had done some deliberately eyebrow-raising things during that campaign, and, when the mood was on him, continued to titillate the public with his unorthodox behaviour. It was more than just appearing in the House on occasion in sandals without socks and a scarf at his open throat, instead of the conventional tie. It was more than sliding down a banister in London while attending a meeting of heads of Commonwealth nations, and more than publicly dating a series of beautiful young women of the international set. He thumbed his nose in the House at an Opposition member who had irritated him with pressing questions. From the rolled-down window of his new, bullet-proof silver Cadillac, he told Quebec unionists, picketing the Hill: *"V'au diable!"* He outraged westerners by asking rhetorically, "Why should *I* sell your wheat?" Some said he had breached protocol by extending a holiday rather than being on hand to greet the Queen in her most recent tour of Canada.

He had always had his detractors. To him they were petty people, unimportant in the grand scheme of things. But the series of tiny shocks to the sometimes stuffy Canadian sense of propriety had weakened his support in the country. How much, he had absolutely no idea. He had surrounded himself, during his first administration, with many of the bright-eyed hopefuls who had managed his leadership campaign and the election upon which he had immediately launched. He assumed that they had a sense of what was happening in the country. Now he knew better. The first campaign had been a triumph, a personal triumph of his own style. The second had been disastrous. He knew that many observers of the Canadian political scene expected him to quit, assuming he would be unwilling to adjust himself to the changed conditions of a minority administration.

He had invited Kathleen to 24 Sussex for a swim and dinner one evening shortly after the election and they had a rare, serious talk over coffee after dinner.

"Kathleen, I know there will have to be changes. We'll have to be more careful – *I'll* have to be more careful. I promise to try to watch my tongue. But I'll be damned if I'll crawl to them. They can decide to support me, or to bring me down, I don't give a damn. But I'll try not to start trouble. Now go ahead, what did you want to say?" He sat back in his chair and looked at her intently.

"Jacques, I think you'll have to go further than that. You'll have to be more conciliatory, especially to the NDP. You can't continue to taunt them by saying that they are nobodies when they are off the Hill! They simply won't stand for it, and they'll vote you out of office at the first opportunity.

"You don't need to go overboard. Nobody expects you to grovel for support. But I think you should see the leaders of the

Opposition parties on a fairly regular basis – just butter them up a little by prior consultation. You don't have to pledge yourself to accept what they say, but you can *listen* to their ideas without compromising yourself." Kathleen paused to light a cigarette and then leaned forward and went on.

"Try to make yourself more accessible to the members. Not just to your own caucus, either. Get rid of that rigid band of advisors around you who keep access to you so buttoned-up. Cultivate a network of people across the country that you can talk over issues with. See a little more of your own Cabinet colleagues, together and separately. And, for God's sake, don't mock the people of the press so openly. You also might start meeting with the party people on a regular basis. They are the core of your support, whatever you think. If the organization people decide to stay home, you're finished. David Kirke, now, has a lifetime of experience in elections. You haven't even met once with him since you were named leader. I think that's a grave mistake. By disrupting the party's continuity, you are destroying the reasons that it has been in office for most of this century."

Jacques had listened, without interrupting her, but now he made an impatient gesture.

"Kathleen, you and Senator Kirke know the party and its people. I don't. And both of you know people you can discuss things with, right across the country. I don't. My best friends are Quebeckers. I don't have the same kind of network that Sinclair had, and there's no way now that I, as Prime Minister, can establish one. How do I know whose advice to trust? How do I know that they aren't just a lot of self-seekers? Aside from my colleagues from Quebec, I'm going to have to rely on you and some of the others. I see now that's a weakness. But I'm glad you agreed to stay on, when you wanted to go. Perhaps you'll bring Kirke by, sometime soon, and we'll start a new approach. Was there anything else?" He turned to pour more coffee.

"Maybe it's not very important, Jacques, but I have an idea that could serve to set a new tone for the incoming Parliament. We used to hold a dinner and a ball, at Rideau Hall, for all the new M.P.s and their wives. Traditionally it was held on the night before the opening of Parliament. I wish you would think about holding one this year. I'm sure Their Excellencies would approve, and the members would certainly be enthusiastic."

Jacques looked at her, considering the suggestion.

"If you like, I'll be glad to make the arrangements," Kathleen pressed on. "And the other party leaders should be involved right away. Makes them feel important. And we will certainly need their good will this session."

Kathleen had been surprised at his ready acceptance of the plan, and even more so when Jacques had insisted upon supervising the arrangements himself.

When the ball was but a week away, Kathleen suddenly realized that Jacques had not, as he usually did, asked her to act as his hostess at the function. Embarrassed, she had raised the question. Most uncharacteristically, he had hemmed and hawed before saying, "Umm, I've, ah, made my own plans, Kathleen. You are free to make other arrangements."

Kathleen had been irritated. What kind of "other arrangements," as he put it, was she likely to be able to make at this late date? There was one possibility – an old friend, now living in England, who had escorted her occasionally to formal affairs. But no, he was in Australia for six months and it was ridiculous to think of calling him to come. She really should ask someone, but who? She racked her memory, but no inspiration came.

Out of nowhere came the thought of Andrew Wickstrom. She hadn't seen him since that dinner, almost five years ago. And although she had watched for him at the leadership convention – half-hoping to run into him – he hadn't been there.

She wondered if she dared to ask him to take her? Wickstrom had been a widower, but she had no idea whether or not he had remarried. Remembering Wickstrom was from Winnipeg, Kathleen, on impulse, picked up the telephone and dialled the number of an old friend who lived there. But the friend was out, and Kathleen lost her nerve.

But the next day, she asked Barbara to try to find where

Andrew now lived. She was vague about the reason, letting her secretary assume Wickstrom was to be considered for some sort of an appointment. She suggested Barbara contact someone who could furnish a bio, including personal details, as soon as possible.

Before an hour had passed, Barbara came up with the information, including the home and office telephone numbers. "Widower: three children." There it was.

"How up-to-date is the information?"

Barbara explained: "I got them from the latest *Who's Who in Canada*. But I checked myself to get the phone numbers: Mr. Wickstrom now lives and works in Toronto, not Winnipeg."

All morning the memo sat on Kathleen's desk. From time to time she would pick it up, look at it, and set it down again.

Finally, she ordered a sandwich and a glass of milk for lunch at her desk, and tackled the draft legislation being prepared under her supervision – an omnibus bill containing substantial and highly controversial amendments to the Canadian Criminal Code.

On her return from lunch, the efficient Barbara noticed in the long-distance telephone log-book that no call had as yet been placed to Mr. Wickstrom. She stuck her head around the door to the inner office.

"Shall I place that call to Toronto now?" she asked.

"Um – yes, Barbara," Kathleen answered absently, not looking up. It was only when the connection had been put through that she realized that this was the call to Wickstrom.

At first the conversation went easily. Andrew said that he had followed her career through the media, and had hoped that they would run into one another again. He congratulated her on her new post as Justice minister. He chatted casually, waiting for her to come to the point. She, meanwhile, put it off, asking questions about his children and business. Until finally, so embarrassed that she could no longer make small talk, she did something she had long ago trained herself not to do – she blurted out the purpose of the call.

"Andrew, there is going to be a Parliamentary Ball next week, on Thursday evening. It is black tie. Dinner, too. Would you come with me?" There was a pause. Kathleen suddenly thought Barbara had made a mistake with the bio.

Then Andrew answered. "I've just been doing a little rearranging of my calendar, Kate. Yes, I am sure I can be there. What time shall I call for you, and where?"

When she hung up she realized she had forgotten to ask if he could dance. And then, without even thinking, she found herself buzzing the intercom.

"Barbara, will you phone my dressmaker and ask her for an urgent appointment. Maybe tonight, say after eight? And tell her I want something really special."

Rideau Hall, or Government House as it was often called, the stately stone residence behind the high fence that enclosed its acres of gardens and woods, glowed with welcome. Lights streamed from every window and soft strains of music drifted through the starry night. Among the trees, lanterns flickered; and beyond the portico, the long wands of light with which the Mounties directed traffic moved like giant lightning bugs. Past the sentries at the gate came automobiles of every description – gleaming limousines, battered taxis, dirt-spattered sedans – to proceed up the tree-lined drive and drop passengers under the *porte-cochère*. And from this mixed procession of vehicles descended freshly coiffed women in long gowns, their wraps clutched tight against the chilling breeze, and men in black or midnight-blue dinner clothes.

As each couple or group arrived, they were directed to the cloakrooms on either side of the massive entrance doors. On their return to the foyer, they were invited to sign the guest book to the left of the door, and then were led, by a uniformed aide in the household livery, up a short flight of marble stairs and then along a corridor of highly polished wood to the receiving line in the Governor General's study.

When Kathleen entered with Andrew, she saw heads turn towards them. Tonight, thought Kathleen smugly to herself, I look my very best. So let them stare. And Andrew, in his dinner clothes, is perfect. In the few available days, her dressmaker had done wonders. Kathleen wore a Grecian-style gown of heavy white silk which fell about her in queenly folds. It was unadorned except for her only really good jewellery – a fine string of medium size, creamy pearls. She carried a finely pleated white bag, and her evening slippers were of delustered white satin. On the bag was a single note of colour: a cluster of cream and yellow rosebuds – Andrew's gift. Her hair was dressed simply, pulled back softly from her face to a fat French knot low on her nape. To frame her face, loose tendrils had carefully been drawn from the smooth-brushed mass of shining black. She had protested to the hairdresser that it looked un-tidy. But he had assured her that it was the latest style. And it *was* becoming, softening her plain, regular features.

But it was Andrew, handsome and attentive, who made her feel that she couldn't stop smiling. From the moment he had appeared at her door, they had found themselves at ease, and by the time they had arrived at Rideau Hall, she could sense a spark glowing between them. And as they circulated through the crowd, she felt a new and quite special sensation – that of being part of a handsome and talked-about couple – a focus for the evening.

The guests had dined in splendour, the long tables aglow with a collection of silver candelabra, their graceful branches set with tall red candles. The length of the snowy napery was dotted with silver bowls of heavy-scented, white and red roses, and the carved crystal stemware spangled lights into the depths of the deep red and pale gold wines. The food was superb and beautifully presented by the long lines of black-clad waiters.

Throughout the meal, the uniformed members of the Air Force Band played background music to the babble of the diners' conversation; and after speeches, which had been mer-cifully brief, Their Excellencies led the way out of the long dining room.

Andrew and Kathleen sought out the ballroom. There, they glided onto the floor as if they had been dancing together for years.

And then, with a fanfare, the Prime Minister was intro-duced. He asked that everyone come into the ballroom, where they crowded towards the bandstand. Looking immensely pleased with himself, Jacques introduced a very special guest.

"I want you to meet Evangeline. I know you have heard of her, and many of you know her records. But this is the first engagement" – and he smiled at her – "that she has undertaken in Canada. Will you give her an especially warm welcome?"

Jacques led forward a slight figure, a head shorter than he. Her features were delicate, her huge eyes like topaz jewels, her expression demure. Under a cascade of thick, brown-gold hair falling below her shoulders, her brows were thick and straight. She was dressed simply in a long tunic dress of rough-woven white cotton; about her throat was a circlet of hammered gold. In her hands, a gleaming guitar.

She paused, head bowed. Then, after leading off with a brief cascade of notes from the guitar, she began to sing in a throaty, exciting voice.

> *"Les étoiles étaient dans le ciel*
> *Tois dans les bras de Gabriel*
> *il faisait beau c'était dimanche*
> *les cloches allaient bientôt sonner*
> *et tu allais te marier*
> *dans la premiere robe blanche*
> *l'automne était bien commencé*
> *les troupeaux étaient tous rentrés*
> *et parties toutes les sarcelles*
> *et le soir au son du violon*
> *les filles et surtout les garçons*
> *t'auraient dit que tu étais belle*
> *Évangéline Évangéline."*

Evangeline sang the six verses of the haunting song of the legendary maid of Acadia, separated from her lover Gabriel by expulsion at the hand of the British, more than two centuries before. The story, taken from a Longfellow poem, chronicled the young girl's lifelong search for her lost love, and her reunion with him when both were old, as he died in her arms.

Evangeline's gentle music was world-renowned and as she

began the familiar last verse, the audience joined in, in English and in French:

"*Il existe encore aujourd'hui*/There are still today
des gens qui vivent dans ton pays/People who live in your country
et qui de ton nom se souviennent/Who remember your name
car l'océan parle de toi/Because the ocean speaks of you
les vents du sud porte ta voix/The south winds carry your voice
de la forêt jusqu'à la plaine/From the forest to the prairie
ton nom c'est plus que l'Acadie/Your name is more than Acadia
plus que l'espoîr d'une patrie/More than a hope of a homeland
ton nom dépasse les frontières/Your name crosses the frontiers
ton nom c'est le nom de tous ceux/Your name is the name of all
those
qui malgré que ils soient malheureux/Who despite their unhappiness
croient en l'amour et qui esperent/Believe in love, and hope.
Évangéline, Évangéline   Evangeline, Evangeline
Évangéline, Évangéline   Evangeline, Evangeline"

The Prime Minister stepped forward, taking Evangeline's slender hand in his, his arm encircling her waist. The crowd was still under the spell of Evangeline's song. Jacques looked into her brilliant eyes, and then turned to face the audience.

"Your Excellencies, ladies and gentlemen. You have seen and heard Evangeline, and it is clear that you have been won by her. You will know, then, how proud and happy I am to reintroduce to you *my* Evangeline. My love, my wife."

Chapter Five

Jean Jacques Charles took off his glasses and laid them atop the clutter on the end table. He closed his eyes and with thumb and forefinger pinched the bridge of his nose.

Since he had walked in on Evangeline and Kathleen, two days had passed. In that time he and his wife had barely spoken, and in the long silence, his anger had gradually drained away until now, finally, he regretted his outburst of temper. He could still see himself standing in the doorway of the sitting room, see Kathleen insolent and confident in his chair, feel his own throat choking with rage. To apologize was out of the question. And yet. . . .

It was an early dusk. The day had been grey, the sky full of tumbling dark clouds, with gusts of cold March wind that shook the leafless trees and spattered clumps of snow against the old stone mansion. Now this evening was showing a small burst of colour: a cold glimmering of red at the horizon where the setting sun was trying to promise spring.

Jacques pushed himself upright. On the corduroy sofa, he dropped the limp leather-bound book of the week's messages telexed daily from Canadian ambassadors in their listening posts all around the world. He paced the length of his book-lined study, then he went in search of his wife.

From his study, which was near the entrance of the old house, he crossed the foyer and walked up the short curve of stairs to the private family rooms. In the sitting room the fire was cold and the lights out. From there he went into the bedroom – the bedroom they had not shared for the past two nights. It was the first time since they were married two years ago that a fight had kept them apart at night.

Evangeline was lying down, a light coverlet pulled over her. The room was unlit, but not entirely dark. She stirred at his entrance, but said nothing as he approached their bed. She pulled herself up, bunching pillows behind her, when Jacques sat on the side of the bed and took her cold hand in his.

"Angèle, *chérie*, we have to talk. I shouldn't have lost my temper at you like that. We never used to fight." He waited, but Evangeline said nothing. "You know, I put my work aside and came home last Friday especially to be with you. I was upset about the argument we had the night before. All the way from the Hill, I was going over in my mind what I could say to you. I wanted to understand what happened, to help you understand too, and when I came into the house I was full of love for you. I rushed up the stairs to see you, and then when I got to the doorway, I heard you telling Kathleen my family's secrets. I was shocked. It was as if, while I was planning to make up, you were trying to start more trouble. You know I am a private man. There are some things I would never tell anyone but you, *mon coeur*. I felt betrayed – and to be betrayed by you, Angèle. Can you understand my anger?"

Evangeline reached for him, drew him down to her and stroked the silky, thinning hair across the hard skull. She pillowed his head on her breast, searching for the right words of explanation.

"I am sorry, Jacques. I did it so naturally; I wanted to explain your feelings about abortion. And it was Kathleen I was speaking to. She has been such a good friend to both of us, ever since I came here. And she is used to keeping secrets. She was the only one I could turn to. I was so unhappy, so ill, after arguing all night. And so afraid. I asked her to come to me that morning. When she told me about the vote, I realized how stupid and insensitive I had been, telling you about my pregnancy and my need for an abortion that night, of all nights. I am so sorry, my darling, for being such a stupid wife."

Jacques raised his head, his eyes luminous in the gloom. He bent to her lips murmuring, "Angèle, *mon* Angèle."

Reconciliation is sweet, Jacques smiled to himself next morning, as he sat at his desk in the third-floor office of the Centre Block. He buried in his mind the realization that they had talked no further of interrupting Evangeline's pregnancy, nor had she asked him to reconsider his decision about Kathleen. They had made love and fallen asleep entwined. This morning at breakfast, the subject remained a closed book.

He shook himself mentally, pushing away personal thoughts. The next matter on the agenda was his Monday meeting with his senior aides to go over the day's business. He buzzed the intercom and they entered promptly.

Kathleen drove slowly through the heavy morning Toronto traffic, her thoughts on the meeting she had organized for this afternoon. She had arranged to meet with members of her riding organization in Niagara for lunch.

She was wondering how to explain her sudden resignation. Of course, everyone knew she had been fired, but she didn't want to drag Evangeline's problems into any discussion. She knew that no matter how close her party colleagues had been, she would not reveal such personal matters.

They will just have to assume that he did it because of the abortion vote, she thought, even if it isn't wholly fair. But what we need now is to hunt for a new candidate to take over when the election is called. And I'll have to make them understand that I'll only be a part-time member myself until that happens.

"Damn it," she swore, as a small, dusty car cut in before her. This traffic is terrible enough, moving at a snail's pace, without some of those lane-changing idiots. Kathleen had dressed carefully for this luncheon, and she peered now into the driver's mirror to check her appearance, taking advantage of the crawling speed. Drawing a lipstick from her bag beside her, she outlined her mouth in fresh bright colour. From behind her, someone leaned on a horn, and exasperated, she pulled ahead.

This afternoon, I'm going on a spree. I'll go shopping – maybe for something silly like a new tie for Andrew. Or maybe I'll have my hair cut, or even go to a movie. Something slightly giddy, to celebrate my new sense of freedom. A whole afternoon to myself, to squander as I choose, she thought, lighting another cigarette. What luxury.

And then what? Perhaps I could practise law again. But not in Niagara. The lawyers there were so marvellously supportive during my parliamentary career. I couldn't imagine going into competition with them now.

Maybe in Toronto? Yes, I should look into that, but first things first. Talk to my people, find us a good candidate, then explore the future. But, she realized sadly, they wouldn't be *her* people much longer.

As the line of traffic picked up speed, she suffered a pang of regret which she resolutely put out of her mind, and for the balance of the hour-long drive, she toyed with ideas of how to spend her free afternoon.

The woman had telephoned the Prime Minister's office half a dozen times during the previous week. She was always put off – passed from one nameless voice to another – and because she refused to state her business with Jean Jacques Charles to anyone else, she had always rung off in anger, tired of the smooth-talking run-around. What she had to say, she would entrust to no one else. Everyone knew the Prime Minister had aides who opened and answered all his mail. She had also heard that almost no one ever received a reply to a letter. It was for that reason that she had made no attempt to write to him.

Unable to reach him by telephone or letter, the woman was annoyed but still determined. If she couldn't get to the Prime Minister himself right away, there was at least one other person who couldn't ignore what she had to tell him. He lived, she knew, at the Centennial Hotel. Short, blond, with a cheery round face, he would be easy to recognize.

Early Monday morning the dowdy, thin woman sat down on a settee near the swinging doors to the Centennial Hotel's main lobby. From her vantage point she had an excellent view of people coming and going from the wide entrance doors to the check-in desk and beyond to the corridor of elevators. She pushed her handbag and gloves down beside her and pulled out her knitting, never taking her eyes from the door. She was going to wait all day and through the evening if she had to.

The sun filtered brightly into the sitting room, but Evangeline, dressed in her street clothes and nervously pacing while she chain-smoked, would not have noticed the sky even if it had been turning itself green.

The love-making and Jacques' apology had made her feel better. But in the middle of the night she had woken up, the heel of her hand jammed into her mouth, as if to stifle a scream. It had been the old nightmare again. For hours she had lain still in the bed, trying to draw strength from Jacques' sleeping body. And then, finally, she had slipped out of the bedroom and gone out to the small wallpapered room which was her private study. There, she went to the small desk where she had sometimes sat in the middle of the night jotting down words for a new song. This time, however, she felt guilty, as if she were planning a rendezvous with a lover. Furtively she reached for the telephone.

At first, when Kathleen didn't answer, Evangeline's feeling of desperation increased. And then, when she realized that there was no one home, her anxiety was replaced by relief. Exhausted she had crept back into bed, fitted herself around Jacques' warmth.

But now, with Jacques gone to work, the old doubts were aflame again. In one hand she had a half-smoked cigarette. In the other she had the small notebook with her doctor's telephone number. He was old, and he was Catholic; but he *was* her doctor. And abortions were perfectly legal. Her telephone rang. She reached for it – then stopped. When it was quiet she dialled her doctor's office.

Hume Frazier too was busy that Monday morning. He had already met with his own senior staff-members and gone over the day's agenda. He looked immaculate and bright-eyed, the classic chin freshly shaved, the hair carefully brushed into crisp waves. His suit jacket hung on a nearby chair, his bright blue-and-white broadstriped shirt impeccable. He liked the effect of that shirt, repeating the brilliant colour of his eyes. This morning, as he had noted, there was no tracing of red. That's from going to bed early – and sober, he reminded himself. And from fucking your own wife for a change, he added. And then couldn't help recalling that, although the deed had been virtuous, it was also joyless.

He brought his thoughts back to the three men who had just entered the large office. He waved them into armchairs across the broad, well-organized desk. They were, he noted on his desk calendar, the presidents of three of the major Canadian insurance companies. They wanted to discuss the effects of indexing pensions. Crybabies, like every special interest group, but such people could be useful in the future and he resolved to be at his charming best.

"Now gentlemen, you wanted to see me about something specific? Perhaps we should get right to it."

The well-tailored businessmen leaned forward in their chairs. They liked this man – no nonsense about him – just straight to business. Hume Frazier certainly would make a good prime minister, too – crisp, efficient, decisive. At least, he would give them a sympathetic hearing, something they didn't often get from Jean Jacques Charles or the other ministers.

While Hume was closeted with the insurance company presidents, Molly moped at her desk in the outer office. Hume hadn't come back on Thursday night, nor had he come into the office at all on Friday. And he hadn't called her over the whole weekend since.

Even by Hume's lax standards, this was inattentive behaviour, and she wondered if he had someone else on the string – or at least someone new. She couldn't imagine Hume spending a weekend at home with his houseful of brats and his ice-maiden wife.

Molly knew that her careful attention to herself, combined with her natural attributes, had led her to be considered one of the truly beautiful women on the Hill. She also knew it wouldn't be hard to find another patron to replace Hume. There had been plenty of offers from other members, even one or two ministers over the years. But in the meantime she was far from giving up on him. And besides, she had seen enough of the Hill to know that if she started switching from one man to the next, she would be only weakening her own position. She had even, in the more optimistic days – before Hume's marriage – thought of such women as call girls who typed. Now she wasn't so sure.

The next day the woman was at the Centennial Hotel again. And the next day. Everyone in Ottawa knew that on Wednesdays Parliament rises at six o'clock. The thin woman with the knitting bag in her lap had taken up her position a little after five. The clerks, busy checking in dozens of people for a beer salesmen's convention, did not notice her.

The woman's vigil was rewarded when, a little after seven, she saw the man so clearly pictured in her mind, as he pushed through the entrance door. He carried a fat black briefcase, wore a black caracul wedge hat and a salt-and-pepper tweed coat, the collar pulled up around his face. As he entered, she rose and sidled toward him. He picked up his evening newspapers at the newstand, unbuttoning his coat to reach into his pocket for change.

As he walked away, holding the newspaper open before him, he nearly collided with the woman, who was standing foursquare in his path. With a muttered apology, he made for the bank of elevators. She followed right behind him and stepped into the elevator on his heels. He studied his newspaper as they were whooshed to the thirteenth floor.

The man with the briefcase stepped out, still engrossed in his newspaper. The woman stepped out behind him, and before he had gone more than a pace or two, she called out.

"Mr. Jamieson? Mr. Jamieson, I must talk to you."

"Damn," Boots Jamieson, the Prime Minister's principal secretary, muttered under his breath, "can't I ever get away from them?" He turned back toward her, a pleasant smile on his cherub's face, noting the thin material and unfashionable cut of the coat, the knitted woollen cap, the mittened hands clutching her handbag and what looked like a large, full knittingbag. As she advanced towards him, he took a nervous look at that worn bag.

"Yes, ma'am. What can I do for you, Mrs. . . . ah?"

"The name doesn't matter, young man. I must talk to you. I have a message for the Prime Minister. Now don't look like that. If you don't think it is important, then you simply won't tell him, I suppose. But you have to hear it first, don't you?"

"Can't you tell me here?"

The woman glanced around her, along the hotel corridor. The elevator was whining its way back up to this floor and very probably there would soon be a bellboy and guests to overhear.

"It's pretty confidential. You live here. Can't we talk in your apartment?"

Jamieson hesitated, then heaved a sigh as he made his decision. If there was something lethal in that bag, he was going to be in trouble, but there seemed nothing else to do, unless he wanted to make a fool of himself by running down the corridor to escape her. She's probably harmless, he thought. If I let her in, I'll get rid of her damned quick.

"This way, but it can't be for long. I have a busy evening of work ahead."

As he put his outer clothes away, Boots Jamieson observed his visitor in the hall mirror. She had gone directly to the sofa and sat down, precisely in the middle. She perched at the edge, twisting the handle of her handbag nervously, the knitting bag propped against a boot.

"Now, madam, you have the advantage of me. You know my name, you know where I live, and you know what kind of work I do, and for whom. And I don't even know your name."

"All in good time, Mr. Jamieson." She reached down and pulled something from the knitting bag. Jamieson held his breath, until he saw that in her extended left hand was clutched what looked like a white file card. "First, I want you to look at this."

He took the oblong of white cardboard, turned it over and glanced over the typed lines and the signature.

"I don't understand. What is this card? I can see that it has something to do with a hospital and that it is a consent to surgery of some kind, but what's its significance? So far as I can see, the patient is Mary Jane Smith, and the signature is probably that of Mr. Smith, although it's pretty hard to decipher. Why have you brought this to me? And why do you think the Prime Minister would be interested in it?"

The woman sat very straight, her eyes bright, spots of colour burning high on each cheekbone.

"Mr. Jamieson. Look closely at the signature. Don't you recognize it? Not the name – not Smith – I mean the hand that wrote it. Surely you've seen that handwriting before?"

He looked again at the scrawled signature. Was it Jean Jacques' hand? No, most definitely not.

"No, it means nothing to me," he said, handing back the card. The woman, still looking triumphant, took the card from him.

"Now, madam, you are going to have to come to the point. The last thing I need is someone waylaying me as I come home, and then handing me a puzzle. I really don't have any more time to give you unless you can tell me exactly what's on your mind."

"I thought you would be smarter, young man! I thought you would recognize something signed by your Minister of Finance, whatever name he used."

"The Minister of Finance? Hume Frazier? What has he to do with that signature? Why would he sign himself as 'Smith'?"

"That Hume Frazier signed that paper pretending to be a Mr. Smith. He signed it to authorize a surgical procedure. An abortion. He pretended to be the woman's husband. No, their names aren't Smith, at all. I happen to know her, and she's a married woman, but her name's not Smith. And Hume Frazier is certainly not her husband. It's a fraud, all the way through. They used phony names, and he gave a phony consent so that the woman could get an abortion. And to think, he was once Minister of Justice, and they say that sometime he'll be Prime Minister! Why he's just a common criminal, and that card proves it! He ought to be in jail. I know what the Prime Minister thinks of abortions. The papers have been full of it for the past week. Well, what do you think he'll do when he finds out that Hume Frazier, his own Minister of Finance, is mixed up in such a crooked business? I think he ought to throw that Frazier out, and that's why I have brought this card to you."

Boots Jamieson had the wind knocked out of him. He found it hard to believe what he was hearing. It wasn't difficult to imagine Frazier getting mixed up with a woman, even getting her pregnant – but surely to God he had enough experience and brains to keep his trouble legal. And away from Sybil and the Government.

Jamieson settled back into his chair and tried to make his voice cold. "I wonder if you know what you are saying? You are charging a serious crime, and you are suggesting that it was perpetrated by the second most important man in the government. What proof have you that Hume Frazier signed that card as Smith? How did you get it? Who are you, anyway?"

The woman's thin face stayed composed. "I work in the hospital, part-time, as a volunteer. I help arrange flowers and take books and things around to the patients. I was near the receiving desk when that woman – Mrs. Smith, she called herself – came in and signed in for surgery. She didn't even see me, and I'm her neighbour, down the block. Too nervous, she was, I guess. Anyway, when they said her husband had to sign a consent she went back out the door, and came back in with a little bag and this handsome man with her. Who wouldn't recognize him? He's always in the papers. I was going to speak to them, but they didn't look as if they would welcome that, just then. Frazier just picked up the pen and signed, walked her to the elevator, and then got out of there as quick as he could."

She put the card on her lap. "I couldn't think of any reason why those two should be together – and especially not at a hospital admitting station. It just seemed so suspicious. A little while later, while the receptionist was on her coffee break, I took a peek at that card. I was shocked, I tell you. Her having an abortion, and him pretending to be her husband!"

"So you stole the card?"

"Not then, I didn't. No, I knew the hospital authorities

would be looking for the card for their records. I just made a note of the false name and the date, and last week, when no one was looking, I got it out of the files. And I didn't *steal* it. I'm not that kind of person. I borrowed it, that's all."

Boots grimaced at her attitude of outraged virtue. "Just being an upright citizen, doing her duty, eh?" he said, eyeing her.

She nodded, with apparent pride and satisfaction. "That's right. And I thought Mr. Charles should know about it. I tried to reach him by phone, but those people in his office simply wouldn't put me through. You know how they are. Then I remembered you, and just waited for you in the hotel lobby. I was here every day this week, but somehow missed you," she said, standing up and pulling her coat about her.

"Now, will you tell the Prime Minister?" she demanded, sure of herself.

Boots Jamieson nodded slowly, thinking to himself that Jacques would go right through the roof when he heard.

"I'll have to check it out first, to make sure that your story holds up. This is a very serious matter." It had better be more than just the work of a meddling gossip, or it was going to end right here, he thought grimly. But if it was true, the P.M. would have to be told.

"I'll show you out now. I really must get to work."

And the woman had gone, pleased with the effect her bombshell had made on the complacent young man. She refused to give her name or address, but Boots knew he could easily learn her identity from the records of her volunteer association, should there be any need.

As the door to the hall closed behind her, Jamieson reached out his hand for the telephone. It was Wednesday evening when he made that first call, and by early Friday afternoon, Jamieson had it all documented before him: The woman's real name, and her husband's name. A statement by the woman. A statement by her husband. A statement from the doctor who had attended her, and performed the abortion. A statement from the admitting clerk. An affidavit from Wednesday's visitor. And sheafs of documents, bearing Hume Frazier's signature, for comparison.

Jamieson had been discreet in his enquiries, and the Mounties even more so. So far as Boots knew, nothing had leaked to the press or to the parliamentary rumour factory. Now he had to tell the Prime Minister.

Mondays were usually hectic days for the Prime Minister. This one had been particularly bad. In the morning paper there had been a cartoon showing a cunning likeness of Jean Jacques Charles as a terrified rabbit, ready to jump in any direction that might prove popular.

The mood in the golden office was sharp, and Boots, had he dared delay it, would have put his revelations off until a better time. But with this there was no choice, and ready for the worst, he launched into his story.

When he had finished, Jacques cursed voluably and at length in English and French. Then to Boots' relief he had pulled himself up short.

"Okay, leave the damned thing with me for a couple of days. And make sure that Hume Frazier is in Ottawa tomorrow so that I can send for him. In the meantime, make sure that Christianne puts a copy of the Criminal Code in my briefcase. And, Boots, don't, under any circumstances, discuss this with anybody till I talk to you. Abortion, abortion, I've had my bellyful of it. Damn Hume, how could he be so stupid? Anyway, this should end all the ridiculous 'heir apparent' talk, once and for all."

It had seemed like hours in the waiting room but finally Evangeline had been asked into the office. After the examination, the doctor motioned her to sit down in the chair opposite his desk. He was an erect, white-thatched, white goatee'd man in his early seventies, and when he smiled he looked so sad, Evangeline knew the news must be bad.

"Why didn't you call me sooner?"

"I did," Evangeline said. "I meant to. Almost every day for the past week I've picked up the telephone. And then I felt like such a traitor I just hung up. Twice I waited for it to ring but when your secretary answered I –"

"That's all right," the doctor said. "It would have been too late anyway. You see, the pregnancy is now quite far advanced. I know it doesn't show much, but you should be gaining more weight. I'm afraid that it would mean a more complicated operation now. With your high blood pressure and the toxemia it would be very dangerous. I am sorry, *madame*. But with good care, I'm sure that we can bring your condition under control before the babies are due. You will have to take very good care of yourself, however."

"But –"

"You could ask another doctor. But I don't think –"

"Yes, doctor." Evangeline was out of her chair and on her feet. "Excuse me, doctor. I must go. Thank you."

In the past week and a half Kathleen and Andrew had grown closer, and she had come to a decision with respect to her own immediate future. She had lunched with a number of her legal friends to explore the possibility of an association as counsel with a downtown firm. She found, however, that she was ill at ease in the high-rise jungle of downtown Toronto; nor did she have any taste for the kind of office politics she encountered in the enormous law partnerships that had become the fashion.

After considerable thought, she had decided to open a small office of her own, and she had begun to search Toronto for exactly the right place. A Toronto office would be a kind of halfway house for her. She was eager to resharpen her skills as a counsel, and could hardly wait to plunge back into the legal world.

The day she found an office that suited her needs, she and Andrew celebrated with a dinner out. Andrew listened to her plans without enthusiasm and Kate sensed his disappointment.

"I'll still have plenty of time to spend with you," she said.

"Look, Kate, I'm not being selfish or chauvinistic. It's just that I want you to be free to pick up and come with me whenever I have to travel. I don't want you to be tied down with a job, or even a house. We could buy a condominium here, and maybe have a house in the Caribbean or in the south of

France when I retire. We could even keep an apartment in Stockholm, or in London, too, whatever you want. I want us to be as free as birds to do what we want to do, when we want to do it. I'm not a poor man and I've worked hard to be able to enjoy retirement. Tage is about ready to take over from me. When I'm free, I want you to be free."

Kathleen understood Andrew's desire to travel, but she knew that she depended on work. She had always had a job, since she was sixteen years old, and she wasn't at all sure that she could – or wanted to – handle such a complete decompression, especially after her busy and productive years in Parliament.

The evening ended on a sour note, with neither of them entirely certain of their future relationship.

Hume Frazier was presiding over a meeting of the Commissioners of Internal Economy, a housekeeping committee of members on which the Minister of Finance would not ordinarily waste his time, but Hume had a continuing interest in the matters under discussion. He defended squandering time he should have spent profitably elsewhere. "It isn't such a bad idea. You never can tell how much money those members will spend on themselves if someone from the Treasury isn't around to curb them," was the way he explained it. Today, the Commissioners were meeting in Hume's office. They had been joined by a number of private members who formed the Standing Committee on Management and Members' Services. The committee was comprised of members from all parties in the House. They oversaw the petty things about which members constantly complained – the formal parliamentary restaurant on the sixth floor of the Centre Block, the cafeterias and coffee shop, members' perquisites, such as free long-distance calls and mailings, office equipment from furniture to typewriters, the gymnasium, the sauna, the pool room, the tailors and the barbers. The Speaker was the regular chairman, but today he was busy elsewhere. The agenda was routine.

Hume sat at his desk, acting as chairman *pro-tem*, but he was only half-listening to the argument among the other members. It centred on food – that perennial complaint.

"Well, damnit, it *is* high time we had some decent food on the Hill. We're all too busy to take time to go somewhere else at mealtime. Isn't that why the facilities are here, and subsidized as heavily as they are? But all we get is meat and potatoes, meat and potatoes. Look at us. Every member gains weight from the minute he arrives, with all that starchy food, and us sitting on our butts all day and half the night!"

Hume was amused. He remembered making the same complaint in almost the same words – or at least with the same import – when he had first been assigned to this committee, back in the early days of the Sinclair administration. Although he had been irritated to receive what he thought of then as a mere housekeeping assignment, he came to enjoy it.

"May I suggest, members of the committee," he said calmly, "that we resolve this question by appointing a small subcommittee, say two or three members, to take up the matter with the chef? Perhaps those of you who feel the strongest about it?"

Hume smiled to himself as he remembered that he and Kathleen had once been assigned to just the same job. Kit had been senior to him – a member of the committee since Sandy Sinclair's days in Opposition – but she had stayed on after she had been called to the Cabinet because she was interested in food and nutrition. The two young members had drawn up a list of regional foods which they thought should appear – in season – on the menu of the parliamentary restaurant.

Hume remembered how confident he and Kit had been when they faced the excitable Swiss who had ruled the parliamentary kitchen. What they had not been told was that the chef had been known to wield his trusty kitchen knife when harassed. It had taken the two of them months of cajoling and pleading with the insulted chef, before he reluctantly agreed to try a kind of *cuisine minceur*, fresh regional food, artfully presented, and low in the calories that plagued everyone in the House.

And even after that fight was won, Hume continued to drop in on Kathleen from time to time, just to chat. Gradually, she assumed a special role toward him; they called her his "den mother." She had, he acknowledged, taught him a lot. She would listen to his ideas, and make suggestions and let him try out speeches on her. He didn't need that kind of help any more, but, damn it, he missed her.

Hume adjourned the meeting hurriedly. He didn't bother to leave his chair behind the desk to see the committee members out. There was a lot of work on his plate, just now. Still, as he shuffled papers, his memory lingered on that wild and wonderful evening when Kit had brought together all the other single people in both Houses to toast his graduation to married status.

It was one dinner that more than met the expectations of the food-fussy members of the Bachelor's Club. The Speaker had loaned Kit his beautifully decorated private dining room, part of his suite off the north corridor, and over forty members and senators had made the rafters ring till early in the morning. There were presentations and songs and Charles' hilarious rendition of a slightly off-colour ditty. It had been great fun, and so far as he knew, Hume had been the only member so honoured. He still had the plaque they had given him, predicting he'd be a future prime minister.

And then he remembered the aftermath. Sybil had been angry and petulant when he had told her that the invitation was for a members-only dinner. Afterwards, when she learned he had gone anyway, she had surprised him by losing her cool, ranting and raving about discrimination. Of course, it had been a tempest in a teapot, but the unfortunate result was that ever since she had disliked Kit, and had done her damndest at every opportunity to put the knife into the woman parliamentarian.

Hume's face darkened at the thought of his wife.

"The lovely Sybil" was what he called her, ironically. The marriage had been a mistake from the first, he now knew. Why the hell didn't Kit stop me, he asked himself resentfully. She might have thought of something – after all, what was a den mother for? But he knew that the marriage had taken place, as Sybil planned it to, because he didn't have the guts to stop it while there was still time to avoid a distasteful scandal by jilting her.

And, of course, the marriage hadn't been all bad. Although she had borne a child every year, Sybil had taken care to keep intact those cool, perfect looks. She was a gracious hostess, and she kept the spotless house filled with influential and important people. Not alone, of course. She had always had help since they had married and taken up residence in the house that her father had bought them.

Hume made a gesture of irritation. The thought of the servants, which were beyond his salary, never failed to annoy him. And since her father had died, Sybil had kept the purse-strings tight. So he had the frustrating sensation of living close to money, but never having any of his own.

There were other women, of course. Always had been, almost from the first, touch-me-not night of their honeymoon. So I have a man's needs, was the way Hume always put it to himself. If a man can't get it at home, he's entitled to look elsewhere. Even though he knew that he was taking risks, especially for a man with an ambition to be prime minister, Hume felt he was safe enough. The press might be aware of his foible, but they would never report it.

He didn't, however, think that Sybil knew; at least if she did, she had never said anything. And he could be pretty sure that the public wouldn't believe it, not when he appeared with the lovely Sybil on his arm.

He tried to be careful, only picking up "nothing" girls on his travels – one-nighters – most of whom had no idea who he was. And there always was good old Molly whenever the itch overcame him. Now and again, he had even gone to bed with Sybil, to allay any suspicions she might have.

The big mistake had been when he had broken one of his own cardinal rules and gotten involved with a married woman. Then, worse, she had been careless enough to get pregnant. And told him he would have to make arrangements for an abortion! For weeks he had been frightened that someone would find out; but now it was past. Gone, he said to himself, it's over. And just you remember it, Hume-baby. No more married women! And make damn sure you make no more babies – not even at home. Hear?

When Molly came in with some letters for his signature, Hume absently asked her to drop them on the desk. He didn't even look up from the columns of figures in which he was engrossed.

Molly stood waiting for an extra second or two, but when Hume paid no attention to her, she sniffed and left the office.

Well, she said to herself, if he won't even look at me, to hell with him! Someone else can tell him that the Hill is ringing with rumours about him. Someone else can tell him – not me.

A little after six o'clock, Hume went home for dinner. This was unusual, but he was too restless to stay in the office. His entry surprised the cook, who was reading in the kitchen, waiting for the children to finish dinner so that she might clean up. Madame was not expected for dinner, and no one had mentioned to her that the master might be in. Hume sat at the head of the gleaming table, chatting with the children, a tinkling glass of whisky and water in his hand.

He had emptied and refilled his drink by the time the resourceful cook placed a shallow plate of canned consomme before him, sliced avocado and sprinkled herbs masking its origin. She followed that with a billowy, puffed omelet, bursting with mushrooms and oozing with melted cheese, and a crisp Romaine salad with hot, buttered rolls. After dinner he took a large brandy, which he then poured into a big cup of aromatic coffee.

By then, the children had been excused from the table. He followed them up, to say goodnight – something he knew he did far too seldom.

Then he shrugged into his overcoat, reluctantly preparing to go back to the House. He was on House duty tonight, something he disliked intensely. It seemed to him that every time the Minister of Finance walked into the House, especially during the slow-paced evenings, whoever was making a contribution to the debate would add some fresh, pointed sentences, complaining how stingy the Minister was in refusing to find money for this or that pet project. And without fail during the evening, two or three of his own caucus members would make their way, casually, to plunk into the Prime Minister's seat beside Hume, to lobby for their constituency where, with just a few new handouts – what the Prime Minister called "candies" – the member would be assured of re-election.

On the point of leaving, Hume was called to the telephone. "This is the Prime Minister's office, sir. The Prime Minister wishes to see you urgently, at 24 Sussex."

Hume explained that he was required to be in the House. The disembodied voice promised to arrange for another minister to take his duty. Well, thought Hume, I'd a helluva lot rather sit snug in Jacques' study and shoot the breeze.

"Please tell the Prime Minister that I will be there directly."

Hume left a message with the cook for Sybil: "Don't wait up for me – I've gone to an important meeting with the Prime Minister."

The red-haired maid opened the door to Hume.

"Come right in. The Prime Minister is expecting you." She helped him to remove and hang up his coat, and took his rubbers from him. "This way." She directed him to the study door, stepped in, announced, "Mr. Frazier, sir," and disappeared.

Jean Jacques Charles in a maroon velvet smoking jacket and ascot tie, sat in the club-chair facing the entry. He set his pipe in the ashtray and motioned Hume to the sofa against the near wall. In a noncommital voice, he enquired whether there was anything Hume would like.

"Yes, sir, a long strong whisky and water, please." The drink appeared almost immediately, and Hume asked permission to light a cigar.

"Go ahead," said Jacques, "it's your funeral." The Prime Minister rarely smoked anything but his battered pipe, but appeared not to care when others did in his presence. He himself had asked only for a mineral water. He sipped from his glass, his eyes on Hume.

There was no doubt that Hume was handsome. It was no wonder that the women fell all over him. But what amazed Jacques about Hume was his utter single-mindedness. It was both amusing and irritating to Jacques that Hume's one goal in life was to have his job, to be prime minister.

And yet, despite the driving ambition, Hume had no apparent political or personal philosophy. As a minister he had been competent enough in his various portfolios, but certainly not spectacular. Aside from some good appointments to the bench, Jacques could think of not one significant measure that Hume had sponsored. Or wanted to sponsor. Even the press had occasionally made comments on his low profile in Finance. Yet, somehow, Hume Frazier had become popular in the country; he wanted to lead it – though no one knew where – and the press had been happy enough to dub him as Jacques' crown prince.

Hume was growing faintly embarrassed under Jacques' silent scrutiny. He felt the need to move, to break the steady gaze upon him.

"I was told you wanted me for something urgent, Prime Minister." He tapped the solid ash from his cigar.

"Yes, Hume. Thank you for coming so promptly."

Another silence, which Hume punctuated determinedly. "Some kind of crisis, sir? Of what nature? No one told me anything further."

"No, no one yet knows the subject of our talk. It's about your resignation, Hume." He had spoken in such a flat, casual tone that Hume scarcely credited his ears.

"My – ah – resignation, sir?"

"Yes, the one you must tender this week."

Hume swallowed. The Prime Minister didn't appear to be joking.

"Jacques, what are you talking about? What's on your mind?"

The fact that he had called the Prime Minister by his given name – something very rarely done by Cabinet ministers to their first minister, no matter how long or close the previous association – betrayed Hume's surprise and shock. The subtlety was not lost on Jacques.

With visible regret, he placed a folder on Hume's knee. He sighed. "Look, Hume. I have no desire to be an executioner, but unless you have an explanation for this, you are going to have to resign, and to do it with a full public statement."

Hume snatched up the file and opened it, scanning the documents inside. A dull flush began at his neck and spread upward, suffusing his face. Beads of sweat broke out on the wide brow.

"Where did you get this stuff? It's a pack of vicious lies! Who are these Smiths? What kind of proof is there?" He tried furiously to figure out who could have betrayed him. Surely not Allison – she had as much to lose as he did. He reread the documents. His heart sank. There was everything here any law officer would need to lay a criminal charge – maybe more than one.

"Is that your considered answer, Hume? That this is nothing but a frame-up? That you are innocent of the whole affair?" The voice was grave. "Is that what you expect me to believe?"

Hume looked at his leader. He was on the point of protesting his innocence again, of holding to his story that it was untrue, but when he saw Jacques bent forward intently, as though about to pounce, he realized that no prime minister would face a senior minister with gossip that hadn't been thoroughly checked – and certainly not on such a serious charge.

His shoulders slumped and the light went from his face.

"No, it's true. It's true. But the affair has been over for a long time now. And I haven't seen her since I took her to the hospital. So far as I know, she and her husband have been getting along well enough. I'm sure he never even knew. But I'm not the first minister who has committed adultery, or made some stupid woman pregnant! Why should I have to resign?"

"It's not the adultery, Hume. Nor even that you were mixed up in an abortion, though you certainly ought to know how I feel about that! It's passing yourself off as her husband – even signing a name that isn't yours! You've been Minister of Justice. Surely sometime you have taken a look at the fraud and forgery sections of the Code? Whatever made you do such a stupid thing? And right here in Ottawa? How could you dream that it would never come out?"

"It wasn't deliberate, Jacques, believe me. I had made all the hospital arrangements, and I drove her there, just to see that everything was all right. And then they told her she would have to have her husband's consent. How was I to know? That's not part of the law, but there wasn't time to haggle over it. I just signed the damn thing, and they took her off to have the abortion. That's all there was to it. I never thought about breaking the law. It all happened so fast. And no one else knew."

"It's all there in those papers, Hume. Some woman recognized both of you, and made it her business to do a little checking. She reported it to one of my staff, who has made careful enquiries." Then, his tone changing, he looked at the younger man, slumped on the sofa. "I think you'd better freshen that drink." He rang again and, with a gesture, asked for another round.

When the maid had come and gone again, he said: "And Hume, it seems to me that you are hitting the bottle a bit too regularly. From now on, that's your personal business, of course, but I think you should be aware that people notice."

"Then you insist I resign?"

"I think that best."

"No alternative – a tour to the foreign financial circles? An appointment, maybe? Maybe until the next election? There is a minority government, and you have already lost Kit."

As soon as he mentioned Kathleen, Hume knew that he'd made the final mistake. Jacques' eyes flashed. His tone was cold now, quite at variance with the half-regretful, gently probing accents in which he had spoken up till now.

"No, Hume, and that's final! For a change you're going to have to take your medicine like a man. You've been skating on thin ice for years, with all your women. Do you think such things are not reported back to the Prime Minister? Well, you've finally gone over the edge.

"It isn't immorality we are talking about. It's *illegality* this time. Illegality – and from a former senior law officer of the Crown! I won't put up with it. The public won't put up with it. I won't try a cover-up. You deserve what you have brought on yourself.

"You'll have to resign in the House itself and make your explanation. I want no rumours about why you are going, like those about. . . . Never mind, you will have to do it – tomorrow – right after question period, or the next day at the latest."

He stood up, terminating the interview. "Now, goodnight."

Hume drove straight home to the pillared, white Colonial home bought with his father-in-law's money. When he had presented the young Fraziers with the deed, Sybil's father had said it represented the family's faith in a brilliant future. "A brilliant future," Hume repeated to himself, shrinking from the thought. "My God, it's all over now. There *is* no future. A whole lifetime kicked away, all by one stupid, stupid mistake. How bloody unfair."

At this moment, he suddenly realized, he probably had less than a thousand dollars in the bank. No job, and after this, no prospects. Until his interview with Jacques he had felt absolutely confident that his ambitions would be realized. Now his whole life – from his mother's manoeuvring to get him into the right schools to his marriage to Sybil, the perfect prime minister's wife – had been torn apart like a paper doll.

And Sybil. How could Sybil be told? She would be angry and more. And she would throw him out soon enough. No job, no home, no wife, no kids.

He bent his head to the wheel while tears ran down his face. When the bout of gulping and weeping had passed, he turned the key in the ignition, backed out the drive and drove straight to Molly Paradis' apartment.

He let himself in with his key. Molly took one look at Hume's state and poured him a stiff brandy. Then she led him to the bedroom. They didn't talk as they undressed. She held him, pressing his handsome face to her swelling breasts. After a long time, the tears abated, and Hume slept.

Chapter Six

The House was unnaturally still – no rustle of papers, no background hum of voices, no members moving in and out. The Minister of Finance had the floor on a question of privilege. He was in the front row, to the right of the Speaker, and as he stood behind his desk, preparing to speak, he was aware of the Prime Minister beside him. Jacques sat motionless in his own place, his head on his hand, his arm braced against the side of the chair farthest from Hume. His eyes were hooded, his granite face without expression.

Hume shuffled his papers, uncomfortably conscious of the curiosity of the members, and aware, too, of the glaring eye of the television camera which would carry his humiliation across the country.

Voice trembling, and tears insistently welling to his eyes, he began to read his letter of resignation. As Jacques had demanded, Hume read the letter in its entirety, the Hansard reporter's flying pen recording his every word.

Somehow he got through the whole *mea culpa*, laying bare the facts so that the rumours would be ended. He pleaded with the House and with the press not to seek out and harass the woman involved. He said that it was his duty to shoulder the blame; and that he knew he might yet be the subject of criminal prosecution. But as he spoke he knew it was this public declaration that was the most difficult thing – facing the men and women who had been his friends and admirers, facing the country – and admitting that he had let them down so badly and so stupidly.

When he had concluded, he looked around the broad green chamber with its rows and rows of desks, behind which sat silent, grave-faced members. To them all, he whispered: "I'm sorry," then stumbled from the Commons. The tense hush continued unbroken, each member touched by the unprecedented drama of a powerful minister who had just committed public *hara-kiri*.

Then the Prime Minister was on his feet, his voice soft, the tone bland. He bowed to the Speaker, and announced that he had a statement to make regarding a constitutional conference to be called in the following month.

Kathleen saw Hume resign on the six o'clock television newscast. She found herself feeling utterly unsurprised by the development. Though she had never anticipated such an event, now that it had happened it seemed his weakness for women would *have* to have been politically fatal. She was torn between sympathy for his embarrassment and the death of his life-long ambition and anger at him for being stupid enough to get caught in such a situation. Of course, it wasn't entirely his fault alone, Kathleen thought. The woman must have known better than to leave herself vulnerable to pregnancy. Her price for the escapade would be a shattered marriage. But Hume's, she thought, would be worse. At least what he did was gallant; he stuck with the woman. One had to give him credit for that.

Then suddenly, while still distantly analyzing Hume's actions, Kathleen realized why he hadn't been able to vote, one way or another, on the abortion bill. Poor Hume! What a tragedy it was that someone so full of promise could be so easily forced out of public life. And Sybil – what a terrible blow to the icy woman's pride to have the whole world know about Hume and another woman! Could she possibly stand by him? Or would she be so angry at the shattering of her own ambitions and the façade of the perfect marriage that she would leave him? At least, Kathleen thought wryly, Sybil won't come out too badly: she has all the money, the kids, and the house.

Kathleen got up from her chair and switched off the television set. Hume would need a job now; maybe Andrew could help him. She thought of the way other political friends of hers had fallen, of the silent and fascinated way those who survived always watched the departure of those who hadn't. Then she went to her desk, took out deckle-edged monogrammed sheets and an envelope, and swiftly penned Hume a sympathetic note.

The night Jacques had confronted him, Hume had drunk himself into oblivion at Molly's apartment. The next night had been a repeat performance. He had phoned her at the office and asked her to pick up more brandy on her way home. And that evening he kept drinking until he was almost unconscious, with just enough will to reel into Molly's bed, a sodden, bewhiskered, stinking mess.

Molly wrinkled her nose and spent the night on the daybed in the living room.

Before she left for work in the morning she had dragged Hume's sagging body to the bathroom, stripped him and hung up his wrinkled clothes. She stuffed him into the shower stall and turned the cold water on full force. Then she flicked on her electric percolator and went out the door to work, in disgust.

An hour later, she telephoned Hume to remind him that the Prime Minister was expecting him to make a speech at two P.M. that day. Hume had shaved with shaking hands, wolfed half a loaf of toast and emptied the coffee pot. Then he managed to concentrate on the speech he must make. When it was written, he took it to the office for Molly to type and duplicate.

This was one time he was grateful that he always kept a fresh change of clothes in his office. As he knotted on his tie, the trembling had abated, and he was able to call his executive assistant and his Deputy Minister and break the news crisply.

Now, returning from his ordeal in the House, he felt freer than he had in a long, long time. Purged, for the moment at least, of his ambition and of his guilt. It was done! It was time now to face Sybil – and to find out what future their family would have.

As he was leaving the office, he hesitated, then turned back and shyly thanked Molly. Then he was gone. This time, she didn't know whether or not Hume would be back.

When Hume arrived home, he found Sybil in the drawing room. She was immaculately dressed, as if she had been expecting this conversation. And as they sat down in the pastel velvet chairs, Hume felt a sudden admiration for her, for the composed way she awaited what was obviously to be bad news.

She heard him out without interruption. When he haltingly begged her to forgive him, and not to leave him, she nodded slowly. Her face flushed briefly and that was all he ever saw of her anger. The next moment she was talking as if she was giving a very rational summary of a committee meeting.

"We'll stay together, Hume. You are all I have – you and the children. We'll simply have to pick up the pieces as best we can, and put on the best possible face. Perhaps we should go away for a little while, until the dust settles. Would you like to go to England? It will be spring there soon – a good time for a fresh start."

"England would be fine," muttered Hume.

"You understand, of course, that I intend *never* to suffer another humiliation like this. I want your word on that, and then the subject is closed between us. In England, we can work out a plan for the future. You're still young, and everyone knows you're very talented. We'll just give them time to remember that, and to forget the other. Do I have your word?"

At Hume's nod of humility, she rose and left the room.

Although the resignation of Hume Frazier had been highly dramatic, the public reaction was ambivalent. The resignation made all the newscasts, and was repeated on television programs where press pundits and politicians discussed it at length. For the first few days, reporters scrambled to dig out further facts. But soon their editors decided to drop the matter on the basis that all parties concerned had already paid enough. No one could reach the Fraziers. All that could be learned was that the family, including the children, were on an extended overseas trip. That did not prevent a rash of stories in newspapers and magazines bemoaning the very considerable loss of a brilliant young man often hailed as the next prime minister. In these stories Hume's political shortcomings seemed entirely forgotten.

Conversations in living rooms and boardrooms across Canada often turned to the Frazier scandal, and the question of whether he had transgressed so mightily that his future in politics was smashed beyond repair.

In the offices and lounges of both Houses of Parliament, the same topic held centre stage. Most members liked and respected Hume Frazier. They had overlooked his consuming interest in the opposite sex – there were too many of them who lived in the same glass house to be eager to throw the first stone.

Despite the sympathy, however, there were many people – in Parliament and in the country – who condemned Hume because of the revealed adultery. And there were some who disapproved of his involvement in an abortion, even though Kathleen's bill to decriminalize such procedures had now become law. There was even enough public concern about the apparent criminality of Hume's acts that the Attorney-General of Ontario initiated his own enquiry before announcing that he did not intend to proceed with criminal charges.

Not only was the Attorney-General's compassionate act greeted favourably, but there were even some who championed Hume for having done the right thing in helping the woman through their mutual problem. They were ready to excuse what looked like forgery as being an unpremeditated act performed under pressure and designed only to help the woman. Within a week, there was a groundswell of sympathy for Hume and the public appeared ready to forgive him.

With Hume forgiven, it was towards Jean Jacques Charles that the animosity was directed. Jacques was blamed for the swift retribution; and he was especially disliked for insisting that the Minister of Finance resign in public, before the fascinated gaze of the whole country. No minister, for any reason, had ever before had to suffer standing before his peers to confess his sins publicly, and the members began to believe that Jacques' decision had been unnecessarily savage and personally motivated.

In her two years with Jacques, Evangeline had always felt close to him. But as the mood of the country turned against him, and the references to him on radio and television and in the newspapers, gradually changed from admiring to critical, and even at times contemptuous, she felt her own distance from him increasing.

Every day she telephoned Kathleen's apartment to get the name of another doctor. But Kathleen, of course, was in Toronto; and although Evangeline knew she could reach Kathleen by calling Andrew Wickstrom, she felt it would be intruding to telephone her there.

Finally, leafing at random through the telephone book, she picked out the name of another doctor and made an appointment, under a false name. Feeling ridiculous, she dressed herself in a trenchcoat and dark glasses. She left the house by the garden door, but of course the Mounties outside recognized her. They said nothing but as she pulled out of the drive in her little car, she saw them right behind her. Even when she pulled into a parking garage, they followed. She hid a while in the public lavatory of a large downtown department store, and then with satisfaction, decided she had given them the slip. The game was silly, but she dared not let Jacques know where she was going. She finally made it to the doctor's office, out of breath but elated.

She took off her dark glasses and settled down comfortably. He seemed like a nice man, much younger and more modern than her regular doctor.

"Madame Charles," he began.

Evangeline fled.

April arrived, and snowdrops and crocuses began tentatively poking through the thawing ground. The sky arched blue behind the Peace Tower, fat fleecy white clouds blowing, their shadows racing across the melting snow on the broad expanse of the lawns on the Hill.

But as the days grew brighter and the weather milder, the mood of the House of Commons grew darker and more ominous for the Charles administration.

At a regular Wednesday morning NDP caucus, a fiery young member from a Vancouver seat began the process.

"I want to say, Mr. Chairman, that I believe there has been a very serious breach of privilege of the House – and of all its members. Let us review the events of the past month: first we have the abortion bill. The Prime Minister made no bones about his opposition to it. Indeed, he led the fight against it. And then when his own Minister of Justice beat him at his own game and split his caucus, he fired her, just like that!

"Now that was a free vote – as we all know. That's supposed to mean we vote the way our own conscience tells us – not the way the party, or the leader, may want us to. But this Prime Minister fires his own minister because she dared to promote the bill – and it was a Government bill, don't forget – and then voted according to her own conscience!

"And now he fires the man who is supposed to succeed him – again over abortion. And makes him stand up there and spill his guts before the whole world! I think Charles has finally gone too far. He's goading us into getting rid of him. From what I hear, some of his own caucus are talking revolt. Why in hell don't we try to throw him out? We've got the votes. Let's face him with it, now, and get rid of him! I think we'll have the public with us on this one."

The idea, to the surprise of its originator, was immediately and unanimously agreed to. After discussing the implications with his party organization, the NDP leader instructed his House leader to make discreet enquiry among the other parties in the House to discover how many members they might carry with them if they moved to bring Jean Jacques Charles down on this issue.

Len Avery reported back that there was considerable interest among the other parties. Within hours, the rumour raced through the House that a wave of dissent was building, a wave designed to knock Jean Jacques Charles from his high perch.

The Prime Minister, insulated behind his swollen staff, heard nothing directly. The rumour first came to the attentive ear of Boots Jamieson, the P.M.'s principal secretary. Much as he disliked being the bearer of bad news yet one more time, he knew that someone would have to bring the matter to Charles' attention before it got out of hand.

He raised the matter during the following morning's scheduled briefing.

"Prime Minister, there's going to be trouble. This afternoon, someone is going to bring up a matter of privilege involving the whole House."

"A matter of privilege? What on earth for?" demanded Jacques.

"It's about firing Kathleen and Hume, after the free vote on abortion – that's about all I can tell you. But I think it could be very dangerous. You know the House is getting very cranky these days."

"Well, head them off. Don't let them get recognized. Squash it." He dismissed the matter with a wave of his hand.

"There's no way that can be done, sir." Boots was again surprised at how little the P.M. had learned about the rules of the House. "If the speaker allows the motion, they can keep flogging it forever."

"Then have a word with the Speaker. We put him there. Remind him of that, and lean on him a bit. Ludvic will understand."

The young man was aghast. He sputtered: "But . . . but if I did that, he'd have me thrown out of his office, and rightly so. The Speaker is the servant of the members, not of the Government. That is not only highly improper, but also unconstitutional, I – "

"Unconstitutional, is it? If you are so squeamish, Jamieson, I'll speak to one of the ministers about it. He'll see that the fuse is put out before anything catches fire. Now, anything else for today?"

Question Period was tumultuous. But that day no motion of privilege was attempted, and Jacques congratulated himself on his decisiveness. There was a crisis every half-hour, it sometimes seemed, but for once one had been easily resolved.

"A question for the Prime Minister: Can the Right Honourable gentleman advise the House which of his ministers is next on the chop list for opposing his views on abortion?"

For an instant Jacques' temper flared, and a sarcastic retort was poised on his tongue. Then he pulled in the reins on his anger and sat silent. But he flashed a furious glance at his questioner, who sat back, triumphantly. His dart had gone home.

Every day there was a similar, pointed question from another part of the House. Jacques kept himself under tight control, refusing to rise to the bait.

But on a Friday morning, when the House as usual sat at ten A.M. to wind up its business by five o'clock for the weekend, he was taken by surprise when a young member rose from the last tier of desks opposite and raised a question of privilege.

The young Opposition member argued earnestly that the privilege of every member to vote according to his conscience had been breached by the Prime Minister's actions toward his two senior ministers, who were also members. His voice trembled with passion and nervousness.

As he sat down, Len Avery, the NDP House leader and an acknowledged expert on the House Rules, rose to make his contribution in his dry voice. He made a compelling case. The leader of the Official Opposition followed. Sherwood had misgivings about this, but he sounded very firm. And so it went. Very few Liberal members rose in defence.

The Speaker was troubled. This was going to be difficult. He was impressed with the Opposition's argument, and still smarted from the affront of Findlay's visit. He knew that if he found a *prima facie* case of breach of privilege, the Government would be in real danger. It was unlikely they could muster enough speakers to drag the debate until five o'clock, nor enough votes to save themselves if it came earlier. And that, of course, would also cost him his speakership and maybe even his career if an election followed. He wrestled with his own conscience, and then firmly put aside personal concerns.

Stephan Ludvic ruled that there was a *prima facie* case of breach of the members' privilege, and the debate began in earnest.

For a moment there was a huge rush of panic. Then, gritting his teeth, Jacques prepared to fight. There was no likely source of help in the debate among the few scattered members of his caucus who were present. The rest were already off to an early start to their weekends. He twisted in his seat to speak to the Whip.

"You'll have to make sure we have enough members around to keep the debate going. Unless we can win it, we can't afford to let this come to a vote."

Then he began scribbling a note: "Find Bonnie for me and send her into the House as quick as you can. And the House leader. See if you can locate him." He snapped his fingers for a page, and sent the note off to Boots, above him in the officials' gallery.

All through the morning, across the lunch break from noon to two, and into the afternoon, the Whip's office worked feverishly. They located all the Liberal members still in Ottawa on this fine, early-spring afternoon, and demanded their immediate presence in the House. As the afternoon wore on, more and more faces appeared from behind the gold velvet curtains. The press gallery was almost vacant, its only occupants a couple of sleepy, junior wire-service reporters. There were only a scattered handful in the public galleries. It would have taken an experienced student of the parliamentary process to sense the building tension, to be aware that an unusually large number of members occupied their desks on this unseasonably warm April afternoon.

Even Jacques, who was not normally known for his compulsive attendance in the House, stayed in his seat. All afternoon his hopes rose and fell. The Whip was constantly assuring him that enough members could be mustered to win the vote, but after the abortion vote Jacques was not confident of the Whip's predictions. However, as the hours wore on, the feeling of being betrayed and surprised gradually gave way to the sense that this crisis, like the others, might finally be weathered.

It was half-past four. The Whip was nervous. He was having difficulty finding enough speakers to join in the debate, no matter how briefly. And the slips of paper accumulating under his hand, reporting the growing Opposition strength, were disquieting.

"There are just too many if it comes to a vote!" he muttered to himself. He chewed his scraggly moustache, desperately trying to make the projected totals come out differently.

The silence suddenly penetrated his concentration. The Speaker was on his feet. Wildly, the Whip looked about him. All the Liberal members in the House had already spoken. The rules permitted only one speech per member. There wasn't time to call in another. He had fallen into the oldest of parliamentary traps.

"Now we're for it," and he cursed under his breath. "Shit! Shit! Shit!"

The Speaker called for a voice vote.

"Those in favour?" A mass of Opposition members rose together.

"Those opposed?" and the Government members rose from their seats. The Government seemed hopelessly outnumbered but the Whip was on his feet at once, the words leaping from his mouth. "On division," he shouted.

The Speaker stood. "Call in the members."

The Speaker sat down, and through all the rooms and corridors of the cluster of stone buildings, the bells began to ring out the call for a recorded vote.

The Chief Government Whip had done his utmost to bring in all the Liberal members in Ottawa. But it wasn't enough. There was only one solution to his dilemma and that was to keep the bells ringing until five o'clock. That would only postpone the inevitable, because on Monday morning, the Commons would resume the business of the House where it had left off. Of course he would wire and telephone all the Liberal members to have them in their seats, but this was a minority parliament, and defeat was inevitable.

Jean Jacques Charles felt his iron control slipping. He looked down at his white-knuckled hands on the desk before him, and fought to keep down the bile rising in his throat. "*Sois tranquille. Calme-toi!*" he urged himself, and gradually, the flood of fury receded. The Prime Minister hated emotion above all. Reason was the only guide a man should follow. Logic, thoughtful discussion, and a careful assessment of the implications – that was the way. Jacques had always sneered at those guided principally by their passions. "The head must always be the master, not the heart. I must heed that now."

Crisply, he spoke to his assembled advisors: "You have obviously all given up. I haven't heard a useful suggestion yet. But we are still the Government, and we have the weekend ahead to design a solution that will keep us in office. I want to explore the possibility of doing what Alexander Sinclair once did. I want you," he turned to the ashen-faced House leader, "to draft a motion in time to get in on the Order Paper as the first order of business on Monday. Or on Tuesday, if it requires more notice. In that case, we'll have to adjourn the House on Monday on consent as soon as we meet. And we must be able to muster enough members to support us. The motion should offer the House another chance to vote, to reverse itself if it defeats the Government. You know how to phrase it – look up Sinclair's motion in Hansard. I am sure the House only intended to administer a rebuke to the Government. They don't want an election now. And we certainly don't. We are totally unprepared. If you come up with some clever wording, it will enable everyone to save face and back off from an election."

The House leader's eyes were veiled. He had no stomach for this work. He had always thought that Sinclair had resorted to a cheap trick, an unconstitutional manoeuvre. The defeat Sinclair had faced had started as an Opposition stunt. But this time he was sure the Government couldn't get away with it. This was no prank. This time the Opposition meant business. And the members – even some of the Liberal caucus – were in a mood for change. They were ready to dump Jacques, who had been too arrogant for too long.

"Well, what are you waiting for? Get to work, and let me

111

have the draft as soon as it is ready." He flipped up his calendar. "Let me see. I notice I have a speech on Monday at that convention of women. Better cancel that. Send Bonnie, if you can find her.

"I'll be at home all evening. I'm going to take Evangeline to the country tomorrow. The spring air will do her good. You had better alert the staff at Harrington Lake that I am to be expected. And call me if anything turns up. Now cheer up and don't look so glum. And have a nice weekend," he added ironically. "We're not through yet."

But the Prime Minister was wrong. When he arrived home that night, the messages had already begun to pile up.

He locked himself in his study and began to make phone calls. Soon it became clear that the other party leaders would not allow him to put through any business in the House on Monday. They were taking the position that the debate must continue on Monday to the vote, and that if the Government lost the vote and fell, they would insist that he, Jean Jacques Charles, must make the traditional call on the Governor General to advise dissolution of the Government.

It was eight o'clock before he left his study and went to face Evangeline. She was sitting in the same room where he had caught her with Kathleen a month earlier.

"Angèle," he said, sitting beside her and taking her thin hands in his, "I'm sorry but we won't be able to go to Harrington Lake this weekend. There is going to be an election. I don't want one and the country doesn't need one, but there's no choice."

"Oh no," Evangeline murmured sympathetically. "Are you afraid of an election?"

He looked down at her, surprised. "Afraid, Angèle, afraid that I might lose? No, I don't mind that." But there was something. She was right: the prospect of fighting an election on his personal popularity was hardly pleasant. The media would be full of gleeful columnists and announcers waiting to broadcast his downfall. His only consolation was that the Tories were even more disorganized than usual.

"No," he finally said. "I'm not afraid. But I'm not looking forward to it either. Not the way I used to." He paused. "But they won't force me out, the bastards, they *won't*."

Evangeline smiled. "You'll win," she said. "I know you will."

By Sunday Jacques had reached the seven people who were the heart of the Liberal Party organization, the men who had stood behind the scenes and made sure that the Liberal Party stayed – if not in power – near enough to grasp it quickly back again.

As they arrived at 24 Sussex, Jacques realized that he scarcely knew their names, and he now recognized that he had made a grave mistake. Despite their longtime service as the movers and shakers of the Liberal Party organization, he had virtually ignored The Seven since he had romped to victory at the leadership convention. As Prime Minister he had kept on his young, untried aides in the election he had called on the heels of his leadership triumph, and they had Charleston'd across the country, sweeping the opposition before them. Jacques had stuck with those same people in the last election, too, discovering too late the shallowness of their campaign experience. He now blamed them for the minority situation which had just collapsed.

The seven men sat waiting for him to announce the purpose of this hurriedly called meeting. They didn't, Jacques realized, look pleased to be here.

"I have meant for months to call you in," he began, apologetically, "to ask you to organize for the next campaign. I am sorry that I have not done so earlier, but it has been a busy period. There isn't much time to put together the kind of campaign you usually run. But I ask your help, for the party's sake. Will you take on the campaign?"

After a brief discussion, during which Jacques found himself in the uncomfortable position of being told what he must do and how he must behave, they accepted. They would do it they said, "For the party's sake. For Canada's sake." No one mentioned that it was not for the Prime Minister's sake that they had agreed to take on the thankless task.

Sunday evening Kathleen was at her home in Niagara Falls. She had put the house on the market and was having Andrew for a sort of farewell dinner before moving to an apartment she had taken in Toronto.

When the meal was prepared and she was still waiting for Andrew, she sat down for a few minutes in the living room to have a drink and read the papers. It was only then that she noticed the report on the debate on privilege. It appeared in a small box on an inside page of the Saturday paper.

"You know," she said to Andrew later, "the Government will be defeated on Monday."

Andrew, startled, looked across the table at her. "What? I didn't see anything about that. How do you know?"

"It was in the papers," Kathleen said. "Practically hidden. I just happened to notice it." She explained the point of parliamentary procedure.

"Will there be an election?"

"I don't know," Kathleen said. "Sinclair got away with a defeat once; it depends on how serious the motion is considered to be. I know Jacques won't want an election now. He's entirely unprepared. I don't see how he could keep office."

Andrew quizzed her on the constitutional point of a Government keeping office, even after a defeat, and then, after a leisurely coffee, they forgot about politics and engaged in their favourite vice – a fierce backgammon battle.

The next day, back in Toronto, Kathleen was lunching at Winston's in downtown Toronto with a valued old friend, a distinguished, silver-haired former Minister of Finance in the Sinclair administration. She was very fond of Carter Warden, and they had kept up contact over the years since they had served in Cabinet together.

Deep in conversation, they gradually became aware that the suave proprietor was hovering over them.

"I thought you would like to know that there has been a radio newsflash that the Prime Minister has just come from the Governor General, and is on his way to the House to announce the resignation of his Government. The election is expected in June."

Matthew Lyon shifted his finely tailored bulk behind the scarred desk at the Liberal Party Headquarters in Ottawa. He was a British Columbia businessman, and more importantly, he was the chairman of the Liberal Party of Canada. He ground out his cigar as he dropped the telephone into its cradle. Then he looked up at the two people seated across the desk from him.

"Davie, this is a tough one. Aaron Shapiro tells me there's not much money around in Winnipeg. The picture is a little brighter in Quebec, or so Fernand LeMesurier reports. Peregrine Melton thinks he will make out all right on Bay Street; though they don't like the Frazier firing – he's their white-haired boy, you know – but they don't have confidence in the Opposition, either. Anyway, it's clear that we'll have to run this campaign on a shoe-string. No fancy polls, mind. We'll need the money for the candidates and the national campaign."

At the mention of polls, David Kirke winced. He had a well-deserved reputation for proposing a few opinion samples when in doubt. The shaggy-haired, stoop-shouldered Senator Kirke had been through enough political campaigns, however, to know the importance of financial considerations.

"There's no time for them, anyway," he said, "even if there was enough of the long green around, Matt. We're just going to have to wing this one. I don't like to fly by the seat of my pants like this, but what choice do we have? Imagine letting the party machinery run down this way! My God, this office was on skeleton staff when the Government fell! Charles doesn't deserve to win again! But like you, and the others, I'll do my damndest to pull it all together. I got Brian Scotland to take on the job of finding candidates, but we had to promise him a Senate appointment to do it. Jacques was none too keen. But he'll have to take the flack. There's simply no time to worry about bending the rules a little. Hell, if he wants to come back as Prime Minister, he's going to have to learn to *fight* an election! Kissing young chicks isn't going to get him anywhere this time. And he can't afford to glide about like the philosopher king, as he did in the last campaign. This is a fight, an uphill fight." Senator Kirke paused. He was letting his own anger show through and knew now was not the time for it.

"I wanted to pull out all the stops on Evangeline," he went on. "Have her with him all the time. Canadians just can't get enough of her, and that sure doesn't do Jacques any harm. But he says no; she isn't up to it physically. Apparently she's in bed most of the time with a rough pregnancy. They expect twins. Did you know that?" He looked at the others, eyebrows raised.

The wealthy westerner shook his head. "That's a bad break. I was counting on Evangeline to pull in some votes. But if you can't use her, how about working that song of hers into the campaign? Maybe some blow-ups of her at every major rally? Build some sympathy for Jacques, if nothing else."

Bonnie Costello, seated next to Senator Kirke, nodded her head. "That's not a bad idea, Matt. Evangeline seems to touch everyone, not just women. And I'm sure she'll do everything her health allows. Maybe we could tape some radio interviews. Even television. Or she could sign a big batch of letters and we could send them out."

Senator Kirke looked across at the vivacious speaker. Bonnie was no great looker – her nose was too long and heavy, and her ankles were more like the proverbial piano legs – but she made up for it with enthusiasm, and after the first few meetings he'd forgotten her looks and been utterly charmed by her.

Bonnie, Jean Jacques Charles' parliamentary secretary in the just dissolved Parliament, had come up to Ottawa for a few days at the chairman's request. She had already whipped her own organization in Toronto Beaches into shape, and now she was making herself available for a national speaking tour, to give a hand to other ridings. She was the liaison member from the parliamentary caucus, and the chairman was grateful for her quick, creative mind.

Years ago, he remembered, there had been another bright, eager newcomer who had given of herself unstintingly when the party needed her. This girl is a lot like Kathleen was then, he judged, regretting that Kathleen wasn't here this time to give them a hand. But under the circumstances, she couldn't be asked to do anything this time. If only Charles hadn't fired Kathleen and Hume – his two most popular ministers – they wouldn't be in this mess now. It was another symptom of Charles' foolish pride. He shook his head at the thought.

"Have you by any chance seen Kathleen Marshal in Toronto? I hear she's there most of the time. Do you know if she plans to take part in the election?"

"No," Bonnie answered. She walked over to the coffee pot and drained its dregs into her cup. "I don't think she expects to do anything but help the new candidate in Niagara. I saw her the other day, to thank her – she'd sent me a campaign contribution." And then she added: "Do you think it's fair to ask Kathleen to do anything more? After the way the P.M. treated her? She's taken enough from him, in my opinion."

"You're right, Bonnie," agreed Senator Kirke. "But I wonder if she could give Brigadier Melton a hand raising money?"

"Not her line of country, Davie."

"I suppose not, Matt."

"Well, to get back. Who's in charge of speakers? Who is making up the Prime Minister's tours? Maybe there should be someone assigned to keep Jacques' temper down. Seems to me he's pretty unbridled these days. Without Evangeline along to keep him sweet, there could be a potential danger." Matthew Lyon ticked off the questions on the checklist lying before him on the scarred desk.

"It's okay, Matt, we've covered that. I am sending along his principal secretary, Boots Jamieson. We have worked together often before, you know. It was my suggestion that Boots go into the PMO in the first place. He knows Charles, and how to handle him. Hopefully there will be no problem on that score." Kirke referred to his list of personnel and their assignments. "And as for the speakers' desk, I've arranged to borrow Kathleen's secretary, Barbara Hepburn. There isn't anybody more efficient anywhere. And the P.M.'s tours will be handled by Gordon Neville, who was Kathleen's executive assistant. They are both crackerjacks, and we are lucky to get them. Right now, also, I'm waiting for a call confirming that Hume Frazier's exec is coming with us. There's Hume's secretary, too

– the blonde bombshell – but she could be pretty disruptive here."

And so on through the list. Finding the appropriate people to staff the dozens of key jobs for the national campaign, and hundreds more for lesser, but still essential, work. The campaign was off to a late start, but it was taking shape as loyal Liberals across the country answered the call to battle. Constituency people, who had been gradually souring on Charles and were dismayed by the near defeat in the House, were starting to feel better. This time, the political pros were back in command.

"Look, Boots," Jean Jacques Charles turned to his aide, "I know that the party insists that we do everything their way, but this pace is killing me. I have no time for myself, or my wife. I have to take some time off."

The two men were sitting in the aging jet, papers littering the table between them. They were in shirt sleeves, their ties loosened, a welcome drink in hand. The plane was not as comfortable as the government's VIP aircraft, but it was the best the party could afford. They had been campaigning for three weeks now, and the P.M. was beginning to chafe at the tight reins that had been placed on him. At first he had also been angered to find Boots Jamieson constantly at his elbow. However, although he knew that the cherubic-faced bachelor was a watchdog assigned by the old pros, Jacques had come to value his political judgement; and the two men had fallen into the habit of intense conversation in the hours they had to while away on plane or trains or bus or motor car. Jamieson was in constant touch with the campaign committee, and each day they discussed the implications of the reports streaming in from every area of the country.

"I'm sorry, Prime Minister. I know that you are worried about Evangeline, but the latest polls show that the party is running neck-and-neck with the Tories. That's not bad, considering the near-defeat in the House, but it isn't good, either. You see, a party defeated in Parliament just doesn't get returned to office, although it has happened once or twice. But what is most troublesome, sir, are these other polls." Jamieson pulled a sheaf of papers out of his briefcase which documented that Charles was trailing the Conservative leader, Richard Sherwood, in personal popularity. "Somehow, we've got to get that trend reversed. If we can't, there goes the ballgame."

"Okay, I'll keep it up, but if I shake any more hands or smile for any more photos, I might as well be replaced by a robot."

Boots laughed. He knew that the P.M. was making an attempt to be popular. Jacques had found it difficult to accept the idea that the party saw him as a millstone around its neck, but he had also realized somewhat belatedly that he needed the party. He had, on the whole, done as he was told, and had redoubled his efforts to be charming to the press people who accompanied him everywhere. He had even made an attempt to remember the names and faces of key Liberals he met across the country.

"Where do we go after Halifax?" the Prime Minister asked. "Regina, I suppose, that's far enough away," he added sarcastically.

"Actually, we're only going to Sudbury," Boots replied. When he saw the look on Jacques' face he hurried on. "You know that the campaign organization decided on a scattergun approach to keep you criss-crossing the country by air."

"Yes, but it's such a waste of time, dropping into Quebec, and then over to Calgary, to Victoria and then right across the country to Charlottetown, then doubling back to Kingston, then Winnipeg, Toronto and Saskatoon."

"But this way we get the maximum publicity in all the provinces. You must appear to be everywhere at once."

Grudgingly, Jacques accepted Boots' advice. The campaign had been exhausting, both physically and emotionally. There were no massed thousands at his rallies, no sign that the old magic still existed. But though the audiences were lukewarm, even skeptical, he was at least reassured to see that most of the halls were full. What he didn't see, Boots knew, was the effort that had gone into making sure that the faithful crowded in.

The spring had been a long and lonely one for Evangeline.

After her visit to the second doctor, when she had fled his office, she had walked about downtown Ottawa in a state of utter depression. As she used to when she was on tour and felt too depressed to cope, she dropped into a bar. Not so much to drink – she had seen too many drunks as a child to be interested in drinking very much herself – but just for an anonymous place to sit and think.

And, in the comfortable darkness of a downtown Ottawa bar, she had toyed with a glass of wine and tried to think reasonably about her future. She would not, she now knew, have the nerve to go to yet another doctor to seek an abortion. Kathleen had left Ottawa and there was no other friend she could turn to. Jacques had taken her silence on the whole issue to be agreement, and had now taken to making remarks about how things would be "when the babies come."

There was nothing to do, she knew, but to go ahead and have the babies. If this was to be her fate – let it be.

But as April wore on, it became clear that the pregnancy was not going to be an easy one. Her blood pressure was still high and her health had deteriorated. The doctors had made her take to her bed in the hope that she could carry the twins to full term. Jacques was away all the time and Evangeline was lonely and bored in the stone mansion by the Ottawa. The nightmares came less often, but each time they did and she awoke to find herself alone in the large bed, she struggled anew with her fears and her growing sense of fatalism.

She missed Kathleen desperately. She regretted now that in the two years since she had married the Prime Minister of Canada, she had had so little opportunity to make a wider circle of friends. But she had been content to share her hours with her new husband and with Kathleen. Now, when she most needed it, there was no one for her to be close to.

When Jacques had broached the subject of helping in the campaign, Evangeline had been enthusiastic, glad at last to have some significant role in the political fight of her husband's life, and glad, too, for something to fill the empty hours.

They brought in television cameras, and, dressed in a delicate lawn robe touched with lace, a large double bassinet beside her, and a tangle of knitting in her lap, she gave interviews. She penned letters by the hour – bright, cheery notes to people she had met across the country – and placed endless long-distance calls for a brief chat, to hundreds of people from the lists the party supplied her. She sat for new photographs, to be enlarged and used at party rallies. And there were poignant photographs of her and Jacques, hands entwined.

Everything she did seemed to succeed and, desperate, the party exploited her more and more. "The Song of Evangeline" was heard everywhere, and her records and tapes were handed out freely at party functions. Evangeline's popularity grew, and the affection that poured out to her across the country began finally to influence Jacques' standing among the leaders.

But as the campaign wore on, Evangeline's appearance was transformed: always slight, she lost weight until she was almost wraith-like. Her slender, expressive hands were pale and blue-veined to the point of translucence. The smudges below the great topaz eyes never faded, and the thick, dark-gold cornsilk of her hair seemed to have lost much of its former vitality.

In the end the party regulars held out some hope that Evangeline had been able to turn the tide that had been running against her husband and the Liberal Party.

Early on election night, Jacques dropped in to the untidy hotel suite where the leaders of the campaign team had gathered to learn the results of their efforts. The Ontario polls had just closed, and they were watching the early returns from the Maritimes. Those returns – touch and go – were a vanguard of the long night when the fortunes of the Charles Government teetered this way and that. Feeling useless, Jacques left after less than an hour, as Quebec's early returns began to flood in. His own province was supporting him as he had hoped.

Later, Jacques and Evangeline lay together in the big bed, watching the television set which had been pushed to its foot. Beside him, the radio, tuned low, gave him reports in French. They snuggled together as they had not for months, and joked a little, playing games with names for the unborn twins. He was alarmed at how wan Evangeline looked, and murmured plans to take her on trips, promising to be by her side evermore. He talked of his joy at the birth anticipated by early July, and promised her that he would complete this term as Prime Minister, if re-elected, and then retire so that they would have time for themselves and their children.

Her head on his shoulder, his arm encircling her, Evangeline was content. This tender Jacques was the man she had married. He had been purged, it seemed, of the wild anger of months ago. She was glad that she had helped in the campaign – glad to have been there when he needed her. Evangeline dozed, awoke to whisper and kiss her husband, and dozed again. Even Jacques slept in snatches as the night wore on. The Liberals had strengthened their support in Ontario and Quebec, slipped back disastrously in the prairie provinces. British Columbia would tell the tale.

At midnight, it was not yet resolved. Jean Jacques Charles pulled his arm from about his sleeping wife and got up to turn off the television.

"What does it matter, anyway? Tomorrow is soon enough to know whether I am to remain as master of this house. There's nothing anyone can do now. It was decided hours ago when the polls closed. It may be morning before all the results are in. I'm tired, and Evangeline is tired. She looks so frail."

Before he climbed back into bed, Jacques dropped to his knees in the dark room. "Please, God, keep my Evangeline safe."

The election resulted in a tie between the Conservatives and the Liberals. For several days, many asked whether the Government had a right to hang on in office, or whether, denied a majority again, the Prime Minister should advise the Governor General to ask Richard Sherwood to form a Government. Then a recount in a distant B.C. riding added another Government seat, and the Liberals stood at two members more than the Conservatives. Jacques would at least be allowed to meet the House, to discover whether he would be supported by enough of the Opposition to carry on.

The Cabinet was recalled. Jacques made only a minor shuffle, necessary because of the loss of a handful of ministers. For the moment, he took back the Justice portfolio himself. It had proved too onerous for Stan Findlay, already overburdened by the responsibilities of Transport. The dispirited Cabinet began the process of drafting a new Throne Speech.

Jacques woke with a start. The big old house was still – too still. Something was wrong, but what? Then he realized that, although he strained in the darkness, he could not hear Evangeline's soft breathing, nor feel her slight weight in the bed beside him.

He snapped on the bedside light. Three o'clock. The sheets beside him seemed still warm, but where was she? Pulling on his robe, he stepped from the bed into something sticky.

"My God, it's blood! Evangeline, Evangeline." Then he saw her, collapsed in a heap on the floor. A dark wet pool was seeping across the floorboards from beneath the still, crumpled figure.

Frantically, Jacques pressed the buzzer to summon help. He knelt to gather her in his arms, tenderly raising her head to pillow it against his chest, as he murmured her name into her ear. She was so white, so limp, but he was sure she still lived.

After what seemed an eternity, the ambulance had arrived and sped the Prime Minister's wife to the hospital through the silent, pre-dawn streets of Ottawa.

The doctor was already at the hospital. The old man sighed deeply as he met Jacques in the waiting room. "This is what I feared most. I'll have to do a Caesarian section immediately. I can't promise anything. Her blood pressure has stayed high, and her heart has weakened under the strain. Couple that with toxemia and there's bound to be trouble. It sounds like a massive separation of the placenta. I'll do everything I can, Prime Minister. Everything."

The next morning, only two weeks after election day, the Prime Minister's office issued a brief press release:

During the night the Prime Minister's wife, Evangeline, was

delivered of twin girls by Caesarian section. The children, as yet unnamed, are doing well. Madame Charles died in childbirth.

Chapter Seven

Kathleen was sitting with Andrew in his living room when the news of Evangeline's death was broadcast. For a moment she was too shocked to believe it. And then, as the announcer explained that the twins' lives had been saved by a Caesarian section, but that their mother had died only hours later, Kathleen gradually realized that it was true. Evangeline had died in childbirth. Just as she had feared.

That night they had been invited out to meet some friends of Andrew's. But Kathleen found herself so upset that she cancelled the dinner and went home to be alone in her apartment.

Evangeline, dead. In these months away from Ottawa she thought that she had forgiven and forgotten everything bad that had happened in the capital. But this news brought it all back. Evangeline, totally distraught, turning to her when there was no one else. And Jacques, arrogant and proud, unable to let anyone know him beyond his controlled exterior.

During the months since that bitter scene at 24 Sussex when Jacques had ordered Evangeline to have nothing further to do with her, Kathleen had become increasingly concerned about Evangeline. But it was only in the last month of the election campaign, when Evangeline's pictures began to appear in newspapers and on television, that Kathleen realized that her friend was under great stress. She had been greatly disturbed by the visible changes in Evangeline's appearance. But since Kathleen herself knew little about bearing children, she tried to convince herself that Evangeline's obvious exhaustion was something any woman might expect with a difficult pregnancy. There had been no call for help, no hint from Evangeline, personally or in her television interviews, that she was less than serene about her approaching *accouchement*; and in the photographs with Jacques, her face glowed so luminously with love that Kathleen thought Evangeline must have overcome her fears and become reconciled to bearing the twins.

Kathleen poured herself a drink. And then she sat down and wrote a long note to the Prime Minister. She knew that he must be devastated at his loss.

Kathleen and Andrew flew in Andrew's company plane to the Montreal funeral. Without direction from the Prime Minister, his aides had made the plans to lay his wife in his family plot in the old cemetery, with its gray and toppling gravestones. The priests in their white vestments celebrated a mass of joy at the ascent of Evangeline's soul. At the funeral Kathleen caught only a glimpse of Jacques. Head bowed, he moved like an automaton, unaware of hands reaching out for his, or of snatches of whispered commiseration.

Over the summer, there were the usual newspaper photographs of the Charles twins: tiny wrinkled human morsels with their mother's heart-shaped face, wisps of golden down on their round little heads. When an adult was included, it was always a crisply uniformed nurse in white. There were no pictures of the Prime Minister with his small daughters.

In July, it was announced that the re-opening of Parliament would be delayed until late fall, and in the torpor of the Ottawa summer, reporters scrambled for crumbs of political news. There was little. The leaders of the other parties were themselves tired. Their forces were in need of regrouping, and they sensed the sympathy that welled from the Canadian people for Jacques in his loss. They were content to bide their time. Jacques himself disappeared from the news. If the staff of the PMO knew were he was, they refused to say. The ministers left to their senior officials the unfinished work of drafting the new Throne Speech, and themselves sought relaxation from the rigours of their June election campaign.

It was summer and the whole country seemed willing to drift. Everyone was content to enjoy the unusually good weather, the long string of bright hot days that melted into cool and perfect nights.

Kathleen had postponed the opening of her office until after Labour Day, and she and Andrew spent much of the summer relaxing together.

In July, Kathleen badgered Andrew into driving to her cabin in the mid-Ontario highlands. There, he pitched in like a veteran cottager, helping her to straighten and clean after the winter's closing. To her amusement, he displayed a knack for cooking breakfasts of fresh-caught bass and thin-sliced new potatoes, raw-fried. They strolled around the lake while she pointed out its beauty spots; and on the pine-crowned ridge they sprawled on the deep mat of fragrant needles to watch the sun set across the rippling water.

Taking Andrew to Secret Lake was a kind of test. The long, twisting lake had been a part of Kathleen's summers since her childhood. It had a deep hold on her, crowded with memories. Something in her responded to the peace of the place, and she knew that if she were to marry, it would be to someone who was as vulnerable to the appeal of the lake as she was.

Despite the strong attraction between them, Kathleen and Andrew remained circumspect about sex, and had never shared sleeping quarters. Although Kathleen was not a virgin, she had hardly been a woman to tumble into bed on first meeting an interesting man. The mainstay of her adult life had been work in law and politics – both places where women were very much in the minority. And although she had occasionally taken lovers, no man had ever remained important after the first months of infatuation.

At the lake, she gingerly explained her past to Andrew, who showed no interest whatsoever in knowing who the men had been. He talked a little about his long-dead Swedish wife, Astrid, and how the loneliness of the intervening years had been alleviated by pleasure in his children and the success of his publishing business.

They returned to the lake for the Labour Day weekend, and

as they lay sunning themselves beside the water, stretched out on rustic chaises, Kathleen reached a decision. She sat up and reached for Andrew's tanned hand.

"Drew, darling, when do you want to marry me? I have just come to the conclusion that it is stupid to put it off any longer. Look at the time we are wasting. Who knows how many years we have left? I've been thinking about Evangeline and Jacques. What a tragedy that they had only two years together!"

Andrew looked at her, elated.

"What about the office you're opening on Tuesday? Have you thought about that? The announcement cards are out, and your staff is raring to go. It isn't like you to change your mind that way. Are you sure, Kate?"

"Yes, I am sure, Drew. But you're right. I don't want to give up the office. But I assumed that you wouldn't mind if I worked until you retire. I thought I could go ahead with the office, at least until then. Who knows? It may not be a success. Perhaps there'll be no clients. God forbid! And my lease is only for a year. Anyway, I do need to do something. I've had no income since the election, except for my parliamentary pension, and while I have loved this lazy summer, I'll go crazy if I have nothing to do all winter."

Andrew swung his legs off the slatted lounge.

"And that's how you see marriage to me – as having nothing to do?"

Kathleen looked at him anxiously. He had turned his back to her and she detected an edge to his voice.

"Oh, Drew, don't be so bloody sensitive! You know what I mean. For a while at least, I need the mental stimulation. My mind is getting flabby. And, I suppose, I need to prove something to myself. Maybe that I can make a success of a new life, on my own. That will give me more confidence to take on the awesome job of being your wife." She touched his shoulder.

"How about a compromise?" he said, turning to face her. "Let's say you tackle this job until, say, Christmas? New Year's? In the meantime, I can set things in motion for retirement. My sixtieth birthday is in December. That will be just about perfect. We can take a few weeks out for a honeymoon somewhere in the south and then you can come back and grind away in your office till the lease is up. And then we'll talk about it again. Suit you?"

She threw her arms around his neck. "Oh, Andrew Wickstrom, you're a darling! That's perfect! Oh yes, everything fits. Thank you for understanding."

On the day after Labour Day, Kathleen had opened her office. That evening, as she waited with Andrew to receive guests he had invited to a small reception to celebrate her re-entry into the profession, he slipped a magnificent solitaire pearl ring on the third finger of her right hand.

"This is something very special that I have been saving for two long years, Right Honourable Madam! Here's to us, Kate, my love, and a long and happy life together."

"Oh, Andrew, it's beautiful. I love it. But why on my right hand?"

"An old Scandinavian custom. They wear it there all over Europe, I think. Makes me feel just a little more secure about you. Do you mind?"

"Of course not. It will give me more opportunity to flash it around. Discreetly, of course. Oh, Andrew, I'm so happy."

Kathleen lay on her back on the wide bed in the cool, spacious bedchamber. She glanced fondly at the quietly sleeping form facing her. Fingers of early-morning tropical sunlight reached through the slatted blinds to stroke him, gilding the bright fuzz of body hair, moulding the ropey shoulders and powerful legs, tangling in the close-cropped hair of the well-sculpted head.

"Kathleen Marshal. Kathleen Marshal Wickstrom. Kathleen Wickstrom. Mrs. Andrew Wickstrom."

She rolled the names around on her tongue, savouring them, testing the feel of them on her lips, listening to the sound of them. "Kathleen Marshal" sounded fine, familiar. There had been more than fifty years of Kathleen Marshal. But the other names sounded strange, somehow wrong. Except for Kathleen Wickstrom. Kathleen Wickstrom. That was a name she might get used to.

Yes, I think I like the sound of that – Kathleen Wickstrom. But it isn't me. Not yet, anyway. But then, it's only been me for a day.

Does every bride feel so odd? she wondered. It isn't like a new dress, or a new hairdo – those are such temporary changes, and underneath, you are still you. But this woman – this Kathleen Wickstrom – she's never existed before. She's a brand new person, just since yesterday.

Yesterday. Had it only been one day?

Kathleen hated big weddings – the white dresses and matching attendants – the whole circus. She had always dreaded the engagement parties of her youth – the showers where the bride-to-be struggled to untie the knotted ribbons, the false cooing over yet another tasteless gift. She much preferred the little dinners and cocktail parties tendered them last fall by Andrew's friends and associates.

She was determined that she wasn't going to parade down an aisle on a stranger's arm in a big church, turning into a public display the very private and significant moment of pledging between Andrew and her. So they had been married at noon in Andrew's comfortable living room. Kathleen had no illusions; she thought herself as a big, plain woman, but she had felt beautiful in her pleated grey chiffon dress, her arms overflowing with yellow roses and sweet-scented sprays of white freesia.

Now she stretched her arms out before her, turning her hands to catch the beams of light. On the third finger of her right hand was a broad band of beaten rose-gold and, next to it, the glowing pearl.

She laughed to herself at the shock it was going to give everyone on the Hill when they heard the old maid had finally taken a husband! She wondered what Jacques would say. Parliament – she hadn't thought about it for months and now it was filling her mind on the first morning of her honeymoon. As if anything in Ottawa could be traded for this morning in Bermuda.

Kathleen tenderly traced the outlines of the sleeping face beside her. Andrew's eyelids trembled, and his eyes opened.

Those deep blue eyes that reminded her of changeable northern lakes, ringed round with golden reeds of long, sun-tipped lashes.

Very gravely he said, without moving, "Good morning, Mrs. Wickstrom."

Kathleen was startled. It seemed as if he had read her thoughts! "Good morning, husband."

Andrew reached for her, pulling her into the circle of his arms, pillowing her head on his shoulder and holding her close. Kathleen lifted her head and kissed him. Her husband drew her close, their bodies touching at breast and thigh. Gently he kissed her hairline, her nose, her eyelids, and then deeply, her parted lips.

"*Vass goot*, Frau Wickstrom?" he murmured into her ear when it was over.

"*Vass goot*, Herr Wickstrom," she replied. "But not perfect."

Andrew lifted his head in surprise.

"I think we should spend this day in bed, practising to be perfect," she said solemnly.

Andrew grinned, a wicked gleam in his eye. "You shock me, Mrs. Wickstrom. What a suggestion from a respectable married lady who is, shall I say, past her first youth!"

"No, you shall not say that! I was born only yesterday. Do you realize, Drew, that there never was a Kathleen Wickstrom before yesterday? I am fresh-minted, sir, and feeling very randy-dandy. And you are a very superior lover."

"Superior? Is that all? I can furnish better testimonials than that!" Andrew grinned at her again, as she made a face.

"What – with that old thing? It must be all of sixty years old."

"What blasphemy! Anyway, let's get up now. I want a shower and a shave. How about sharing a shower? That's something we haven't tried yet. Then you, my bride, may scrub my back. Maybe I'll even introduce you to the mysterious rite of a man shaving." He rolled her away from him with a playful slap at her buttocks. "Oh I like that." He grabbed her and patted her bottom again.

She squirmed out of his grasp. "Drew, I'm not so sure *I* like it," she said hesitantly.

"Like what?"

"That butt-slapping, it's really a chauvinist's gesture, you know. And I don't know about sharing a shower. I'm not used to living with someone, and that kind of intimacy will take some getting used to."

Andrew looked at her in surprise.

"Intimacy? After what we have just been doing? Sometimes Katie, I think you are a little nuts."

He moved to her, catching her by the upper arms, until she turned her face to him.

"Kathleen, remember I love you. Very much, and I want our lives together to be full of joy. But we are both old enough to need some space in this marriage. We can't be together every minute, and we shouldn't be. We would both find it stifling. But we shouldn't be embarrassed being together, in any kind of intimacy. Darling, will you give it a try?"

Kathleen sat on the edge of the bed. She was a little surprised at the serious tone of Andrew's remarks. Yet it was true that she had harboured misgivings about marrying so late; she had been afraid she would be suffocated by living at close quarters with a strange male creature. It flashed through her mind how well Andrew could read her.

She cast her eyes down, and said demurely: "Yes, my husband. I'll try, but you must be patient with such a newly graduated old spinster." She sneaked a look at him. Andrew's expression lightened and he laughed. The awkward moment had passed.

In the next three weeks Andrew and Kathleen covered nearly every square foot of the tiny, flowering island of Bermuda. The weather was a miracle. Instead of the windy, rain-driven days they had been prepared for, it was unseasonably balmy as they walked and cycled and picnicked, cruised in a glass-bottomed boat and a fast, spray-flinging cutter. They played a little lazy tennis. They sunned on the slivers of sheltered beaches, but shunned the too-cold waters.

In the three weeks of their honeymoon, the Wickstroms floated in a space out of time, responding to no regimen but their own. Their marriage took on shape and depth. They grew to a new intimacy as the secrets of the other, body and mind, unfolded in harmony.

It was an idyll, and it had to end. They stuffed themselves, their luggage and their purchases into a minute taxicab and gaily waved goodbye to the now-familiar trees overhanging the highway and to the glimpses of coves and beaches, assigning to each a special remembrance of their happy hours there.

At the airport, Andrew's company plane awaited them. As they entered the plane, bronzed, relaxed, and happy, the crew could see that the union of these two, no-longer-young lovers was off to a rousing start. At their request, the pilot circled Bermuda after takeoff for their last, lingering view of the island paradise; and then Andrew opened the bulging briefcase and Kathleen eagerly immersed herself in the pile of Canadian newspapers.

It was a shock to their eyes, still filled with the greens and pinks and whites of the island and its surrounding azure seas, when their descent to Toronto revealed the forgotten vistas of snow-piled fields. Sharp blasts of frigid air buffeted them, and they were glad to scramble into the warm car that awaited their arrival. When they reached Andrew's sprawling Rosedale home, they were suddenly happy to see the eager faces of the housekeeper and of Andrew's three grown children, who had arrived to welcome Kathleen to her new home.

Later that evening as they were preparing for bed, she turned to him and said, "It was just that, you know, Drew: a homecoming. They are such wonderful kids. They have been so kind to me. They do like me, don't you think?"

She was seated at the dressing-table and Andrew stood over her as she plaited her hair into thick, loose braids.

"No, darling, they don't just *like* you. All the Wickstroms *love* you. We are already a family, with grandchildren and all."

It was now almost exactly a year since the last election, when the wise men of the party – and, most of all, The Seven – had pulled off the miracle whereby Jean Jacques Charles had been returned as Prime Minister – a minority Prime Minister, once again, but still Prime Minister.

Now The Seven were meeting again. They had come together for a grim purpose: to dethrone a king. But the problem was to find his successor. In the last months, they had talked by telephone several times, but they found such communication far from satisfactory. Now, in mid-June, they were gathered in the gloomy old Toronto mansion that was the home of Brigadier Peregrine Melton, retired.

"I figure that the Opposition won't let him survive much longer. I know the NDP leader made that promise to the nation last year – that they would support the Government for at least a couple of years to avoid yet another election – but they'd love to bring him down. I would say we have no more than another year, at most, and maybe not that long. Remember what happened last time. And Charles, despite his election promises, hasn't been making himself any new friends."

The speaker was their host, the retired brigadier. He swung his balding head around, his glance resting on each of the others lounging in deep armchairs, drinks in hand. Melton was the oldest in the room, with the possible exception of Carter Warden, once Sandy Sinclair's doughty Minister of Finance. The old soldier's faded blue eyes caught the slight nods of agreement of the others: Senator Aaron Shapiro of Winnipeg, chief party fund raiser; Fernand LeMesurier, responsible for the French-speaking party wing and for raising money in Quebec; Senator David Kirke, the chief party organizer; Matthew Lyndon, from British Columbia, the chairman of the federal Liberals, and Senator James O'Rourke, the short, round, pink-skinned pixie with the fringe of stiff white hair, a former premier of Nova Scotia. In the corner's gloom, beyond reach of the dim lights, were two specially invited guests, Bonnie Costello, M.P., and Boots Jamieson, the Prime Minister's principal secretary.

"I suppose this is difficult for you, Jamieson? Would you rather be excused? You can't enjoy being present while we plan a palace revolt. You are so close to the Prime Minister every day. Suit yourself, but we won't hold it against you – unless, of course, you should decide to tell him." The courtly Brigadier's tone had hardened at his last words. There was a hint of a threat, Jamieson felt.

"Yes, sir, this is making me squirm. But I'm a party man, first and foremost. I rather like Jacques; he isn't always the ogre; and I guess I excuse some of the things he does because he really hasn't recovered from the loss of Evangeline. But I do agree that he's become totally ineffective. He's just got to go and I think my place is here, sir, really I do, if I'm to be of any help."

Senator O'Rourke murmured approvingly. If Boots' reply hadn't been expected, they would never have permitted David Kirke to bring the man to this meeting. The essence of this operation was total secrecy. No one could guess what the Prime Minister's reaction to their insurrection would be, but Jacques was certain to see their actions against him as nothing less than high treason, and no one could doubt his retaliation would be swift and cruel.

Matthew Lyndon, the impeccably garbed chairman, crossed his legs, bringing into view the pebble-grained white loafers that marked him as a Vancouverite. The Brigadier, seeing Lyndon's shoes, couldn't help shaking his head. Wouldn't be caught dead in 'em, was the way he put it to himself, but he was at least consoled to know that none of the older, more conservative men in the room would have disagreed.

Bonnie Costello broke the silence. "I suppose you're also wondering about me, sir. After all, I was Jacques' parliamentary secretary in the last Parliament. But I helped Kathleen and the others with the abortion bill and I suppose the P.M. didn't approve of that. This term he didn't reappoint me; and as far as making the Cabinet goes – well –"

It was Lyndon who answered the young M.P.

"It was my idea to invite you here, Bonnie. I don't know what we would have done without you during the campaign last year. You've already proven that your credentials are good, so far as loyalty to the party is concerned, so don't worry about that."

"Thank you," Bonnie replied. "From everything I've heard lately, the public in Toronto has reached a high level of irritation with this Government. That first wave of sympathy for Jacques just melted away when the rumour started that

Evangeline's doctors had initially advised an abortion, which Jacques refused to let her have. Even the pro-lifers have swung against him."

"What you say about feelings in Toronto goes in spades for the west coast," Lyndon agreed. "Abortion has always been a hot topic out there. We took a lot of flack in the election but the public seems to approve of that bill.

"All kinds of people in my circle have made nasty cracks about Charles – condemning his wife to death, as it were. Added to the mess of the economy, the sick dollar and growing unemployment even while the welfare ripoffs continue – well, you have to look around mighty hard to find anybody who wants to 'do the Charleston' now. If Angel had died before election day, and all that medical stuff had come out, we wouldn't have had a prayer, and you know how vital those last couple of seats in B.C. proved to be."

"Same picture in Winnipeg," added Aaron Shapiro. He had white hair that hung to his shoulders, but his dark eyes sparkled and his face was amazingly unlined. "Jacques has never been what you might term Manitoba's favourite politician, but they sure liked Hume Frazier; and they haven't forgiven Jacques for dumping him so savagely over that affair." Some of the others nodded in agreement; like every prime minister, Jacques had gained support with a strong Cabinet. In firing Kathleen and Hume, he had only hurt his own credibility.

The Honourable Carter Warden, slender and spectacled, was dressed as usual, despite the June day, in a dark, pin-striped suit, his stiff collar caught by a gold collar bar.

He had been out of electoral politics for more than a decade but he had maintained an enormous circle of friends. There was nothing formal about Warden's network of contacts. People just called him up for lunch, or dropped into his office to talk politics, or kept in touch by mail. He probably knew more, from day to day, about Liberals in every part of the country than anyone else did.

Now Warden pulled off his glasses and played with them absently; then as usual he went straight to the heart of the matter:

"The problem, gentlemen, is that we cannot face the Prime Minister and demand a new leadership convention until we have some idea who the next leader will be. There is just no point in leaping from the frying pan into the fire. We'll be forced to stick to the devil we know until we have a credible alternative. There are some damned able people we had hoped to elect but they were just too scared to run in last year's election. Two or three of them might have the makings of a prime minister – I'm thinking of that former mayor of yours, Matthew, or maybe our former university president, Peregrine, and there are a couple of other high-profile people – but they aren't elected yet, and they have no parliamentary experience whatever. And since Kathleen and Hume have gone, there's nobody left in the Cabinet of any weight or following.

"If we could hold off on this for another year, some of those new people might get into office. With a little seasoning they would give us a much wider choice. But we can't wait. I think Peregrine is right when he says time is running out. Gentlemen," with a nod of apology to Bonnie, "we are, as the saying goes, up the creek without a paddle."

Fernand LeMesurier was a man of considerable elegance, tall and lean with a distinguished bearing, the scion of an old Quebec City family.

"*Mademoiselle*," he enquired of Bonnie, "what is the position of the caucus toward our Prime Minister? In particular, what are you perhaps able to tell us about his support among the Quebec members?"

The young M.P. thought for a moment and then faced her questioner. "I know that they have been having meetings. I think they are unhappy with Jacques' leadership. But there are several cliques, some of them at cross-purposes with the others. But the Quebeckers are quite, ah, secretive – if you'll forgive the word. They keep to themselves. You understand, sir?"

"Ah yes, I am afraid I do," he said. "What you have described is what I have been told by my own sources. Some of them are fiercely supportive of the Prime Minister. They assess any suggestion that he should be asked to step down as a slight against every *québecois*. Others would be glad to see him go. They are all a little frightened by him, I think."

There was a pause, and then Aaron Shapiro broke in.

"How about Hume Frazier? The press still mentions him as the heir apparent, despite that fiasco. I hear he is doing very well for himself with SilverTinCo. They live in Toronto now, and are pretty social. It doesn't seem to have hurt his career in business, anyway. And he's liked in the west."

Aaron Shapiro was a particular fan of Frazier's. He liked Hume's crisp, staccato style; and their infrequent meetings while Hume had been a Cabinet minister had left him with admiration for the young man's organizational flair. Shapiro had often prophesied that Hume Frazier would make a splendid prime minister.

But James O'Rourke, the former premier of Nova Scotia, was less than happy with the idea of Hume Frazier as prime minister.

"Frazier? Oh sure, he'll jump in just as soon as he hears there's to be a leadership convention. You can bet on that. And I suppose Frazier still has some support in the country. But I, for one, wouldn't want to see him win. In my part of Canada, it takes a long time to live down that kind of disgrace. And it makes a lot of people wonder about what kind of judgement he has. I don't mind saying I'm one of those people."

Senator O'Rourke was worth listening to. They all knew that the former premier had a sensitive ear for public reaction, not only in his home province, but among the other Atlantic provinces.

"I don't suppose Kate –" began Bonnie Costello.

"You couldn't pry her loose from Andrew, no matter what," interrupted Carter Warden. "No, those two still behave like honeymooners. She's just loving it – running that little office of hers and being Mrs. Wickstrom, married lady. Too bad, Bonnie, Kathleen would certainly be my first pick, but she just isn't available."

"Why not ask her, Carter?" This from David Kirke. The veteran party organizer had been going over in his mind a long list of possibles, but none of the other names he was prepared to bring up for consideration seemed exciting election material. There was, he knew, only so much you could do with salesmanship and organization. You had to start with a viable candidate. And one that had a spark with the public.

"It would be a waste of time, Davie. No, we'll have to think of someone else. I have to confess that I simply have no idea at the moment. Has anyone else?"

There was an uncomfortable silence.

"Then it appears we'll have to keep searching," Matthew Lyndon said. "But are we agreed that as soon as we find the right candidate, we'll face the Prime Minister and ask for a leadership convention?"

Heads nodded in agreement.

"Davie, you had better scout out possible convention dates. It seems to take longer every time to find space when we want it. We'll probably be in the hands of the big convention centres. It's likely we'll have to take what we can get."

"Does it have to be Ottawa, Matt? Or can I check out Montreal, Toronto, maybe Vancouver?" Senator Kirke jotted down a note to himself.

"I think not." As he spoke, Lyndon looked around at the others. "Maybe the other parties hold their leadership conventions elsewhere, but it's our tradition to hold them in Ottawa. Right?"

Matthew Lyndon stood up. "Then that's everything for now. Please keep in touch. Let me have any bright ideas as soon as they occur to you. But remember, there isn't a lot of time. We must have a new leader, or it's ballgame over." The party chairman closed his file and stubbed out his cigar.

As the members of the group stood, collecting their papers together, their host announced: "Mrs. Melton has laid out some cold cuts and things – nothing very fancy – for anyone who can stay for a while. It's this way," and he led them into the dining room, where trays and platters of meats and shellfish and salad awaited them.

It was while they were eating that Carter Warden approached David Kirke.

"Davie, I've been thinking of Kathleen. If we don't ask her, who do we have?"

"No one," Kirke admitted.

"We can all go home and stew for ages, but we're not going to invent anyone new." Carter set down his glass and took out an ebony cigarette holder into which he fitted a cigarette. "If we don't ask Kathleen, one of two things is going to happen: either we'll settle for Hume Frazier, who would probably lose the election – and anyway, I'm not sure I want to betray Jean Jacques for Frazier – or we'll get so discouraged that in the end we'll do nothing, and then we'll find ourselves running another campaign for Charles."

"No way," said David Kirke. "You can count me out for that."

"Well then," Carter said, "maybe we'd better think about Kathleen again. She's all we've got."

"What about the fact that she is a woman?" the Senator asked. He was reluctant even to raise the question, but his political instincts told him that it was a troubling matter.

"That's the big question mark all right, Davie. I can't tell you the answer. Not how the delegates will react at the convention, much less the voters in an election. But for the delegates, like us, I think it will come down to this: they want a winner. And it will be our job to convince them that Kathleen can be that winner.

"You and I know that there never is a perfect candidate. There's always some shortcoming. But Katie has never lost an election. She's widely known through the party and across the country. She's been in Opposition, she's been a minister, she's even been the prime minister for a time. Now, candidates just don't come any more experienced than that. And it's a fresh idea – a woman leader. Let's think positively on that score."

"Yeah, Carter, I guess you're right. Everything considered, she's the best."

Chapter Eight

It was another hot, still day. As soon as she woke Kathleen was aware of a smothered feeling – the harbinger of a temperature that, like yesterday's, would climb well into the nineties. Until yesterday each day of her two-week holiday had dawned bright and sunny. Now the humidity was making her feel claustrophobic and she wished a storm would come and clear the muggy air.

The thick-walled old log cabin, built by her father and his friends as a fishing camp during Kathleen's early teens, was still, after almost forty years, in habitable shape. Every morning, it was dark and cool. The sun rose behind the ridge above the cabin, and it was only in the late afternoon, toward the end of its daily swing across the sky, that its rays reached the cabin's lake-side porch.

Every morning, Kathleen slept as late as her body would permit. For the first few days Andrew had been with her, then he had suddenly been called to Vancouver on business. Instead of going with him, or back to the city, Kathleen had decided to stay at the cabin herself until Andrew returned. And now, alone, she found the time passing slowly. She used to love spending time alone at the cabin; now she was amused at herself for being restless and for missing Andrew's presence.

Kathleen took the red enamelled coffeepot off the boil, and poured herself a large glass mug of the dark brew. She tied her robe about her and padded from the lean-to kitchen, through the messy cabin and out to the shaded porch.

On the porch was a rocking chair they had planned to redo

on this trip. Now she tried to convince herself she would enjoy doing it herself: first sanding down the old hickory wood, then covering it with a fine oil finish.

The hickory rocking chair had lived most of its life on Kathleen's grandmother's veranda in Chatham. She could remember rocking in it the night she got sick from eating too many green apples. That was more than forty years ago. And on the porch, too, was her grandmother's old rug. Looking down, she scuffed her slipper over the faded, hand-braided oval beneath her feet.

Kathleen sipped her coffee and smoked, her gaze resting on the lake. The view was changeless, yet ever-changing. She had spent hour after hour these past two July weeks sitting in this chair, drinking coffee in the mornings, iced tea in the afternoons and a long drink of brandy in the gathering dark of evening. She smoked, and watched the lake, and let her thoughts take her where they would. In the whole time since she had left politics, this seemed like the first real solitude she had had.

Today, the rounded hills across the lake, clothed for full summer in various shades of green, were drenched in gold. Heat shimmered near the water's edge on the far shore, blurring the familiar shapes of the headlands.

The lake at her feet was still, without a ripple. Today, there was no gurgle as the water moved against the ramshackle dock. The two flags that signalled that Kathleen was in residence at the cabin – above, the red and white Canadian flag, below it, the scarlet banner of Ontario, with its Union Jack and coat-of-arms – hung limp on the peeled sapling at the end of the dock.

She missed the sound of the flags snapping as they streamed from the mast before the playful breeze. Far off, there was a dog baying. It echoed around the lake, and when it died, there was nothing to break the breathless silence but the buzzing of a trapped fly and the intermittent penetrating song of the cicadas.

Watching the limp flags, she knew the day would be a scorcher. She went into the cabin and changed into a pair of denim shorts and a creased cotton halter that she dug from the clothes-chest. Then, finally hungry, she walked through the cabin to the kitchen, where she searched through the refrigerator until she found an iced tin of consomme, which she dumped out and seasoned with a dollop of sour cream from a nearly empty carton, and a squeeze of lime. From the breadbox she took a handful of crackers; and soupbowl and spoon in hand, she went back to the rocker facing the lake.

Rocking gently, she took up her vigil over the lake. Life with Andrew was sweet. She had long gotten over any embarrassment at living close to a man; now she was so attuned to his presence that even the bittersweet feeling of missing him was welcome. Yes, to miss him gently for a few days was almost as nice as being with him. But to be really separated – to have the emotional tie broken – she couldn't imagine how that could be borne.

Suddenly the perfect silence of the breathless morning was broken. Kathleen caught the sound of heavy vehicles labouring along the rutted dusty road that circled the lake. They passed through the belt of pine trees on the ridge, and then she heard the sound of engines dying and slamming doors on the hill behind the cabin.

She stepped outside the cabin to peer upward through the trees, wondering who might be her unexpected visitors. Around her, butterflies, brown and gold, flew up from the long grass thick with wild phlox and starry white daisies.

She heard several voices, but the words were indecipherable and so, curious, she walked a few paces up the path.

The scene she encountered was utterly bizarre. From two sleek and powerful black automobiles the sunlight glinted. Only thick layers of dust from the rough trail marred their perfection. Two chauffeurs in dark pants and white shirts stood talking, brushing away flies in the heavy heat. And down the path came a solemn procession. An odd impression flashed through Kathleen's mind; they looked like a scene in a film of Mafia bosses filing in to attend a Family funeral! Each of those now picking his way with care down the steep, rough path to the cabin was dressed in city black – black suits, black socks, black shoes, and each of the men either wore or carried a sober black hat. The woman in the group was bareheaded, but she, too, was dressed in a neat black cotton, sprigged with faint tracings of white.

"It's Matthew Lyndon! Whatever is he doing here, all the way from Vancouver? And Jim O'Rourke, and David Kirke! And Carter – I must be dreaming."

But Kathleen wasn't dreaming, and the first four were followed onto the now-crowded porch by Bonnie Costello, the elegant Fernand LeMesurier and a panting Peregrine Melton.

"Brigadier Melton, please sit down and catch your breath. It's a hard climb when you're not used to it. And Bonnie, dear," she kissed the young woman, "how nice to see you. And Carter, my old friend. This is just about the last place in the world I would expect to see you! Fernand, I never realized how primitive this place is, until I saw you sit down in that rocker with the peeling paint! Please forgive the mess."

She disappeared into the kitchen, then came back with a tray of ice-filled glasses and a pitcher of clear iced tea and lemon slices. As she passed around the sweating glasses to her unexpected guests, Kathleen was vastly amused at the picture they made; all those dark, stiff city clothes, so out of place here in the casual comfort of her pillow-strewn porch.

"Now what on earth brings you all here? Or have you just come to pay a social call? What a tremendous surprise."

Her guests looked at one another. How to begin? They had discussed various approaches to their subject on the long drive to the lake, but in neither air-conditioned car had anyone hit on anything but the baldest of explanations. "After all," they had reasoned, "Kathleen will guess at once by our very presence that we have come on political business."

Senator O'Rourke put away his big white handkerchief, his reddened face mopped of perspiration, and took a long gulp from his frosty glass.

"Ah, that really hits the spot." He smacked his lips, appreciatively. "Fact of the matter is, Katie-girl, we've got a problem, and we've come to ask your help." He looked around like an embarrassed schoolboy. "Is – uh – Andrew around?"

"No. He's away on business." As soon as she said this, she saw looks of sheepish relief being exchanged among the men. There was a long pause. Finally Kathleen turned to Carter Warden.

"All right, Carter, what's up? And quit looking so guilty, you're making me curious."

"Kathleen, my dear. First, we must apologize for disturbing you here, when you have obviously come such a long way to be alone. And you may well consider it presumptuous of us, but . . . " He looked around, hoping one of the others would take over, but when no one did, he continued: "We know, Kathleen, how hard you worked for the party, how inconsiderate Charles was with you, and that you have now made a new life outside of politics. You can be sure we wouldn't intrude on your privacy in this way unless the matter were urgent. And it is, Kathleen. Very urgent. We are forced to risk offending you by coming here, but we are in agreement that there is no other way."

"Your visit does come as a total surprise, but you are all old friends, and welcome. So what, exactly, is the nature of the mysterious urgent matter? Perhaps, Brigadier Melton, you would like to tell me?"

"Uh, well – actually, I think Matthew had better start – he's the party chairman. Kathleen, would you mind if I take off my coat. It really is deuced hot."

"Of course, how thoughtless of me. Please do. You should have brought your bathing suits." Glancing at her own bare legs, conscious of her near-nakedness in the skimpy halter, she laughed. "As you can see, we don't dress formally here at Secret Lake."

"Kate, let me be blunt." Matthew Lyndon discarded his jacket, pulled loose his tie and rolled up the sleeves of his monogrammed shirt. "We have come to the conclusion that Jean Jacques Charles will be the death of the Liberal Party, and maybe even of Canada, unless we can get rid of him quickly. We are prepared to do that, but we must first be sure that we have a viable alternative. We want you as that alternative."

Her astonishment was obvious to all.

"Me? To go back to politics? Oh no, I'm finished with all that! Why I have a new life, with a wonderful husband. . . . "

There was silence.

"Kate. We are all sorry, Kate. We know you must be happy to have escaped to a new life. But we are shoved for time. Just listen to us, Kate. Please hear us out. We've come a long way to talk to you. Please let us tell you why it's got to be you."

Fernand LeMesurier spoke then. "*Madame*, perhaps you have not followed the government's progress so closely over the past year or so, since your departure from the Cabinet. I must tell you that our Prime Minister is on a disastrous course. Whole segments of the country are disaffected. And we have reason to believe that the two-year moratorium on elections promised last year by the socialist leader may not be honoured. The Government may be defeated at any time.

"Jacques has lost the ability to be flexible. He taunts the House as if willing his own destruction! But if they bring him down – and they will if he continues to treat them with such naked contempt – it may be the end of the Liberal Party. In my view, that is not acceptable. I no longer have faith in our leader, and I, like the others, have concluded he must go."

Kathleen had listened intently to the suave Quebecker, but now she turned her head at the intervention of Bonnie Costello. The dark-haired young M.P. pursued the point.

"Kate, it really is as bad as he says in the House. The members talk about it all the time, even those who are still supporting Jacques. He abuses the Opposition and ignores the Liberal caucus. It's so frustrating. And lately, he even seems openly contemptuous of his own Cabinet. Last week, on his return from the summit meeting in West Germany, he suddenly demanded television time to make a speech on the economic situation. Most of his Cabinet ministers knew nothing at all about it in advance – not even the Minister of Finance! He treats his associates as if they were children, but it's he who acts like one. You know, those things are bad enough when there's a majority, but right now, in the second minority in a row. . . . He's just so different since Evangeline died. He's so isolated – so arrogant and quick-tempered. He seems to be relying, increasingly, on that redneck, Stan Findlay. It is as though Jacques just doesn't give a damn. It's as if he were daring the Opposition to vote him out. And if we are defeated in the House, the party won't stand any chance. I don't think we would come back with a single seat in Metro.

"Look, Kathleen, I don't like to sound disloyal, but it seems impossible for anyone to get through to Jacques. Caucus meetings are a shambles. He just gets on his high horse and walks out when he's offended. And that's happened too many times already. Mind you, there are those who will fight for him, no matter what. A lot of the Quebeckers fall into that category, and there are others, led, of course, by Findlay. They just can't imagine anyone beating Jacques. That's why there has to be someone credible to take his place."

Kathleen had been listening intently, her thoughts racing.

"But I. . . . There must be others you can approach. Why must it be me?"

Senator Kirke leaned toward her: "But there aren't, Kate. Just try to think of someone else. We've been talking for weeks, canvassing the country. There is just no one who is ready. There are some possibilities on the horizon, but it's too soon for them. You're the only one. You have the experience, you have a national name. You know the party and it knows you. You're popular."

Carter Warden put down his glass. "Kathleen, you top everyone's list. You always did, ever since we started to put together this cabal. We wanted to ask you before, but we didn't dare intrude on your marriage. But now we must take the chance. Send us away if you must, but please listen first. You have Andrew, your husband. You have your law office. And, of course, you have Andrew's children. But none of them needs you as much as the party – and Canada – need you. I hate to put it to you so brutally, Kate, but if you were a man I'd say: Look, don't you think it's your duty to put your country first?"

Kathleen studied her old friend. Inside, she felt panicky, wanting to run from the burden they proposed that she should shoulder. Then, with a flicker of hope in her voice, she announced, "Hume! What about Hume Frazier. It's been his life's ambition to become prime minister. Surely he would do it."

"No doubt he would, if we were to ask him. But we won't. We have discussed Frazier. A little over a year ago, he would have been the obvious choice. Despite your experience as prime minister, he would have been, perhaps, a safer bet. No one really knows yet how the country will react to a woman leader. They've never had the chance to vote for one. There *is* a big question mark about public confidence in a woman, but we have already faced that problem.

"It may be stupid, but there it is: your sex may mean that the gamble we are all prepared to take will be a losing one. But we are all agreed. We would rather face that problem, with you, than go with Hume Frazier, knowing that every time his name is mentioned it will evoke that scandal. In time, the public may forgive him, as they seem to be forgiving Senator Ted Kennedy for Chappaquiddick and even Nixon for Watergate. But this time out, I think Hume just isn't viable. I'm sure he'll run anyway, but not with our support."

"Is that what you all think?" she scanned their faces.

"All of us *here*, Kathleen," Senator O'Rourke added: "You know Aaron Shapiro, from Winnipeg. He is one of The Seven but he couldn't come today. He's with us all the way in getting rid of Jacques, but, you know, he's always been a supporter of Hume Frazier, and he might very well decide to back Frazier if he runs."

"But all the rest of us are for you, Kate, and there'll be plenty more beside, as soon as it's known that you'll run." Bonnie was full of enthusiasm, excited at the possibility that the woman who had been her longtime political model might consent to contest the leadership. "I'm not one of The Seven, but they just couldn't keep me away when I learned they were coming here today. Oh, Kate, if you only would."

"Does Jacques know about this? Is he prepared to step down, or will he fight? Surely, the Liberal Party has no precedent in asking for the resignation of the leader while he is prime minister? I remember the Conservatives attempted it a decade or more ago – but have we ever done it?"

"There were some pretty strong hints directed at Louis St. Laurent – after he lost the 1957 election – but he wasn't actually prime minister when the convention call went out. I suppose that's the closest precedent. Not many people remember that," pointed out the aging Peregrine Melton.

"No, Kathleen. Jacques knows nothing about this, as yet. We decided that we wouldn't face him until we knew we had someone waiting in the wings. If you accept, as we hope you will, we must then tell the Prime Minister. We will advise him to announce his resignation and to permit us to call a nominating convention as soon as possible. And even then, there is the gamble that the Opposition might grab its chance to throw out the Government before we have elected a new leader."

"No," Kathleen said thoughtfully. "From what I know of those men, they would never do that. Besides, they know the public would consider it dirty pool. If it's announced that Jacques is stepping down, and a new leader will soon be named, the Opposition will just have to grit its teeth and take whatever he dishes out. But it's certainly going to be no picnic for those of you who have to bell the cat. I don't envy whoever has to take on that job."

Carter Warden grinned, although the prospect of facing Jacques was not one he looked forward to. "Kathleen, we are prepared for that responsibility. We are the ones who are the current power in the party. He must know that he owes his election last year to us; and that without us he would have been defeated. Technically, I suppose, he could refuse to resign as prime minister, but I really think given our concerted demands, that is inconceivable."

"What about funding such a campaign? I have very little money, and it would be very costly. I couldn't ask Andrew for money. And staffing it? Remember, I am not a member of Commons now. I would have to look around for an available seat, and get elected."

"All in good time. We understand that if you agree to run, you will need all the support we can muster. But don't underestimate just how much that may be. We are not only the heads of the party apparatus, we are also the principal fund raisers for the party, and we believe that there would be no trouble in putting together an adequate kitty and experienced campaign team."

"I don't even speak French all that well. How do you feel about that?" she asked of the elegant LeMesurier.

"Anyone can improve if they are prepared to work at it. It's only a matter of lessons, and there will be time," he responded smoothly.

"Well, Kathleen?" Chairman Lyndon asked, after a pause. "Will you do it?"

"I don't really know, Matthew. I can't give you an answer today. But I do promise to think about it. And I'll talk to Andrew, too. We'll have to decide this together."

"The sooner the better."

"Andrew won't be back in Toronto for a few days. Before he comes I'll have to do some thinking. And then, even if I agree and he agrees, I'll want to talk to some people in the city. I'll call you as soon as I can. That, I'm afraid, is the best I can do today."

They accepted Kathleen's answer, encouraged that she had not given them a flat "no." When she offered them some sandwiches, they surprised her by bringing from the cars an elaborate picnic hamper. It was crammed with cold herbed chicken, carrot sticks and celery, fresh fruit, cheese and rolls, and cool bottles of a still white wine. They dallied for an hour or so in the heavy heat of the porch to talk of other things, and then, the food and wine consumed, they trailed back up to the waiting limousines.

That night, the sky roiled with greasy black clouds. Streamers of bright pink unrolled across the sky, and the brilliant spark of Venus did not appear. Thunder growled and lightning flickered; all the night long there was a rush of slashing rain, pouring off the rooftop and pounding at the lake.

As she lay in bed that night, a debate raged in Kathleen's head.

Remember campaigning? Pounding the pavement, knocking on strange doors, grabbing for handshakes, standing at bus stops and before plant gates, the endless round of coffee parties, the speeches, the speeches. On the go, from dawn to midnight every day. The exhaustion. Ah, but don't forget: the good, warm feeling of comradeship, the teamwork, the fun of planning the campaign, the excitement of winning.

Remember Parliament? Long hours and those hateful night sittings, the dull speeches, the interminable wrangling. And sometimes the meanness, the pettiness of people. The jealousies. The gossip.

Ah, but don't forget: that's where the action is. That's the centre. And sometimes the high drama, history in the making, and the sense of being a part of it. You're *making* history, every day.

Remember the loss of privacy? The nutty phone calls, people stopping you in the street or stores to ask for an autograph, or to pick a quarrel. The constant demands for donations. The necessity to show up at even the most minor community event, the endless travel to and from the constituency. The erratic schedule with no chance to plan holidays in advance. And the loneliness. No real, lasting friendships, nobody who gives a damn about you. The constant sniping and criticism.

Ah, but don't forget the joy of meeting so many interesting new people, of getting to know the movers and shakers of the world, and of being one yourself. And don't you secretly *like* to be recognized wherever you go? Don't you like to be asked for an autograph? Don't you like to feel important, like to be sought after? Don't you like the trappings: the staff, the government planes, the special treatment?

C'mon, Kate, be honest with yourself.

And then a sly little voice in her head spoke up: This time, *you'd* be the boss! Isn't that what you've always really wanted? Isn't that what every politician wants?

By morning the air was fresher and the storm had passed. Kathleen prepared the cabin for the winter, and with a last look around, closed it up and headed for Toronto.

Hume and Sybil Frazier were dressing for a party. The spanking white dinner jacket lay ready on the bed, the gleaming black patent pumps aligned below. Hume struggled with his tie before the bathroom mirror, and Sybil, seated at the frilly dressing table, carefully applied the final touches to her make up.

Slipping on his supple leather shoes, Hume walked to where his wife sat. He pressed his lips to her smooth blonde head, and held before her a small, black velvet box.

"A little present for my bride."

As her fingers fumbled with the catch, Sybil blushed with pleasure. On a bed of white satin lay a tiny diamond heart, and as Sybil lifted the heart from the box by its delicate chain, she twisted towards Hume.

"Oh, Hume, it's so lovely. It's the one I admired so much in the jeweller's window. But, Hume, it's very extravagant. Can you really afford it?"

"I've always told you, Sybil-baby, stick with me and you'll wear diamonds! Sorry it's taken so long to get you the first one, but there'll be more, you better believe it. You've been such a brick this past year. Since we came back from Europe everything has gone so well. We're meeting so many new people; we're even having fun. I've never been this social before, not even while I was single. And you seem so happy with this new house, and so busy with all your new friends. Even the kids like their new schools and camps. Yes, sir, the sun's in its heaven, and all's right with Hume Frazier's world."

As he fastened the glittering bauble around her neck Sybil watched him in the mirror. The truth was that Hume *did* seem more content out of Ottawa and away from politics. And she herself found the people in Toronto far more interesting than the Rockliffe crowd. Here they lived the way people ought to live: Hume got home after work instead of having to hang around the House of Commons all night. They gave glittering parties. And they certainly made a lot more money.

Not that Sybil had ever worried about money. While she was growing up there had always been money for whatever she wanted. During her father's lifetime, he had always made sure that she had enough household staff and enough money in her chequing account to live comfortably, especially during Hume's low-earning years in Parliament; and she had inherited a very substantial trust fund after her father's death.

But now, since they had moved to Toronto, Hume had been able to take over all the household bills at last, and it had done wonders for his pride. To Sybil, it was significant that her husband now felt confident enough, financially, to present her with the diamond heart. "The first diamonds since my engagement ring," ran through her head as she adjusted the swinging pendant to fit the hollow of her throat.

She thought regretfully about Hume's ambition to be prime minister – he had wanted it more than anything – but soon even he would have to admit that he was now better off in every way.

Sitting at the dressing table admiring the pendant, Sybil was able to assure herself that Hume, although he still noticed every pretty woman in the room, had stopped having affairs.

And, in fact, what his wife believed was true. The Hume Frazier of the past year since his forced resignation had been a badly frightened man. In the two drunken days after Jean Jacques Charles had given him his marching orders, Hume had faced the possible loss of his wife and children as well as his career in public life. It was the loss of his family, he had finally realized, that he most feared; and he had, while lying hung over in Molly's bed, promised himself that if Sybil forgave him this time he would truly change his ways.

He had drastically cut down on his drinking, substituting mineral water or the occasional glass of white wine for whisky and brandy. His head continued to turn to mark the passing of a beautiful woman, but he did nothing about it, content to look, but not touch. Perhaps "content" was to put too strong a word on it, because he had to fight the desire for sweaty, enthusiastic sex with a writhing, vocalizing partner; and, as he pumped away over the dutifully pliant Sybil, he often fantasized a full-blown, athletic, scratching sexual virtuoso. If only, he wished, she would open her eyes, or move, or even say something! If only it were possible to suggest how many more things there are to do in sex – so many positions – so many different experiments. After all, there're a thousand ways to scratch a perfectly natural itch! But Hume found that the only thing Sybil wanted to do was to lie there and be respectable.

Sometimes he felt like a gas station attendant – just servicing her. And the worst part was that he knew she thought she was doing *him* a favour, the kind of favour a wife is supposed to endure in a ladylike way.

To combat his gnawing sexual needs, Hume did everything he could. In desperation he tried a regime of cold showers, only to discover that they only aroused his urge to pick up and vigorously bed the first blatant, experienced woman he could find. Finally he settled on trying to dull his senses by exhausting himself, and he again took up tennis and squash and handball, finding no dearth of partners among the successful men he had met recently. SilverTinCo expected its senior executives to circulate socially. Many a deal had been concluded at the nineteenth hole or at the end of a fast hour of handball. It was good business to appear often in the exclusive places where other important people congregated; and many of them were there for exactly the same reason. The vertical mosaic was a movable feast, and the Fraziers fitted in easily with such circles, both those of staid old inherited money and those of the upwardly-mobile.

When he thought about it, Hume, perhaps naively, was surprised at how easy it had been to fit into the financial community. He had considered various offers on his return from Europe – and even the possibility of setting up his own consulting firm, which might have seemed like a conflict of interest so soon after leaving the Treasury. But the advantages of SilverTinCo had won out.

At the end of that summer he had joined the company as its president and now, almost a year later, felt himself well-established in the corridors of corporate power.

His salary of $150,000 a year was basic. To that were added stock options, bonuses, and a generous expense account which included, as a matter of course, memberships in the best clubs Toronto had to offer, together with a wallet stuffed with credit cards. The company furnished both Hume and Sybil with a new car each year, and a driver-mechanic for his. He had the use of one of the company's private planes when needed, and of apartments in Paris, London, Geneva and New York. He was expected to travel – to South America, the Middle East, and Japan – wherever the interlocking interests of Silver-TinCo might direct him.

For the first time in his life, there was plenty of money coming in – money that he himself had earned, and he revelled in a new sense of financial independence – the first he had ever known.

Not that Hume was a stranger to the presence of money. His mother, after she had been widowed many years, had married a squat, scarred immigrant to Montreal – Sergio Massimo Allessandro – who was a count in his native Italy and a very rich merchant prince in his adopted country of Canada. Together his mother and her new husband had made sure that Hume was exposed to superb schooling, and that he acquired the social graces. With his lithe, athletic figure, his crisp waves of black hair, the collar-ad face with its cleft chin and piercing blue eyes, Hume had been much sought-after by palpitating daughters of the wealthy. But, following the careful game-plan his mother had worked out, Hume had steered clear of an early marriage. After a few years with an established law firm, he had launched himself into federal politics, under the leadership of Alexander Sinclair, who was a childhood friend of his mother's.

From his first election, Hume had never swerved from his determination to become prime minister. But for one careless episode, he would still be the front-runner to succeed Jean Jacques Charles, who was himself surely due to be succeeded.

As he and Sybil drove to the party, Hume found himself thinking about his final interview with Jacques and wishing once more that somehow the secret could have kept. He glanced at Sybil. Never once had he detected an expression, or heard a word, intended to recall the circumstances of his resignation. He wondered if she could really have forgotten, when it still gnawed at him.

Sybil sat serenely in the cloud-soft seat, her features limned by the dashboard lights. She stirred, feeling his eyes on her.

"You're quiet tonight, Hume darling," she said as she lightly touched scarlet-tipped fingers to his black-clad knee. "Anything special on your mind?"

"No Syb. Just counting my blessings. You, first among them."

In the dark, she flushed with pleasure. He had sounded as if he really meant the compliment.

"We're almost there, Hume. I've checked and there are some new people to meet tonight. Richard Sherwood, the leader of the Official Opposition, will be there. Now, don't let him drag you off to talk politics. There will be a lot of other people who can do you much more good than he can. I don't think you need to be rude to Sherwood. You never can tell, he might come in handy if there's a change of government – as there certainly ought to be – at the next election.

"Gay – that's our hostess, Mrs. Blair White, and you certainly know him, the financier – Gay suggested that we should be sure to meet the Ambletons. He's in mining. And Macbeth, that new bank president, and Tage Wickstrom. He publishes weekly newspapers. Let me see. Oh yes, a very wealthy lawyer from Winnipeg – Aaron Shapiro. Fancy, a Jew invited to the Whites! I suppose it's for business reasons. But Gay said she thought you would particularly want to talk to him tonight. Any idea why?"

"No, not that comes to mind right away. Shapiro, from Winnipeg, did you say? That seems to ring a faint bell. I may have met him while I was in the Ministry. Oh well, if I have met him before, he'll be certain to bring it up. You know how pushy some of those people are."

Hume Frazier was a little surprised to find himself dissembling. And he didn't know exactly when he had begun to make anti-Semitic remarks. He had never been guilty of discrimination in all his years in politics, and he had curtly broken off any such conversation that had tried to include him; but lately it seemed even to his own ears that he had begun to echo the attitudes commonly expressed by people in the circles he now moved in.

That was probably the reason why he had denied knowing Aaron Shapiro. Of course he knew him. Shapiro was much more than just a wealthy lawyer from Winnipeg. Hume Frazier was very aware that the dark little gnome of a man, with his thin fall of prematurely white hair and intelligent black eyes, was one of the powers behind the Liberal Party of Canada – and one of the innermost circle. Aaron Shapiro was one of The Seven.

It was, he thought, a symptom of Sybil's altered ambitions that she no longer remembered Aaron Shapiro's importance. And despite her dislike of the idea of his being cozy with the only Jew invited to the party, Hume resolved to make a point of saying hello to Shapiro.

"Here we are. It's that big white modern place set back in there. And it looks like a big party. Now smile, often, Hume. Your smile is so attractive! And don't forget to be charming to those people I mentioned. Gay says it isn't easy to meet them any other way. My, isn't the house big? And hear the music? Maybe there'll be dancing. It's been worth being nice to Gay, to finally be asked here."

The airy rooms were filled with candlelight and music, and massed bouquets of white flowers of every kind perfumed the air. The dead-white walls blazed with brilliant abstract paintings, and the furniture, aside from the ebony satin finish of a grand piano – its shining surface crowded with silver-framed photographs of their host, Blair White, the business world's boy-genius shaking hands with the great and the near-great – was all angular modern, overflowing with fat puffs of white cushions. Two black standard poodles lay before the black-marble fireplace, watching with disdain the movements of the guests as they passed to and fro, admiring the costly paintings, the expensive furniture, the air of easy luxury.

After drinks, the guests were led to an enormous dining room ablaze with candles, crystal and silver. While Hume made polite conversation with the flattered women on both sides of him, he was restless to make contact with some of the important people Sybil had mentioned earlier. And even as he charmed the women with what appeared to be his concentrated fascination with each, one level of his mind kept busy plotting how he might casually effect those encounters after dinner.

At his hostess' signal, the women rose together and drifted

off to "freshen up." Blair White led his male guests beyond the broad French doors to settle on the terrace overlooking the pool. After the perfect airconditioning of the spacious house, the out-of-doors seemed oppressively hot; and when the women returned, Gay suggested that they go back inside.

Aaron Shapiro saw his chance. He cornered Hume as the guests entered the elegant living room. Gesturing energetically in the few moments they had alone, Aaron spoke quickly. At first Hume was surprised by Shapiro's remarks; but then he carefully smoothed from his face all expression as the short, swarthy financier with the flowing white locks continued. And then the host arrived with two other guests in tow.

The interruption came at just the wrong time. It was impossible for the two men to complete their conversation after the new introductions were performed. Soon Aaron Shapiro made his excuses and left, content that he had sown a seed. Whether it would flourish into life depended upon the other man's ambition. For the moment, the Winnipeg financier was content.

Later that night, when Sybil and Hume were lying in the dark of their bedroom, listening to the music of the softly falling rain, Hume whispered: "Syb, are you still awake?"

"Mmmmmmmm," she reluctantly murmured. "Why?" She turned over to face her husband who lay on his back, hands crossed behind his head on the pillows.

"Am I a dead duck, politically, do you think?"

"Of course not, darling. What makes you bring that up, tonight?" And with a thought dawning: "Don't tell me Richard Sherwood made you an offer – to run as a Conservative?"

"No, that's not it, although I suppose that wouldn't be too hard to arrange. It isn't as though I would be uncomfortable with his people, but I'd have to think hard about crossing the floor. Canada isn't England, and I'm not Winston Churchill. The custom isn't much appreciated here, and no one here has ever made a success of it. Political people are too suspicious of turncoats. Besides, what would be the point of joining forces with Sherwood? It wouldn't be any better than being second banana to Jean Jacques Charles."

"But you are smarter and more experienced than anyone he has with him, even better than Sherwood himself," his wife said, punching her pillows behind her, as she sat up and switched on the bedside light. "If it wasn't Sherwood, then who did start you thinking about politics tonight?"

"It was Aaron Shapiro, that fellow from Winnipeg. He told me some very interesting things. I haven't heard a whisper of this around anywhere else, so, Sybil, I don't have to say this, but I'll have to count on your absolute discretion. Promise you won't breathe a word of it, not even hint at it, to anyone?"

Sybil bridled. "You know I wouldn't! Now what is it that the little Jew told you?"

"Another thing, don't say things like that anymore. 'That little Jew' is not the kind of remark that goes down, politically, no matter how often you hear it on Bay Street. I really don't like it, and I want you to be careful, whether anything in politics should materialize or not. And his news doesn't necessarily mean anything to us. It's just a possibility."

"Well, Hume, what did Mr. Shapiro say?"

"He told me that The Seven have decided that Charles must be made to step down. Apparently they've been making soundings across the country, and they're afraid that if the Government is dumped in the House, the party may never recover. Everybody is angry or disappointed with the Government – just like the people around here. There is a real wave of discontent with the Government's record on the economy; and there's a personal distaste for Jacques which dates back at least to when he fired Kathleen and me, and Evangeline's death. The Seven, Shapiro says, were the ones responsible for pulling the fat out of the fire in the election last year while we were away.

"Shapiro says that they did it, in effect, by running Evangeline and down-playing Jacques. Now that she is gone, and the people have learned that he could have saved her by agreeing to an abortion" – the word, even now, made Hume wince – "they are angry, and they blame Jacques for her death. Shapiro says the party has to dump him, now, before he's defeated again in the House, and find a new leader."

"Oh, Hume, do you think they can?"

"I don't know. It seems that they haven't gone beyond the stage of canvassing for support for their plans. They haven't yet faced Jacques."

"What are they waiting for?"

"Shapiro says they won't move until they have a candidate they're satisfied with."

"And he asked *you* if you would stand?"

"No, not exactly, though, you know, in the old days, he used to be a great supporter of mine, and he certainly sounded positive about my chances should I decide to enter the race. But he didn't ask me to in so many words. He just said that The Seven have no candidate firmly in mind at the moment.

"What do you think, Syb? Should I follow it up, maybe nose around a bit about my chances? I doubt they will have forgotten . . . well, you know . . . and I suppose they won't appreciate the fact that I wasn't around for the last campaign. But if, as Shapiro says, they are stuck for a candidate. . . . Just think of who is left in the Charles Cabinet – a bunch of faceless nothings! They won't find a candidate there to take on the old man. Maybe they'll just *have* to come to me. I think we ought to consider it, very carefully, just in case."

Sybil now was sitting straight up in bed, intently weighing every word. "All right, darling, we can stay home tomorrow night, to be alone so we can talk about it. I'll find some excuse to get out of that dinner party, and we can have something sent in. Anyway, I'm sick of getting dressed up every night to go out in this heat. Would you like that?"

"Sure, Sybil, that will be great." Long after she had turned on her side again, facing away from him, Hume lay on his back, his gaze fastened on the darkened bedroom ceiling, his thoughts racing with his rekindled ambition to be prime minister.

Chapter Nine

"Drew, do you have time this morning to talk to me about something quite important?"

Andrew lowered his morning paper. It was two days since he had come back from the west, and ever since she had picked him up at the airport, he sensed that Kathleen had something on her mind.

"How important?" he asked, looking at her through the top part of his bifocals. "Earth-shaking? Or only us-shaking?"

Kathleen, across the table, had been toying with her eggs, her gaze on her plate. "Us-shaking, maybe," she admitted reluctantly.

Andrew thought her admission ominous. Folding his newspaper and putting it aside, he said, "What is it, Kathleen? Out with it. If it's that important, I'd better hear about it now."

Haltingly, Kathleen told her husband about the visit of The Seven. Even as she recounted it, she herself found it hard to believe. It had the eerie quality of a dream. Andrew didn't help her. He sat in silence, his face unreadable. She had the uneasy feeling that even telling him about it was a mistake. She desperately wished that she had given The Seven a firm No, so that it would not now be necessary to tell Andrew. But she knew, even as she was speaking, that if he approved – wholeheartedly, without reservation – she would run. I'm just like those old fire horses that at the first smell of smoke are busting to get out of the barn, she thought to herself.

"And what answer did you give them, Kathleen?" Andrew asked her formally, setting down his coffee cup.

161

"I . . . I gave them no answer," she stumbled, and then looking at him, "I only told them that I would think about it, and discuss it with you. I made no commitment, Andrew, except that I would tell them by the end of this month."

"Why didn't you tell them No at once, Kathleen, that you are finished with politics? You remember that very early in our relationship I said I didn't want to play second fiddle to a political career. And I waited, until you thought you were sure. The terms were clear: you were to have a full-time job as my wife. Have you forgotten?"

"No, of course not, Andrew. But this isn't just a little law office, nor even running for Parliament. This is the highest elective office in Canada; and it's the chance to be the first woman, ever, to head up an administration."

His eyebrows raised.

"Oh, not like before." She plunged on. "I wasn't *elected* to be P.M. then. It wasn't my Cabinet, not my ministers, not my policies. I was just a caretaker. It meant nothing. This is something else, Andrew. A chance to do it on my own – to pick my own people, develop my own policies. My dear, think what an opportunity it is – for women, for me." As she spoke, she reached to touch his hand, pleading for understanding.

Her cry echoed round the chambers of Andrew's mind. He was dismayed at what Kathleen had revealed. She wanted to do it, no mistake about that. She wanted to be prime minister. And to get there she seemed ready to go back on her promise to him.

I wouldn't have believed it, he told himself. I was so sure she had her fill of that life. If I hadn't been, I would never have married her . . . or perhaps I would have. His resolve hardening, he stared straight into Kathleen's hazel eyes.

"Tell me, Kathleen, do you really want it?"

"I don't know, Andrew." Then words tumbled out in a rush. "Believe me, I had no intention of ever running for office again, but this is different. A chance to lead, to be prime minister." Her voice broke. "It was a dream – an impossible dream. I never thought it could happen. And now it has, I don't know. . . ." Her voice trailed off.

"I'm asking you again, Kathleen. Do you want to do it?" His voice was stern as he leaned toward her, his knuckles white against the napkin he clutched.

She looked at Andrew, her husband of only a little more than six months. Was she risking losing him? She didn't yet know him well enough to gauge his reaction, but she felt a chill of premonition. Could her marriage already be in the balance, just because she had not turned away her old colleagues with a firm rejection?

She hesitated. "Andrew, I haven't forgotten what you said about playing second fiddle to politics. Does that mean that if I said Yes, our life together would be finished?"

"And if it would?"

Kathleen looked down at her hands. She twisted her rings. The lustrous pearl. She couldn't meet his eyes. She had a feeling that she was at the brink, that their future happiness could well depend on what she said now. She took a deep breath.

"If I must choose between what some see as my duty, and losing you, Andrew. . . ." Her voice faltered and she groped for words.

At the half-completed sentence, Andrew lost his nerve. He was afraid to hear her response. I mustn't lose her – not like this, an inner voice cried.

"Kathleen, let's say no more about it just now. Let's think about it. Sleep on it. And I think we should call in the children to discuss it, before we decide. Before *you* decide." He took her hands, and was dismayed to see that her eyes were wet with tears.

It was Sunday. They sat around the lunchtable with the children: Tage, the eldest, was now president of Andrew's chain of newspapers; Per, the next, was a chartered accountant entirely disinterested in the newspaper business; and Ingrid, the youngest, was married but kept up a career as a fashion photographer.

"I want to ask your advice," began Kathleen. "What I am about to tell you is still a secret. It would be terrible if it should come out in the papers – even in some of our own. But I know I can count on you. And I do need your advice."

They all stopped eating and looked at her expectantly.

"Very soon now, Jean Jacques Charles will resign as prime minister."

Tage half-leaped from his chair beside his father. "Resign? Charles? Wherever did you come by that information? And you expect it not to be printed? That's news, very big news!"

"Tage! If there's even the slightest chance that you won't respect my confidence, I can't tell you any more. You must promise not to print that, or anything else I'm about to tell you. Sometimes premature reporting can kill off a project before it has a chance to get off the ground. This is one of those times. Promise?"

Tage looked at Andrew, who nodded his assent.

"Well, of course, if it's all that important to you. But who says he'll resign? There has been speculation for years that he would, but there was never anything to it, except some wishful thinking. Why do you sound so positive now?"

"Because I know that the most powerful people in the Liberal Party are soon to demand both his resignation and an opportunity to elect a new leader. And, under the Liberal constitution, the leader of the party cannot stay on if its membership wants him out.

"But that is only part of what I have to tell you." She then described the visit of The Seven to Secret Lake.

"They sure had their nerve, bothering you at the lake. I'll bet you hadn't even heard from them since you got kicked out of the Cabinet," said Ingrid hotly.

"My dear, I'm sure they were reluctant, but they felt that they had very little time to spare. A nominating convention takes months to arrange. And, as I explained, they must move rapidly for fear the minority government might be defeated before the leadership is replaced."

"What was your reply, Kathleen?" asked Per, the most stolid of the three.

"I haven't yet given it. I asked for more time, so that I could think about it and so that I could consult with Andrew and you. As you know, I had wanted to leave politics for a long time before I actually did. The fun had gone out of it; and I only stayed on because I was persuaded that I could be useful. Then, with my law practice re-established, and my marriage to your father, the furthest thing from my mind was returning to politics. I felt that I had paid my dues and was entitled to my own life.

"Andrew has made it possible for me to give up the practice of law, if I want to. I don't really. The practice has grown nicely, and the work is stimulating and satisfying. But The Seven have made their offer very hard to turn down. They say it is my duty to the country, and to the party, to stand for the leadership. That's an appeal very hard for me to resist."

"Have you never felt the ambition to be prime minister before?" Tage asked, just a bit skeptical of Kathleen's altruistic talk of duty. "After all, you held the job once."

"No, at least not for many years. Maybe when I was first elected. I thought I could do anything, then." She smiled. "But that was a long way back. It didn't take long to find out that a woman who was able to win a seat in Parliament was regarded as something of a freak."

"There have been a lot of changes since then," Ingrid noted. "Why didn't you try for the leadership after your term as interim prime minister, Kathleen? Wouldn't that have been the natural time to do it?"

"If I had intended to contest the leadership, the Cabinet and caucus would never have chosen me to carry on until the convention. And it would have been underhanded – a real breach of faith – if I had tried to run after insisting that I would not."

"Kathleen," Ingrid pressed on, "what about your being a woman? There was a lot of controversy when you took over after Sinclair's death. The talk wasn't just from men, either. A lot of women didn't like the idea of a woman prime minister. Do you think that's changed?"

"If I don't try, we'll never know. After all, since I was P.M., a woman has made a strong run for the Conservative leadership. Maybe things *are* changing."

"Yeah, and look what happened to her! Why should The Seven think you will do any better?"

"I suppose partly because the public did finally accept me as prime minister, even if only as a caretaker. They say that even after one and a half years out of Parliament, I am favourably remembered. With this Government, maybe absence really *does* make the heart grow fonder. And, to be honest, I don't think they have much of a choice."

"I suppose that scandal killed off Hume Frazier's chances?" asked Kathleen's stepdaughter, changing tack.

"I don't know," Tage interrupted, "no one could be more alive or well-regarded around Bay Street. I met Frazier last month at Blair White's party. You should have seen them – men and women – buzzing around him. His hair is getting quite grey but he's sure a handsome bird, maybe even more so now than when he was in politics. And the scandal hasn't even touched him in business. In fact, he's cutting quite a swath as president of SilverTinCo. He turns up at all the clubs."

"That may be the reaction in your circle, Tage," said his sister, "but a lot of women don't like him, after he was caught cheating on his wife. And his ambition sticks out all over him. And then he has that funny, jerky way of talking, and he uses those queer, nineteen-forty-type expressions. He calls everybody 'baby,' for heaven's sake." She shook her dark-gold head. "Baby!"

"I'm sure that Hume Frazier will run, if he has any encouragement at all, children. He's committed his whole life in that direction. And if he does run, he'll be hard to beat. He's still quite popular in many places, and the public may be ready to forgive and forget."

"What are you going to tell them, Kathleen? What have you decided? Or have you decided?"

"I've been worried about the office. There are only two of us, you know, and if I leave, it will be quite a burden. But that's not the main point. I have to decide on the basis of what's right for me. And I have to consider the party and even the country."

"I want your advice. How do *you* feel about it? How would you assess my chances, particularly you, Tage? You see and hear a lot at the company. What do you think?"

"Well, it takes a little getting used to. A woman prime minis-

166

ter! At least you couldn't be any worse than those women in India and Sri Lanka, but maybe I shouldn't bring them up. Look, Kathleen, to be frank, I am not very keen on the idea of a woman in the top job in the country. But then, Kathleen Marshal Wickstrom is not just *any* woman, and I think I could bring myself to support you!"

"Count both of us on your side." Per spoke for Ingrid, as well as himself. "How exciting! How can we help? I'm not even a Liberal. In fact, none of us has ever belonged to a party" – and he looked at the other three Wickstroms for confirmation. "Does that matter? What can we do?"

"Whoa, you three! I haven't yet said I would run. Am I to take it that's your advice: to tell them I will accept?"

"It sounds like accepting is what you really want to do, Kathleen," Tage said. "And there is no real reason to hold back. I think you can probably carry the party. But don't count Frazier out yet, not by a long-shot. As for your chances in a general election, well, who knows? I can't see the NDP making any headway, and Dick Sherwood, as nice a guy as he is, hasn't given any sign of setting the heather afire. Anyway, if you really want to, you should get in and fight for it. Agreed?"

"Agreed," the other two Wickstrom children chimed in unison. And then they looked at their father, Andrew, who had sat silent this whole time.

"Well, Father, you haven't said anything? Shouldn't we celebrate?"

"There's champagne in the refrigerator. Please excuse me." He went to his study. He had counted on the children to reject a return to politics for Kathleen, but they had not. He had lost.

"Dad, I want to talk to you before I go." Ingrid stood at the study door. He gestured his daughter in. She knelt beside him.

"It's obvious that you don't agree with our advice. What do you plan to do?"

"I don't know. I just don't know. I don't want her to go back. They are just using her, and they'll cast her aside without a thought when it suits them. She may not win the leadership. She may lose the election. She'll be hurt."

167

Gently, she asked: "Are those the real reasons?"

"No," he admitted, "but partly. I know it's old-fashioned, but I am over sixty now and I have been alone a long time – since your mother died. I think a wife should be with her husband. And we *have* been happy together. We had such plans."

She rose and, stooping, put her arm around him. "Dad, she wants to do it. It's in her blood. But you know she loves you; and she made a bargain. She'll tell them No if you insist."

"Do you think she would?"

"Only if you insist. But, Dad, have you thought about what will happen if you clip her wings? She'll tell them No, but what will it do to your relationship? It will never be the same. With your eyes wide open, you married a very political person. You knew who she was, what she was, and you wanted her enough to marry her. Dad, you have to go along, and with a whole heart. Maybe she'll be defeated, and then the problem will be gone. But if you stop her now, I think you'll regret it. Think about it." She hugged him, and dropped a kiss on the top of his head.

They lay silently in the big bed, not touching, not speaking. Then Andrew slipped his arm around Kathleen and held her close.

"Katie."

"Yes, Drew."

"Would one term be enough?"

She didn't understand at first, and then, as the meaning dawned: "I'm sure it would be. There are so many others who need just a little experience before they are ready to take over."

"You're sure?"

"Yes, I'm sure."

"Promise?"

"I solemnly promise."

"Then tell them you'll do it. I'll be with you all the way."

The September day had been beautiful, the air crystal clear sharpened by the warning of the winter to come. In Ottawa, colour had begun to touch the leaves of the trees, and the grounds of the Prime Minister's residence seemed to have achieved a cool perfection.

"Good afternoon, gentlemen. The Prime Minister is expecting you. This way, please." The men walked through the marble foyer, past the curving staircase and to the left into the formal drawing room at 24 Sussex Drive.

The red-haired maid, smartly turned out in her black dress and frilly white apron, the saucy white cap perched on the mass of carroty curls, lingered as the seven men found seats around the room.

"The Prime Minister asked me to offer you refreshment while you're waiting. He'll be just a few more minutes. This is the time he sets aside each day to play with the children. He's with the twins."

For a few moments the seven men sat, drinks in hand, waiting expectantly. Then they began wandering about the room, looking at the paintings on the walls, all on loan from the National Gallery, then inspecting the silver and leather-framed photographs, autographed by world leaders to Jean Jacques Charles.

"Why is it that politicians plaster pictures of other politicians all over their office walls and clutter up their homes with them? Must be some kind of proof they need that they themselves are important, if they hobnob with world figures. Speaking of photographs: look, there's not a single one of Evangeline, or the twins. Funny."

"Are you sure our appointment was for five?" asked Fernand LeMesurier of David Kirke, who had made the arrangements for this interview.

"Yes, that was the time. It took me a whole week to set it up, too. I got the impression that for some reason the Prime Minister was trying to evade seeing us. Can you imagine why?" The Senator swung his shaggy head toward his colleague from Nova Scotia, James O'Rourke. "Jim, have you had any trouble getting to the P.M. lately?"

Senator O'Rourke looked surprised. "Why should I be trying to talk to him? No, I don't know from personal experience, but I did overhear the Senate Leader grumbling that even as a Cabinet minister, he rarely gets to talk to Jacques in private anymore. Everybody on the Hill seems to have the same complaint." As he said this, he darted a nervous glance toward the arched doorway. Even though they were about to ask him to resign, the power of the Prime Minister was such that they didn't want to be overheard criticizing him.

Matthew Lyndon and Brigadier Melton carried on a private conversation about the falling value of the Canadian dollar. They were seated side by side in graceful-legged armchairs, upholstered in the same pale aquamarine brocade as all the other major furniture pieces in the room. The piano bench was covered in dusty rose velvet, as were the sidechairs and the thin pillows on the carved settees. Long sheer curtains hung at the windows, with overdrapes in a deeper shade of the same stiff brocade.

Through the windows they could see across the Ottawa River; and there the leaves' changing colours burst out irregularly, like random shots from an approaching army. The sun's rays were slanting now into this formal and impersonal room, sparkling from a crystal bowl, reaching for a branching pair of silver-gilt candlesticks.

Carter Warden was growing irritated by the delay. "This is all of a pattern with the way Jacques is treating the House and his Cabinet. Damnit, he wouldn't have done this a year ago, when he had to come to us for help in getting re-elected. His insolence is really getting out of hand!"

He went to the door. "Gentlemen, it appears we have time for a stroll around the garden. Let's take a look outside while there is still plenty of light; at least we can see what the taxpayers provide for their Prime Minister these days." While Sandy Sinclair, his longtime friend and colleague, had lived here, the former Finance minister had often been a guest in this house. He noted that there had been changes since then.

Warden led the way through the narrow underfurnished glassed-in back porch, across the close-cropped lawn to the low stone fence between the grounds and the rolling river.

"That's one of the changes, and not a particularly attractive

170

one, either." He pointed out the most modern addition. It had supposedly been paid for by a group of Charles' admirers during his first administration. "They say the taxpayers didn't foot the bill for the swimming pool. Maybe you know who did, Peregrine?"

"Not I, you may be sure. Maybe Davie knows."

"Well, sir, you will understand that, even if I do know, I have been charged not to say."

"Doesn't matter anyway," broke in Warden. "But I think it's an eyesore."

The little maid circulated among them with fresh drinks.

"Please tell the Prime Minister that he has already kept us waiting more than half an hour," began Matthew Lyndon. "Oh no, you can't be expected to tell him that." He tried to think of a message that would not make the girl sound impertinent to her employer. "Please tell him that some of the gentlemen have come a considerable distance to see him, and they have only limited time. We understand that he is dining at Rideau Hall tonight."

"Why not tell me yourself?"

The Prime Minister sauntered out of the house, his still-sinewy, slender body dressed in frayed-bottom denims, his checkered shirt hanging out. On his feet were leather sandals, around his throat was knotted a scarf.

As the maid bearing the tray of empty glasses passed him, he said: "A mineral water please – but not the Perrier."

He turned to his guests. "Won't you come into the house? It will be cold out here soon. Unless you would prefer to discuss your business – whatever it is – standing up. There are not enough garden chairs here for everyone." His tone was cool and not very welcoming.

As Jacques held the glassed garden door wide, The Seven filed silently past. They took up the same seats as before. The Prime Minister threw himself into a settee, where he slid down into a semi-reclining position. Hands locked behind his head, he faced his guests with a trace of petulance.

"Well, what's this all about?"

This time, The Seven were prepared. They had designated

Matthew Lyndon, as the party chairman, to put their case. Despite their apprehension at finally finding themselves face to face with Jacques, each had agreed to chime in, so that the Prime Minister would surely know that they were all firmly of the same view.

Lyndon moved his chair around so that it faced the Prime Minister squarely, took a long breath, and began:

"Prime Minister, we have come to ask for your resignation. It is time that the party had the opportunity to choose another leader. You will appreciate that we have not arrived at this conclusion without a great deal of individual soul-searching and much discussion. We have all invested many years of our lives in the Liberal Party, and we have a continuing interest in its fortunes. It is our considered opinion, sir, that you have become a detriment to the party. If it is to survive to serve Canada, it must do so under new leadership. That is what we have come to tell you."

The Prime Minister had not moved, nor had his expression changed.

Brigadier Melton cleared his throat, and made his contribution. "If things go on as they are, the party cannot count on one seat in Toronto, and the position is not much better elsewhere in the province. If the Opposition were to tip you now, we would be hived forever into a Quebec-only party. We would never recover."

Then LeMesurier added, softly: "Nor do I think our fortunes would be very bright, even in Quebec. And if the Liberal Party is shattered, who is there in *la belle province* to speak for the unity of this country? *Les bleus? Les socialistes? Les créditistes?*

"I most regretfully must inform you, Jean Jacques, *mon ancien camarade*, that we cannot permit this to happen. It is time for you to retire."

Still Charles was silent, motionless but for his eyes which glittered as they moved from speaker to speaker.

Then Senator O'Rourke spoke up, conscious, even as he did so, that he owed his call to the Senate to this cold-eyed man lounging before them.

"We will be wiped out in Newfoundland and New Bruns-

wick, and able to hold only a handful of seats. You know that
we do not form the Government in any province but the small-
est – and we barely hang on there. Nova Scotia's loss was a
disaster. You have to understand, sir; it is necessary to be
practical." The former premier looked sadly at Jacques: "The
facts must be faced, Jacques. The party just can't afford you
any more."

Aaron Shapiro leaned forward. "I am the only one here
from the prairies. Since you became leader there has been little enough support for you. Now, however, the situation is
even worse. For the last decade Liberals in the west were
merely thin on the ground; now they are virtually an extinct
species. Even Findlay is in trouble, and if you can re-elect
Bentley Palmer, Manitoba can sprout mountains.

Jacques' glance flicked from the Winnipegger to Carter
Warden.

"Jacques," Warden began, in the level tone that had carried
him through many a difficult budget night, "it was to us you
turned, last year, when you found yourself totally unprepared,
defeated in the House. We believe the same thing could happen again – any day. Yet you have done nothing since the
election to keep the party apparatus in repair. Not one of us
has been able to get through that wall of staff that surrounds
you since last summer. It is not that we are looking for your
thanks – although we *are* entitled to that.

"Jacques, are you aware of how eagerly the business community of this country awaits your downfall? Do you know how
you have antagonized organized labour? Do you have any
idea how you have turned off the ethnic leaders? How angry
you have made monarchists all over the country by your cavalier treatment of Her Majesty? The civil servants are on the
warpath – and if the Post Office isn't on strike, Air Canada is!
You have lost damn near every constituency that has supported the Liberal Party over the years.

"Young people can't find jobs, women no longer believe what
you say about equal opportunity, civil rights advocates
denounce you – even the police associations are raising money
to reverse your policy of abolishing the death penalty! And

this latest thing – letting Findlay talk about referendums on the noose and on abortion. Why start that up again? You've even lost the support of your own senators with your proposals to reform their jobs away.

"Inflation is approaching double digits. Unemployment is already at crisis figures, and the winter is approaching. The civil service has grown like wildfire. The value of the Canadian dollar falls every day."

Jacques slumped under the tidal wave of words, but his eyes continued to glitter dangerously as he listened to the litany of the sins he was charged with.

Then he turned to the only person in the room who had not yet spoken. "*Et tu*, Davie?"

Embarrassed, the Senator who had fought several campaigns as chief election organizer under Alexander Sinclair, to be rewarded with a call to the Red Chamber, and who had, out of nothing more than loyalty to his party and to the leader of the day, responded instinctively to Jean Jacques Charles' call for help, bringing with him the remaining six of the party's leadership, dropped his gaze for a moment.

Then, raising the shaggy head above the hump of his bowed shoulders, he looked straight at the carved face.

"Yes, sir. You're damned right. Me too!"

The Prime Minister made no protest. He accepted the fact that if they had not been determined they would not have come. He did not argue that all the ills of the nation should not be laid on him, nor point out that the rest of the free world had similar troubles. It was useless to do so. For a Prime Minister, no less than for the President of the United States, the buck stopped at the big desk.

When they requested his formal approval to proceed with preparations for a nominating convention, he shrugged his shoulders in assent.

"I will not, however, resign as Prime Minister. Not, at least, until the leadership convention. And maybe not then. I may decide to run myself. Or maybe not. As Prime Minister, I shall, as usual, conduct myself according to my own lights. I shall make such appointments as I choose, and I will press on with my plans. I intend to pursue my proposals for reforming both the economy and the constitution. If there is nothing else, gentlemen, I am sure that you will excuse me. I would not wish to keep Their Excellencies waiting."

Jacques' anger was held in, but there was no mistaking the signs: the cutting voice, the lip lifted in a sneer, the glacial eyes.

The Seven were glad to let themselves out, relieved to have held their ground as solidly as they had planned, and to have avoided an even more unpleasant scene. They drove away to dine together, and to lay their plans for the campaign and the convention to come.

And Jacques, too, had his own plans to make. Whatever his future, he thought contemptuously, it did not include giving in to the demands of these party hacks.

For Kathleen, the weeks since she had informed The Seven of her decision had sped by. She arranged with a tutor for a cram course in French, and kept at her homework assiduously. Carter Warden had telephoned to report on The Seven's confrontation with Jacques, and arranged for her to meet with Senator Kirke, Matthew Lyndon, and him. After an afternoon of intense discussion, her three old friends went away to flesh out her campaign, reaching into every province to tap contacts for specialized jobs. One or the other of them called every few days to report on the organization of the campaign team as their plans took shape.

At the end of September the Prime Minister held a press conference to announce the calling of the convention for February of the following year. He refused to say whether he himself would be a candidate, turning on his questioners with questions of his own.

"Who knows? Do *you* think I should? Would *you* support me?"

No matter how adroit, journalists could get nothing from him, except glowing talk about his new policies: the Government was making sharp cutbacks in social services, re-allocating funds, shutting down some programs in order to finance new ones without additional money. And he was determined to pursue his plans to modernize the constitution, brushing aside the opposition of provincial premiers and senators alike.

Jacques' press conference was full of showmanship. He was alert, amusing, in turns informative or obfuscating. And instead of the lackadaisical style he had lately displayed, he was coolly in command: every inch the leader with a very personal charisma the country had once so wildly acclaimed.

When Parliament convened in mid-October, the leaders of the Opposition made separate statements, pledging themselves not to rock the ship of state while the Government party sought a new leader. Jean Jacques Charles initiated a more open policy toward the members of his own caucus. He was thus able to probe carefully, to assess what strength lay there, should he decide to contest the leadership. He hadn't yet made up his mind exactly what form his revenge would take against those who had repudiated him by asking for his resignation. He was content to bide his time, and meanwhile to build up his strength.

While Kathleen gathered support and Jacques planned his strategy, Hume Frazier was despondent. For weeks he had made the most carefully guarded enquiries to find out whether The Seven were going to approach him as their candidate. And, to his dismay, he now knew no more than he had already learned on the summer night when he and Aaron Shapiro had held their hurried discussion. Despite repeated telephone calls, the Winnipeg lawyer flatly refused to tell him anything further of The Seven's plans. Without their endorsement, it seemed to Hume that his chances would be hopeless. Endlessly he and Sybil had discussed his possible return to politics, going over his finances, balancing his options. It was clear that without ever expressing it, each felt more and more committed to another run at the leadership.

The night the Prime Minister announced the leadership convention, Hume turned to Sybil with a sigh. "The Seven aren't going to call on me. Let's face it. If I decide to go in, we'll have to find our own support. I think it's time I contacted the people who ran my last leadership campaign – the one against Jacques after Sandy died. Some of those people aren't in politics any more, but there'll be others. What do you say, kid? Are you with me? One last time?"

In answer, Sybil got up and went to the desk. From a drawer she drew a folder containing a long, typed list of names with current addresses and telephone numbers.

"Here's your first campaign contribution, Hume. The names of everyone I could think of who might help. And, Hume, you'll notice that I even located Molly Paradis. You always said that she was the best political secretary you had ever had. And here's something else to start off the campaign." She handed him a cheque: it was for $25,000.

By mid-October, Frazier's Friends, as his committee had dubbed themselves, were gathering support. Hume's announcement fell two weeks after Kathleen Marshal had issued her own statement of intent.

One by one, other, lesser candidates entered the field. The Prime Minister kept his own counsel.

For an intense month in November and then again during January, the party provided opportunities – at annual provincial meetings, at regional meetings, or meetings called specially for the purpose – for all the declared candidates to address potential delegates. Every constituency organization scheduled meetings to elect delegates to the convention. Major political parties in England and the United States requested convention seating for their observers. Ottawa embassies and consulates spoke for tickets.

The leadership contest generated unusual publicity in the newspapers. Both Kathleen and Hume were considered excellent candidates and the confrontation of two parliamentarians, both former Cabinet ministers, both victims of Jacques' temper, focused great interest. The pundits favoured first Kathleen, and then Hume. Special polls commissioned by major newspapers across the country seesawed up and down.

The Seven did not seem too concerned. They assured Kathleen that she had the most experienced and dedicated team it was possible to get together, and that they were concentrating on the bottom line – the delegates who were to make the selection. But Kathleen was afraid her advisors, trying to keep her confident, were being overly optimistic, and she intensified her efforts. Everywhere possible she met the delegates: in bare country kitchens, in crowded, tiny high-rise apartment living rooms, in overheated town halls and in drafty church basements.

Sometimes, the results were disappointing, or even seemed to backfire.

In New Brunswick, as an early snow fell outside the steamy windows of a spanking new library, a delegate attacked her forthrightly.

"Now look, Kate Marshal. We don't want a woman as leader. It's not right. I've been a Liberal all my life, and I never heard such nonsense. Everybody knows that women in their middle years can get a bit silly. So I'm going to put my chips on Hume Frazier, even if he has been a damn fool. He's learned his lesson, and is all the better for it."

Kate was disheartened at the round of applause the veteran Liberal had received from his neighbours, but she was glad that she had not encountered the same kind of prejudice more often. But there was no question, now, that her sex was the biggest hurdle she must surmount, and that the deep-seated bias wasn't confined to rural seats alone. She knew that there were many other delegates who, even if they didn't admit it publicly, shared the feeling that a woman couldn't lead the country.

In British Columbia, she faced a fractious crowd, composed mainly of women. She discovered there that the abortion issue, settled in Parliament at such cost almost two years ago, remained the subject of hot debate. Some of the pro-lifers still continued their campaign, determined to re-establish abortion as a crime. Findlay's talk of referendum had given them new hope. There were hecklers. There were placards demanding she go home. Scuffling broke out after one bout of catcalls, and stood at the podium, unsure of what to do, until it was quelled by the organizers.

Her every hour was filled with activity – travelling, meetings with delegates or rallies open to the public, all-candidate platforms, radio phone-ins and television interviews. It was grim, unremitting work, and the tight schedule was always subject to the mercy of the worst of Canadian flying weather.

In late November, she was scheduled to appear in a small town in western Saskatchewan. It proved impossible to get there as planned by light plane. In a near white-out she was driven to Kindersley. Arriving four hours late, she was not surprised that her audience had already gone home. It was explained to her that prairie people refused to attend evening meetings in the winter, since their cars were likely to suffer "square wheels" when parked for hours, or worse, frozen gaslines.

It was dispiriting to make such effort uselessly; and it was only later that Kathleen discovered that her persistence had not been unrewarded. Word got around that she had cared enough to come, and when the convention assembled, she would find that she carried all the votes of the Kindersley district delegates.

Early in December there was a major rally in Quebec City. It was an all-candidates meeting, and the stakes were considerable. No Quebec candidate had yet declared, and many of the delegates from the eastern region of the province would base their pre-convention decisions largely on the showing of the candidates at this meeting.

"I'm pretty nervous about this, Fernand," Kathleen confessed to the party's chief organizer and Quebec fund raiser.

"But your French has improved considerably. Are you not now comfortable with it?" He had spoken to her in French, and it was an indication of how much her daily studies had revived her fluency in that language that it just then registered on Kathleen's mind that their conversation, all dinner-long, in this famous little restaurant in the old city, had included not one word of English.

Despite the butterflies she felt in her stomach as she sat on the bunting-draped platform with the other candidates, waiting her turn, Kathleen got up and performed at her best that winter afternoon.

Her large-boned figure in the dark, plain dress looked slimmer under the floodlights. Her hair was done in a new, softer way: drawn back smoothly from a centre part, the shining mass was now dressed low on her neck in a French knot. She spoke with strength and conviction about her view of the way ahead. The fact that she spoke entirely in their language, admittedly slower than her usual, rapid delivery in English, and that she sometimes paused to choose the word most appropriate to carry her meaning, went a long way to break down the barriers between her and the audience.

In Quebec, more than anywhere else, Kathleen had expected to encounter resistance on the basis of her sex. But it was not apparent that night, nor at any other of the many meetings she attended throughout the province. Though the proof would have to wait until February in Ottawa, the evening was a triumph for her.

Hume, on the other hand, was off-stride that night in the great, crowded arena. He seemed to be groping for his thoughts. He was perfectly bilingual; that wasn't the problem.

"It was your material," he was told later by his own disappointed organizers. The reason the audience sat on their hands, they said, was because the Quebec delegates now saw him as a representative of the Bay Street establishment, a traditional symbol to them of their repression. They did not add that in family-oriented Quebec, many of the delegates remembered, as they watched the handsome figure before them, the scandal that had forced Hume Frazier out of Parliament.

Kathleen's schedule took her to lunch with publishers, some of them Andrew's business friends. Andrew and Tage insisted on going along to smooth the way. The newspaper people were surprisingly friendly and seemed genuinely interested in her views, but Kathleen concluded privately that their supportive attitude had more to do with the fact that she was Andrew's wife than with their assessment of her own qualifications as a politician.

It's all too true, that old saw: "it isn't *what* you know, but *who*," she thought to herself. The old-boy network operates here, that's pretty clear.

One immensely encouraging aspect of her campaign was the way women flocked to volunteer as workers. Not all were Liberals; but they all saw here a chance to elect a woman leader for the first time, and for that they put aside their own partisan leanings. Many of them had some experience in supporting a woman candidate in the earlier Conservative convention, where they had been disgusted by the double standard of public support and private vindictiveness exposed when their candidate had suffered early defeat. They were determined there would not be a second such failure: if Kathleen Marshal was not chosen by the Liberals it would be many years before another woman would be a serious candidate for the leadership of a major party.

Young people, too, offered their services. Some of them worked in the campaign offices established in each of the provinces, doing the thankless but necessary tasks of any campaign: preparing mailing lists, telephoning delegates, picking up campaign contributions, organizing phone-ins, monitoring media reaction. There was always something for willing hands.

It was a curious campaign. Ultimately directed at the delegates who would come together in Ottawa in February, it had to take advantage of every media opportunity that came along. There was necessarily a lot of overspill, but media attention had the effect of stimulating public interest, and of course, the delegates were a part of that public.

At Christmas the public electioneering paused, but there was little respite for the team that The Seven had put together.

"Kathleen, you must take advantage of the holidays to get a little rest. There are still those two all-candidate meetings in Edmonton and in Halifax. The first is Edmonton, but it's not until the middle of January. Halifax comes almost at the end, ten days before the convention opens. In between, we'll pack in every possible personal contact. You won't have much time off until after the convention is over, so you'll need to build up your strength while you can. And don't forget to keep polishing that French. It's proved an enormous asset. Keep well, and get some rest, hear?"

As she dropped the telephone receiver into its cradle after this conversation with Matthew Lyndon, Kathleen sighed: "Seventh inning stretch, and I can sure use it! Now, what shall we do over the holidays?"

In the end, she passed a quiet, family Christmas in Toronto with Andrew, his children and grandchildren. And on Boxing night, she and Andrew flew off to London for a badly needed week all to themselves.

Although the leaders of the Liberal Party apparatus had endorsed Kathleen Marshal, support for Hume Frazier was growing quickly. Many of those who favoured Hume's candidacy were loyal friends from his early days in the party. During his parliamentary career, Hume had pursued a policy of encouraging pockets of local support, his eye on the future. As a result, he had no more trouble now than he had almost a decade ago, after Alexander Sinclair's death, in attracting dedicated people to join Frazier's Friends.

The movement was swelled by new people: some were leaders in the business communities across the country; others were small-time businessmen or managers who trusted his organizational abilities. They felt that his experience as Minister of Finance made him the ideal person to lead them out of the country's economic ills. Capitalizing on this advantage, Hume gathered a group of economists and academics who prepared policy drafts for his speeches.

With care he chose prestige platforms rather than public meetings where he might encounter embarrassing reminders of the nearly two-year-old scandal. And because he was afraid of the scandal becoming an issue, the media found him more difficult to approach now, less open to interrogation than in his more carefree days. He liked to talk about the theory of the broad policies he would initiate, but he was reluctant to join them in easy joking as he used to. This, they took as an insult, and their previous uncritical admiration became uncertain. It was noticed that the Frazier game plan was to avoid question-and-answer sessions, and although his public pronouncements were well-scripted, the audiences seemed, by journalists' standards, deliberately chosen to be safe.

Sybil, as she had promised when they got engaged, was ready to take on the task of being a politician's wife. On most public occasions she was at his side. But she begged off from travelling with Hume to the smaller, less-well-publicized, difficult-to-reach meetings with delegates. Hume, too, disliked the discomfort of winter travel to out-of-the-way places. To him such meetings seemed a waste of time since so much effort was required to reach so few people, and there was one week in December when he cancelled his appearance at three small events. Disappointed delegates remembered, but Hume Frazier would not know that until February. His campaign team, not as experienced as they were enthusiastic, were naturally chagrined over these cavalier, last-minute cancellations, but not even they appreciated the extent of the damage that was being done. Nonetheless, they were worried, and they pleaded with Frazier.

"Hume, you've got to stop cancelling appearances. Every time you don't show, Kathleen Marshal picks up a handful of delegates." The speaker was Ross Hunter, Frazier's longtime executive assistant. For the duration of Hume's campaign he had arranged a leave of absence from the business leviathan in Montreal where he had found a well-paying and comfortable berth after Hume Frazier's sudden resignation.

"You can't just concentrate on these big-business types alone. They may have the money, and even some influence, but that cuts no ice with many of the delegates, and it's their votes you have to have."

"I won't forget that the delegates are the target, kiddo. But there are ways and ways. Sybil is a helluva lot more effective here, at the centre of her network of society dames, than she is in the boondocks. She doesn't feel comfortable with Ukrainian farmers out west, anymore than she does with the Portuguese in Kensington, or the Chinese patriarchs, or at those basement beer bashes the Italians throw. She hates to be cornered to admire fat, untidy babies with runny noses, and she never knows what to talk about with those silent women who gang up in the kitchens to feed their men."

"Most of them are only shy – and more than a little in awe of her, Hume. I wish she would make the effort. Molly has always been great at that kind of mixing. Despite her looks, the women seem to warm up to her right away. And the men positively drool. If Sybil won't go, why don't you take her?"

"You know better than that, Ross. Molly is doing just a great job at headquarters. People are surprised that she has so much savvy under that fluffy head of hers. But we agreed when she came aboard that she's got to be kept under wraps. It's not good for me to be photographed, or even seen, with any woman but Sybil. It stirs too many memories."

"Well, you ought to get around more yourself, even if Sybil won't go."

Hume paused. He had been in politics long enough to know that advisers didn't tell their candidate anything unpleasant unless they had to. It had been his idea to run his campaign on ideas and policies, but there was no use doing less than his best.

"All right. I'll make you a promise. I won't cancel out on any more of the meetings, although some of them are kind of a farce. Some of those all-candidate meetings drive me nuts. No one gives a damn about the candidates other than Kit and myself; and yet what with the introductions and hearing out the joke-candidates, we sit around all night."

"How are you getting along with Kathleen?"

"Don't see her much to talk to. We rarely sit together on platforms, and in the mingling after the speeches, we're both right out there shaking hands, not lingering about to chat. We've always been friends; but running against anyone tends to drive a wedge. You know what I mean? It's no secret that I'm pretty competitive, and don't kid yourself, old Kit is too."

"Well, it's far too early to tell where you stand, but I have a gut feeling that Kathleen's campaign is gaining momentum. What do you think?"

"Our people say we're ahead. They keep urging me to stick to the game plan, and I'm doing it. Our team doesn't think much of the old-style, scatter-gun campaign she's running. Not very efficient, they say. It's funny, Ross, but at the centre like this, I find it hard to gauge how it's going. But it does seem to me that the newspaper people aren't as friendly. Know what I mean?"

"I agree, Hume. The clipping service has been turning up some critical pieces. Mild, mind you, but I would much rather see a trend develop where they warm up, rather than this cooling off. I don't see much mention of the 'heir-apparent' any more, but that's inevitable now that the leadership race is actually on. In the old days nobody ever took seriously the idea of a woman leader, especially when Kathleen never showed any interest before in seeking the top job.

"Now, here's the schedule until Christmas, and a draft plan for January. Have you made plans for the holidays?"

"Oh, sure, we're taking the kids to the Caribbean for most of the time, and then Sybil has arranged for a very extravagant party on New Year's Day. That's a good time to get people together, and she promises that we'll have some important new support for the New Year."

"Now let's take a look at January. . . ."

While Hume and Kathleen worked, driving themselves day and night, Jean Jacques Charles sat back and watched the progress of the leadership campaign with disdain. In the House, too, he kept a fairly low profile, leaving his ministers to carry the ball on their own legislation. The promises of the other party leaders not to tip his Government until the Liberals had selected their next leader gave him a sense of security, but Jacques was annoyed that the House leaders were taking so long to reach agreement on the schedule of business. He suspected that the Opposition was dragging its feet on some of his favourite proposals, even if they blandly denied the charge.

Jacques himself concentrated his energy on two things: a new constitution for the country and summit meetings with other free-world leaders. The first was a revival of an early political aspiration. He refused to believe that the country was bored with the subject. To him, a revitalized constitution was of consuming interest, and the more the provincial premiers and their advisors resisted his ideas, the more certain he was that his course was the right one.

"But, Prime Minister, the subject has almost no political sex appeal. The public is preoccupied with finding jobs. They want inflation to be wrestled to the ground, they want a strong industrial base, and new economic measures. The weakness of the dollar scares them. Remember what Laurier said: 'The twentieth century belongs to Canada.' The people are still waiting for that Liberal prophesy to come true, and they're getting a little edgy."

"Now let's not go into that again, Boots. I've made up my mind. So long as I'm here the constitution is the thing. And that, you know, may be for quite a while yet."

The group lounging in the gold-suede room stirred, a bit irritated at these veiled allusions to the future. This was a new habit of the Prime Minister – trying to keep his staff on edge by constant ambiguous remarks – and it made even his most loyal friends uncomfortable.

"If he's gonna run, he better get off the pot damn soon, or he'll find he's left at the gate," Tom Shatto, the Prime Minister's chief press liaison officer, muttered to his seatmate near the unused fireplace. Stan Findlay, Minister of Transport and now a habitual attendant at the P.M.'s meetings, looked at Shatto sharply.

"He'll run, all right," Findlay whispered fiercely. "And he'll win."

"Anyway, we are doing the best we can with those other issues, Jamieson," Jacques went on, unaware that his words, which he intended to be mollifying, carried overtones of irritating pomposity. "But the whole world picture affects us. It is difficult to see any real upturn until the American dollar strengthens. But we are keeping our eyes on it, prepared to initiate policies to stimulate the economy just as soon as the moment is propitious. In the meantime, we are concentrating on negotiations with the provinces on the constitution."

"Propitious. Propitious, hell! If something isn't done soon, it may be too late for your precious policies! The Minister of Finance is a helluva guy, but the press are on his heels like bloodhounds. They're tearing him to pieces – laughing him out of that portfolio, and that, by God, won't help the Government's image any." Tom Shatto was getting reckless, thought Boots Jamieson. The P.M. was not charmed by overly critical comment, and Shatto had been around long enough to know that.

As if in reflection of Jamieson's thought, Jacques straightened in his chair. "I thought you were on *our* team, Tom," he said silkily. And then, with an edge: "That's your job – polishing our image. Are you telling me that you are not up to it?"

"No, sir, I'm not. But newsmen aren't stupid, even if a lot of politicians think they are. And if we are going to pull out of this slump, I need something to work with."

The Prime Minister gave him a long, cool look, and then shrugged him off.

"Is there anything in from Bonn?" he asked of Ian Shepherd, his foreign affairs expert.

"Yes, Prime Minister. I put a communiqué on your desk not an hour ago. It is a confirmation of your plans to ski with the Chancellor over the holidays. I understand that there are a number of international matters on the agenda, so it will be quite in order to travel by government aircraft."

Tom Shatto rolled back his eyes. The gesture did not escape the Prime Minister, who snapped: "Have you anything to say Shatto?"

"No, sir."

"Will you be taking the twins with you?" asked Jeanne Dupuis. She was a bright, fortyish blonde who had rushed in to fill the gap left in the Prime Minister's household by Evangeline's death. "Or shall I make other arrangements?"

"My daughters are still a little too young to ski the Alps and I doubt that they would find much of interest in summit discussions," Jacques said drily. "Their nannies can look after them."

"But, sir," she protested. "It's Christmas."

"Yes, but *they* don't know it. They are babies, not two years old. No, they'll be fine at 24 Sussex."

"Well, there's something more immediate. The House rises tomorrow for the holiday break. Will you be attending the traditional Speaker's reception for the members? He would like to know, since it may be the last time –"

The Prime Minister gave her a threatening look.

My God, but Jacques is getting so prickly over everything. Now what did I say wrong? she wondered.

But Charles had already changed the subject. "There is one thing I'd like you to attend to, Jeanne. Will you make appointments for me to see these people." He placed a handwritten list on the edge of the desk, which Jeanne at once retrieved. As she glanced down the row of names, she saw that it included some of the ministers and senators who had been closest to the Prime Minister over the years, although it had been a long time since she had noticed some of their names on his appointment book. At the head of the list were Stan Findlay and Bentley Palmer.

"I would like to see them before they leave Ottawa for the holidays, especially Senator LaCroix."

"In separate interviews, or all together?"

"One at a time, I think." He took up his pipe and filled it slowly.

"And, yes, tell the Speaker I will probably drop in, but not to make anything of it. Who knows whether it will be, as you put it, 'for the last time'?" Jeanne shrank at the barb.

"What about the next day, sir?" prompted Jamieson.

"The next day?" With lifted brows, the Prime Minister waited for an explanation.

"The Christmas party for the kids of the PMO staff. You remember? We have it every year, sir."

"Ah, yes, I remember. There's a box of presents around here somewhere. Jeanne, where are those things you bought? Ask Christianne. She has the damndest knack of hiding things on me. No, I won't be at the party, I'm afraid," he said shortly. "I have other more important things to attend to. But I expect I'll see all of you here over the next day or so. I have a few instructions I'll want to give you."

188

As they left the room, Tom Shatto said under his breath to Boots Jamieson, "No doubt it'll be some lessons on how to fiddle while Rome burns."

Official Ottawa dozed, as it always did, over the year-end holiday period. With the House closed down, there was never much news to report, and most newspapers allowed their staff to take a few days off to be with their families. Everyone who could fled to either the sun or the ski slopes.

On New Year's Day, Kathleen and Andrew dined at the residence of the Canadian High Commissioner to the U.K., a beloved old warhorse from Sinclair's days, put out to pasture early in Jacques' first administration.

Across the Atlantic, in Toronto, Hume and Sybil stood for hours, welcoming an overflowing household of important guests to a party designed to demonstrate how wide was Hume's support.

In both places, the topic on everyone's lips was the same.

In his New Year's Day message televised to the nation, Jean Jacques Charles had announced his intention to contest the Liberal leadership, confident that he would again be chosen. And he had made a powerful argument that in these difficult times it was he who was most qualified to lead. He had excused his behaviour in the last year in office, delicately laying the blame for his shortcomings on his inconsolable grief over the loss of Evangeline. In the final moments of the nation-wide telecast, he had displayed a large photograph of the beautiful sleeping twins, the legacy of that brief marriage. His eyes were luminous with unshed tears, his voice quivering in its appeal.

"To ensure their future, I can move mountains. But it is only you who can give me that opportunity. I beg for that new chance. And I pledge to you that if you give me your confidence, you will never have cause to regret it. Let us go forward together to the happiest of New Years. If you will but let me serve you again, I know that, as the great Sir Wilfrid Laurier promised, the twentieth century *will* belong to Canada. I pledge myself to keep that promise."

Chapter Ten

The nominating convention had been stalled for three hours. In the Ottawa Civic Centre the humidity and the heat grew more and more intense. Candidates, delegates and observers all wilted with the uncomfortable delay. At the rear of the giant hall, the St. John's Ambulance station overflowed with patients who had fainted in the overheated convention hall. The crowd of more than six thousand was hungry, bored, and noisy. The three hours threatened to grow into four; and no one appeared to know the reason for the interruption.

In the far reaches of the Civic Centre, the visibility was limited by the miasma of eddying smoke, and the stink of wet wool and rubber and of packed humanity choked the thousands who clung to their seats. But despite the miserable conditions, very few left to climb down below for fear that they would be unable to reclaim their seats. The people here were of every walk of life, every age and every condition, all drawn by the excitement of history in the making.

The tiers below had been assigned to the fully accredited delegates from each of the constituency organizations of the Liberal Party of Canada. From above, where alternates, special guests of the party, and other privileged people were seated, no one could distinguish individuals among the thousands of jostling delegates. In roped-off sections were other delegates, those who represented no local constituency: lifetime privy councillors who, as former Liberal ministers, were entitled to vote; Liberal premiers or party leaders; current senators, ministers, and members; heads of youth and women's wings of the party.

Six boxes, hung with bunting in the colours adopted by the six candidates in the race, were ranged at equal distance along the west side of the enormous hall. They faced the cordonned-off area of the floor, where the voting booths stood. Along the east side of the room a long, narrow platform had been erected. On it was a line of a half-dozen folding chairs and a table draped in red and white, the Liberal Party's traditional colours.

In the centre of the long platform was a podium with dozens of microphones, each emblazoned with the call letters of a radio or television station. Behind the platform were monster photographs of the twentieth century leaders of the Liberal Party, every one a prime minister.

Lights blazed down on the crowd, adding to the nearly insufferable heat. From time to time, when television lights were switched on for live coverage, it was almost impossible to see through the brilliant glare. But at the moment, there was nothing to see but the crowd milling on the convention floor. Thousands of separate conversations were going on at once, and although a small folk band was playing its heart out from the platform, its music was lost in the monstrous buzz. Meanwhile, because of the long delay, the participants and observers were losing patience.

"Say, George, have you noticed that all the candidates have left their boxes? Must be something up. Do you see either of the chairmen around?"

"Nope. They've disappeared, too. Maybe we'll get some action now. Look at the time! How in hell do they think they can get this election over with and get the new leader on television before eight? We'll have to cut the convention off before the speech. What kind of loony organization is that?"

"Dunno, better let our producer know. If airtime has to be extended, she'll need to talk to the brass. Tell her this is bo-ring; we've got nothing left to talk about. Our pundits have said all there is to say – ten times. And tell her that I'm very thirsty and I want to take a leak."

The two television anchormen were tired and irritable and, like the convention participants, fed up with the unexplained delay.

191

Kathleen Marshal, hurrying to keep up with her chief campaign agent, Gordon Neville, rounded the corner and came upon an angry scene outside room 224, to which they had been summoned by Joey Breen, the convention returning officer.

There was a knot of people in front of the door: Hume Frazier and wife Sybil; Ross Hunter, Hume's agent; the co-chairmen of the convention, Senator Gabriel LaCroix and M.P. Bonnie Costello; and Joey Breen. A uniformed Ottawa policeman stood off at a discreet distance, his face averted but his ears pricked at the noisy exchange.

Sybil Frazier, her face pink with anger, stamped her foot. "I will. I will. I will. You can't stop me. I have a right to be here with my husband. This affects my future, too. I simply won't let you push me away. I'm going to go inside. I am. Hume, darling, tell them that you won't stand for this."

Jean Jacques Charles approached from the other end of the corridor. He was trailed by his chief strategist, the hulking young Quebec M.P., Alcide Morin. Two plainclothes RCMP men followed at their heels.

"What's all this about?" The Prime Minister asked testily.

Joey Breen, a veteran of every leadership convention since 1948, explained with some asperity: "This meeting is for candidates and their agents only, and Mrs. Frazier here" – he gestured toward the ordinarily controlled Sybil, whose eyes now blazed defiance – "she's insisting that she be allowed in, too."

Jacques raised his eyebrows. "What do the other candidates say? Are they here yet?"

"Yes, sir, the others are all inside, waiting. None of them brought anyone but agents, as instructed."

"Well, it's okay with me if Mrs. Frazier comes in. Nice to see you with your *wife*, Hume." Charles smiled at his own clever remark. "No, I don't care. How about you, Kathleen?"

"*D'accord.*"

Jacques glanced at her, amused at the use of the parliamentary expression of agreement.

"Well, then, let's not keep the others waiting. After you, Sybil." He made an elaborate, sweeping bow.

In the small boardroom the ventilation system was turned on full blast, and after the oppressive atmosphere in the convention hall it was almost too cool for comfort.

Kathleen glanced around, noting that the ice storm was still raging outside. Rime coated the room's only window. Around the elongated table, the other candidates sat in relaxed attitudes, their chief agents alert at their sides. The room was already heavy with smoke. Most of that derived from the fiercely puffed pipe of Cy Hurelak, but Barry Anderson's well-chewed cigar was making its contribution.

As Kathleen, Jacques and Hume took their seats, they nodded to the other three candidates: Hurelak, Anderson, and Mary Margaret McMahon.

Joey Breen took a chair at the head of the table, flanked by the convention co-chairman.

"I'll be brief. There's a problem with the voting machines. The tallies are all screwed up. It's worse than the problem the Tories had in Toronto when they decided to use machines to take the vote. The count shows that more people voted than there are official delegates, and that just can't happen. We've gone over our arrangements a dozen times, and there's no way that any ringers could have been added, so it's got to be the bloody machines. We've scoured the city and come up with enough blank ballot books to conduct an old-fashioned, write-in ballot. The City of Ottawa is lending us municipal ballot boxes." He looked at his watch. "They ought to be here now.

"Now the problem is this: Do we release the totals, even if they are wrong? Or do we announce the way the candidates ranked, without the numbers? Or do we scrap the results entirely? I'd like to do that – just burn 'em, and start over."

The first to break the silence was Cy Hurelak, a perennial candidate for the Liberal leadership. Although the burly Newfoundlander never drew more than a handful of votes, this was the third nomination race he had entered and he was the only candidate in the room without an agent. He spoke up in his usual hearty manner.

"I'm for tellin' the whole story to the delegates. They should know what we know. If there's a smell of rotten fish around, it won't help any to bury it. Somebody's sure to dig it up and then the stink will stick to us forever."

Joey Breen nodded, acknowledging Hurelak's shrewd point. "Maybe we should hear from the Prime Minister?"

Jacques, who was with Kathleen Marshal and Hume Frazier for the first time since he had fired them, seemed amazingly relaxed. He was lounging in his chair, one foot crossed over his knee, and at Breen's question he leaned backward slightly, to catch the whispered advice of his bearded agent, Alcide Morin.

Then he shrugged his shoulders indifferently. "What do the other candidates say? They have as much at stake as I have."

Barry Anderson had been born in Edmonton and, until his election, had spent his whole life there. A tall, gangling young man with a bobbing adam's apple, he had only one brief term in Parliament behind him. His candidacy resulted from a tight-knit group of westerners who had badgered him into entering the race. They didn't expect him to win, but his candidacy would ensure that their point of view was heard at the convention.

He blinked in confusion and his large ears turned red. Before he could open his mouth, the pudding-faced Mary Margaret McMahon burst in.

"I agree. We ought to tell them everything, but it sure will cause a lot of confusion. I don't understand it myself." And the doughty little Irishwoman grinned around at the others.

Sybil Frazier, seated behind Hume, poked him in the back and he bent to catch her whisper. Then, turning back to the table, Hume gave his opinion.

"I think we should announce the standings, but not the numbers. They're meaningless anyway. But standings will help shake out the also-rans and maybe shorten things a bit." He jabbed his finger towards the end of the table, where the three lesser candidates sat. "Some of you people have no damned business running at all. It's frivolous, and it wastes time. Everybody knows this is a three-way race, so the sooner the rest of you are out of it, the sooner it will be over." Then, dropping his voice a level, he asked of the co-chairmen, "What about time? Aren't we running awfully tight for television coverage? And what about the delegates? Surely we'll lose a lot of them if this thing drags on. Most of them have planes or trains to catch and that storm out there isn't helping any. The roads are already sheets of ice."

"Just a moment." Mary Margaret McMahon leaned toward Hume, her eyes snapping. "I'd like you to know, Mr. High-and-Mighty Frazier, that any member of this party who can scrape up enough signatures on a nomination paper is entitled to run for the leadership. The Liberals have always done it that way. I damned well don't need *your* permission to run, and you have no bloody business telling me when to drop out! In fact, I just may stay in until the bitter end, the way you did last time, when you ran against Jean Jacques Charles."

"That's right," added Barry Anderson.

"I don't need any help from you, either," she said, to Anderson's embarrassment.

Hume flushed at the exchange and was about to make a retort when Bonnie interrupted.

"We should still have time to finish this evening, Hume. We are doing our best," she assured him in an even voice.

"We all want to elect a new leader in time for live television coverage. It'd be a helluva waste not to and we'll try to avoid it if we possibly can," Senator LaCroix added soothingly.

"Kathleen, do you agree to announcing just the standings, with no numbers?" Bonnie asked.

"Yes, I'll go along with that."

Jacques uncrossed his legs and put his empty pipe in his pocket. "Is that settled then, Joey? You will simply announce the order we stood on that first ballot?"

In the convention hall, Joey Breen stood waiting as Senator LaCroix gavelled for silence. When it was quiet, Breen stepped to the microphones, a piece of paper trembling in the grip of his arthritic hand.

He explained the problem with the voting machines, and the proposed solution. The crowd grumbled but fell silent again as he began to recite, in ascending order, the standings of the candidates on the aborted first ballot.

"Hurelak."

A murmur of amusement from the audience.

"Anderson."

A wild "Yippeeeee" erupted from someone in the crowd.

"McMahon."

Several delegates clapped excitedly, but the audience now held its breath, anxious for the first indication of the comparative strength of the three front-runners.

"Charles."

There was a collective gasp that might have been dismay – or happy surprise.

"Marshal."

For a moment, Kathleen was stunned. She had expected to be first, right from the start. It had simply never occurred to her that this race could end any other way.

Andrew squeezed her hand, but said nothing. This was what he had been afraid of, ever since last summer.

Gordon Neville sat down beside Kathleen. "Well, old girl. Not so good. But I hear you were only a few votes behind Frazier. This is going to be tougher than I thought."

"What about the bandwagon effect, Gordon?"

"I don't know how much being front-runner will boost Hume's chances. I have a hunch that what he has is a big core-vote, but that he can't expect many people to move to him. Your people will hold, never fear. Now, don't lose heart. Remember that old saying: when the going gets tough, the tough get going. I'll be on my way. Gotta keep those deals cookin'. I'll be back as soon as I have something to report."

He adjusted the tricolour kerchief that marked him as one of the Marshal team, checked to see that the red-and-white badge marked "Official" was still in place, and then clattered down the steps and plunged into the crowd.

"Frazier."

There was a roar from the crowd and a flurry of waving placards, most behind and above the green and white bunting that marked Hume's box. As Kathleen watched, she saw a beautiful blonde woman dart forward from the back of the box. She threw her arms around Hume and planted a smacking kiss directly on his lips. He pulled away from her. Hume Frazier's buglers blew a fanfare. His workers were laughing and crying, shouting their delight.

"The voting on the next ballot will now begin," Senator LaCroix announced over the noise.

And then, before she could start to worry, Kathleen found herself under siege by autograph hunters, who laughed and chattered and offered congratulations and waved books, bits of paper, maps of the Civic Centre, even scarves and handkerchiefs for her signature.

A stranger, a square-bodied, jug-eared man with a wheat-stubble haircut, dressed in an unfashionable tweed suit, stepped to her side and began to speak firmly to the people pressing too closely about her. She was puzzled at first, not knowing who he was. Then it suddenly came to her that he was a member of the RCMP.

And for the first time that day realized that whoever was elected was also going to be prime minister. She and Hume would be under RCMP protection, until a winner was chosen.

From the crowd emerged the familiar face of a stocky Ukrainian farmer who had hosted a meeting in Saskatchewan in his spacious, scrubbed-to-the-bone prairie kitchen.

"Atta girl, Katie, atta girl." He pounded her on the back, almost knocking the breath from her in his enthusiasm. The young Mountie moved forward, but Kathleen shook her head and he stepped back.

"You've done well, you'll make it yet," he said in a thick accent. "Where's Gordon? And I don't see my black beauty around either. I suppose they're all out there, nailing down the next ballot. Am I right?"

She laughed at him, delighted at his enthusiasm. "Yes, Gordon's around, talking to delegates. And Barbara's tucked away in the back office, working like crazy as usual. I'll tell them you said hello."

"I'm off then. I'm trying to get through the ropes, to see how Bess is doin'. She's not a delegate, just an alternate, but she wouldn't've missed this for the world. See, over there, she's wavin' at us."

"Give Mrs. Lysenko my best, John," she called as he struggled down the stairway from the box. She realized gratefully he had kept her from becoming discouraged at her first-ballot loss.

With a start, Kathleen remembered that she had not yet cast her own ballot. The plainsclothes officer behind her, she made her way to the crowded floor. When she offered her credentials to the young official, she was waved on with a grin to join the slowly moving line of delegates under "L to R." It took her but a moment to write her own name, her maiden name, under which she was running. She had too much political capital invested in that name to switch to Wickstrom. Once, voting for herself had embarrassed her, but she had long since learned that the gallantry of voting for an opponent was appropriate only in high school.

There were still hundreds in the snaking lines before each voting booth. Grinning to herself, Kathleen remembered that it was the Prince of Wales who said, "Never pass up a chance to pee." Following that royal advice, she led the way out of the hall toward the women's toilets, trailed even on this mission by the young Mountie.

As Kathleen passed by the wide main door to the Civic Centre, it flew open on a gust of frigid air to allow the entry of a pinch-faced figure muffled to the ears.

"God, what a day!" growled the man, as he beat clinging particles of ice from his clothing and stamped his feet in their heavy boots.

"Howzzit going, Katie?" he called, catching sight of her.

She turned, recognized a regular of the press gallery. "You haven't missed anything yet, Brett. Hume's ahead but I intend to catch him."

In the Charles box, aside from the watchful Mounties who stood against the walls, there was no one near Jacques but Alcide Morin, who was talking to him animatedly.

Jacques was listening, nodding, occasionally smiling. He noticed Kathleen stand to smooth down the scarlet dress. The dress was new, and very much in style. She looked very well, he thought approvingly, and for some reason, he thought then of Evangeline, of the long and friendly evenings the three of them had spent together. Then he winced at the memory of Evangeline's loss. The dull pain throbbed through him. His loneliness and guilt still ate at him, and he could scarcely bear the thought of the children, and what they had cost. For a moment, he was almost overwhelmed by a wave of grief. Then with grim determination, he mastered himself and bent to hear his chief strategist, Alcide Morin, but his eyes still rested on Kathleen.

Suddenly, as if she felt his gaze, Kathleen looked toward him, and their eyes locked.

Still seated, he made a mock bow, a kind of salute – almost a friendly alliance of two challengers trailing the front-runner.

She smiled in acknowledgement. Then, finally comprehending Morin, Jacques jerked his head over his left shoulder. For a moment, Kathleen was puzzled at the gesture's meaning. He repeated it, rolling his eyes in the same direction, and she shifted her gaze.

In the packed green-and-white box overhung by a huge photograph of Hume Frazier, there was a very heated argument going on. At this distance, it was impossible to hear anything, but the little tableau's story was clear enough to read. In plain sight of anyone who cared to look, Sybil was engaged in a shoving-match with a beautiful blonde girl with a voluptuous figure.

It was Molly Paradis, Kathleen realized, Hume's former secretary. It must have been she who had embraced Hume after the standings were announced; and now Sybil seemed to have completely lost her head.

In the Frazier box, Hume stood by helplessly as Sybil pummelled the resisting Molly toward the exit.

"Now get out of here, you slut, and stay out! You were hired to *help* my husband, but as a secretary, and nothing else! If I catch you sneaking around here, or ever see you lay a hand on him like that again, I warn you, you'll never know what hit you."

"Shut up, you frigid bitch," Molly screamed. "This isn't your box, it's Hume's! What does he say? He doesn't love you and never did! It's me he loves! Why he says you aren't even a good lay! He . . . "

Hume held his hands over his ears, unwilling to believe that Molly was actually shouting these things at Sybil. Finally he pushed between them, aware that many in the crowd below were already staring at the curious little scene.

"Molly, be quiet. You had better go. Right now. Sybil, you're making a public spectacle of yourself. Pay no attention to anything she says. *Sybil!*" He swung his wife around to face him. "*Let her go!* Get hold of yourself. She didn't mean anything by kissing me. She was just excited, that's all."

Sybil had begun to sob. "She said you loved her! And she said – " But Sybil couldn't bring herself to repeat the phrase that had cut so deeply. "Have you been seeing her again, Hume? Tell me. I must know."

"No, of course not, Sybil." That, as Frazier was queasily aware, despite his hearty tone of reassurance, was not quite true. He had fallen off the wagon, just once, with Molly. But he didn't blame himself for that. She was so lush, so willing, and he had lived in a desert, deprived of satisfying sex for such a long time. "And, Sybil, remember that it was you who suggested that she be on the campaign team."

Hume hushed Sybil, who blotted the tears from her face, and then he led her back to their seats at the front of the box.

"Now smile, darling, and keep on smiling. That's the way, smile. It's all right. I'm sure that hardly anyone noticed. Smile!" And the two of them leaned forward, Hume's arm about Sybil's waist, beaming and nodding and waving to the delegates below.

The returns from the second ballot were expected any moment.

"It's been a tough two days, Kate, but it's almost over now. Hold on, old girl." Andrew and Kathleen had been talking quietly when Gordon came back to the box to report to her that he expected at least two, and perhaps all three, of the minor candidates would be ready to join forces with her immediately after the results were announced.

"Here they come now."

200

The chairman gavelled for attention.

"The results of the second ballot. May I have your attention please? Quiet, please. Are you ready?"

Joey Breen stepped forward as the crowd fell silent.

"Number of delegates registered: 3747. Number of ballots cast: 3567.

"Good, we haven't lost many delegates, despite the delay," whispered Gordon, busily recording the totals in his tally-book.

"From the bottom up as before. Hurelak – seventeen."

A groan from the crowd.

"Anderson – one hundred and twenty."

No reaction from the crowd.

"McMahon – four hundred and nineteen."

Whoops of excitement from those clustered in and near Mary Margaret's box were quickly shushed by the crowd.

Joey Breen paused, removed his glasses and looked over the mass of people. Then he replaced the glasses and again took up his paper:

"Charles – seven hundred and ninety-five."

A deep murmur rose and swelled in the large room. A shrill whistle split the air. With that sound, everyone in the auditorium knew it was over for Charles. Reporters crushed around Jacques' box, their microphones held aloft as they pleaded for a comment from the Prime Minister. He waved them off, leaning forward to catch the next name to be announced.

"Frazier – one thousand and ten."

A gasp – Frazier had slipped to second place! Hume's head was bent to the tally held by his agent, Ross Hunter, who hunched beside him. Sybil clutched his arm, and they turned to look uncertainly at one another.

The response of the crowd was mixed. Cheers, many signs waved, a lot of unreadable background noise; but also there was more than one isolated "boo."

"Marshal – twelve hundred and six."

"That's more like it," said Andrew, squeezing Kathleen. "Now you'll pull away on the next ballot."

Before there could be any kind of demonstration, Senator

LaCroix quickly shouted into the rising current of voices: "Quiet please, quiet! No candidate has a majority. Please get ready for the next ballot. The time is passing quickly, so please do not delay. Use ballot number six, this time, please. All right, let's get to it.

"Hold it." He saw a movement at Mary Margaret McMahon's box. "Have any of the candidates any announcements to make?"

The west-coast woman waved frantically at the chairman and despatched a scribbled note to him. Then she left her box and made a beeline for Kathleen's box across the crowded floor. As she came, she pulled off the huge yellow rosette bearing her own name.

Gordon, on Kathleen's left, wiped his face with his tri-coloured scarf and turned to Kathleen.

"Good for Mary Margaret. She didn't hang on till she was knocked off. Now is the time when it'll do us the most good. We can use the votes – over four hundred of them. Now where is Anderson?"

Mary Margaret reached Kathleen's booth, out of breath. She took the red, white and blue scarf offered by Gordon and knotted it around her throat.

"All right, Kate, now it's up to you to beat the bastards. I'm counting on you, and so are all my people." The two women hugged, and then sat down again, facing the platform where LaCroix was intoning in a neutral voice.

"Mr. Hurelak drops from the ballot automatically, as the low man. I have been officially informed that Mary Margaret McMahon has withdrawn. Anyone else?" His eyes searched the other boxes. He took up the microphone again, but Barry Anderson had pushed his way to the stage and come up behind him to seize it from his hand.

"Me too," he said with a gulp, and left the platform. It seemed he was making his way to Kathleen's box. But when he arrived below, he ducked his head and went on; and when he reappeared he was standing beside Hume Frazier, shaking hands. Tying bright green-and-white streamers around his stetson, he turned and waved to the crowd.

202

"Damned dirty, double-crosser," spat out Mary Margaret, to Andrew's amusement. "I never did trust him. I think he's one of the worst chauvinist pigs in the House. And I don't think his supporters will follow him over to Hume. Kate, you're sure to pick up some of his votes."

The chairman held up his hands for quiet. The number of candidates was now down to three. Heads turned to the box hung with orange bunting. From it Jean Jacques Charles stared straight ahead, his face without expression. Behind him stood Alcide Morin. And on either side were his two main parliamentary supporters: Bentley Palmer and Stan Findlay.

"Then let's get on with it. Ballot number three, but remember to use ballot number six, please. The *pink* ballot."

The lines of delegates began to form again, snaking past the credentials desks, across the floor and into the half-dozen curtained booths where each delegate marked the ballot in secrecy.

"Let's hope this is the last round. Andrew, isn't the suspense awful? I doubt anyone else will cross the floor. From now on, this is a fight to the finish."

"Don't speak too soon, Kathleen. Look who's coming."

Cy Hurelak hove into view at the top of the staircase to her box. The big Newfoundland fisherman picked up one of her scarves, and said shyly: "I'd like to wear your colours, too, if you'll have me, Miss Kate?" and she opened her arms and kissed him warmly.

Kathleen, Andrew, and the two failed candidates talked for awhile together, speculating how the next results would go, watching the delegates below, and then they, too, went down to join the line and cast their own votes.

Kathleen was patted on the back, her hands wrung in quick handshakes. People reached out to touch her, or pulled the tall woman down to whisper encouragement in her ear. Badly aimed kisses landed on her ear, her chin. As she moved on her way, she was pushed and shoved and jostled by people who wanted only to touch her. This would be a day to remember, and they wanted to be able to tell their friends and neighbours back home that they had been there, and seen her, face to face. The poor Mountie struggled to stay near Kathleen, but it was clear that she was in no danger from the friendly crowd.

These were precious moments to Kathleen, that pressing of the flesh that seems to energize every politician – a kind of proof of the public's love.

Kathleen was still on the convention floor, slowly threading her way back through the thousands of delegates, some on their way to vote, and some, like Kathleen, returning to their seats.

She barely heard the chairman, Bonnie Costello, now, taking her turn at the gavel. The young M.P. announced the return of the group of folksingers who had been called upon to entertain the crowd several times already this afternoon. They called themselves Les Troubadours de l'Isle Royale.

They swung into a rousing "I'ze the By," and Cy Hurelak leapt to the platform and began a jig, his ponderous body shaking the boards of the temporary stage.

Kathleen stopped for a moment to watch the sight. The audience roared out the song, clapping their hands in unison.

Then the leader of the group spoke into the clustered microphones and thanked the panting Newfoundlander for his contribution. When the round of applause died, he said softly: "And now for something you all know. Please join in on the last chorus. This is in memory of a lovely lady who had to die too young, and this is to say how much we miss her."

Kathleen stood stock-still when she recognized the opening bars of the song she had first heard that long-ago night of the Parliamentary Ball, "The Song of Evangeline." Poor lost Angel, was her first thought; and just then Andrew came up and put his arm around her. Together, along with a growing number of the delegates and watchers, they began to hum the song.

There are still today
People who live in your country
Who remember your name.
Because the ocean speaks of you
The south wind carries your voice
From the forest to the plain.

Your name is more than Acadia,
More than the hope of one homeland.
Your name is the name of all those
Who despite their unhappiness
Believe in love, and hope.

It wasn't very clear what happened next, so swift it was, and unexpected. It was obvious that Jacques had not heard the song's introduction and that it was only after the haunting strains had begun that he had recognized the melody. For a moment, as she watched, Kathleen was pierced to the heart by the shocked look of utter devastation, the naked anguish that twisted that carved face. The Prime Minister stood rigidly alone, the poignancy of his loss etched deep, tears trickling down his face.

There was a sudden blurred movement: a woman had sprung towards him, catching Jacques by the arm and pulling him down towards her. With her other hand, she clawed at his face, screaming. Her voice was picked up and magnified by the hand-held microphone of a roving reporter.

"You monster! You killed her! You let her die! You killed our Evangeline."

The woman hung on Jacques as the whole Centre went quiet. His face a white mask of fury, Jacques stared down at the screaming woman; and then with the full force of his extended arm, he struck her face with the flat of his hand. The slap echoed around the convention hall, cutting through the silence like a thunder clap.

The woman fell backward, a shower of blood spurting from her nose. She was hustled quickly from the room.

On Jacques' white face, below one glaring eye, blood seeped from the long scratches left by her nails.

Two young Mounties who had not been quick enough to get between the Prime Minister and his attacker now took him by the arm. Jacques shook them off. He looked helplessly around himself, then plunged down the stairs from his box, to disappear from view.

Not every delegate had seen the shocking scene, but within

moments, everyone had heard some version of it. Kathleen was stunned. She let Andrew lead her back through the uproar to her own box, where she slumped, thoughts tumbling through her head of Jacques, and of Evangeline. She could not get out of her head the picture of Jacques in the moment that he struck his tormentor. She had never before seen such naked pain on the face of any human, and she understood then, as she had not before, how he blamed himself for the death of his beloved Angel.

Bonnie Costello stepped back from the podium, giving way to Joey Breen, third-ballot results in hand. The mood of the crowd in the hot, airless room was subdued, and silence came at once when he requested it.

"The results of the third ballot: Charles – three hundred and thirty votes."

Almost as one, the mass of humanity drew in a sharp breath. The Prime Minister had lost more than half his support. Jean Jacques Charles was finished. Whether it was as a result of the violent incident, which took place while voting was yet under way, or because the tide had finally run out for him, would be the subject of argument for months to come. But it was done. The king had been dethroned.

"Frazier – eleven hundred and seventeen."

The audience was spellbound, hanging on the next few words.

"That's it, Katie, we've won," breathed Gordon into her ear. Kathleen scarcely heard him as she strained to hear Joey Breen.

"Marshal – two thousand . . . "

She never heard the rest. A wall of sound smashed against her. For Kathleen, the next half hour would always remain a kaleidoscope of flashing images. It was pandemonium. The brass band played her theme song, and the musicians of the other candidates followed as they formed a conga-line around the floor. Hats and ribboned badges flew through the air. Andrew crushed Kathleen in a bear-hug. Cy Hurelak grabbed the young Mountie and pulled him around in a jig. Mary Margaret laughed and cried together, tears of joy streaming down her face. Gordon Neville caught up Kathleen's hands and squeezed them so hard she had to pull away. Her young supporters were going crazy, waving their placards and turning cartwheels into the mob – for a mob it was now. Hundreds rushed her box, clamouring to reach her.

"Here's the speech, Kathleen," Gordon said, handing her a slim folder. "Just read it slowly. We're right bang-on for television. Now let's get to the platform. There'll be the official pictures with the other candidates, and then – well, the country is waiting to hear from you, Katie-love. It's all downhill from here!"

"Okay, here goes." And she stepped before the eye of the television camera, alert, in control, her face full of light and hope.

As he stood proudly watching her, Andrew Wickstrom became aware of a delegate standing beside him, an uncertain look on his face.

"Do you think we did right? How will it be for the country, d'ya think, electing a lady? Will she do?"

Andrew threw an arm around the delegate's shoulder, looked again at the stage, and said to him slowly, and with utter conviction.

"It'll be great, and she'll do very, very well. Our Katie is a very political lady."